# A PINCH OF
# P·O·I·S·O·N

## FRANCES & RICHARD
## LOCKRIDGE

HarperPerennial
*A Division of HarperCollinsPublishers*

Originally published in hardcover by Frederick A. Stokes Company in 1941.

First HarperPerennial edition published 1994.

*Designed by R. Caitlin Daniels*

Library of Congress Cataloging-in-Publication Data
Lockridge, Frances Louise Davis.
A pinch of poison / by Frances and Richard Lockridge.--1st HarperPerennial ed.
p. cm.
"A Mr. and Mrs. North mystery."
ISBN 0-06-092491-8 (paper)
1. North, Jerry (Fictitious character)—Fiction. 2. North, Pam (Fictitious character)—Fiction. 3. Private investigators—New York (N.Y.)—Fiction 4. Women detectives—New York (N.Y.)—Fiction.
I. Lockridge, Richard, 1898– . II. Title.
PS3523.0243P56 1994
813'.54—dc20                                                    93-39970
94 95 96 97 98 ❖/RRD 10 9 8 7 6 5 4 3 2 1

The characters in this novel are fictional and have no counterparts in life. Pete, previously noted as an exception, is one no longer. Others addicted to cats may share some part of the authors' regret that Pete died in June, 1941, at the estimated age of ten.

# • CONTENTS •

## · 1 ·

Max Fineberg sat on the running-board and the late July heat sat on his shoulders. The heat, that afternoon, sat on everything; it was a damp and steaming burden on the city of New York. The air was faintly hazy but the sun beat wickedly through it. Hot light glanced from the shiny top of Max Fineberg's taxicab and beat back from the glass of windows across the street.

Mr. Fineberg, his head sagging against the support of his hands, was worried and afraid. He wished he were somewhere else, doing something else. He wished somebody would tell him how he was going to make the next payment on his shiny cab and that he knew how Rose was feeling in the hospital and that his, until recently, instructor in economics at C.C.N.Y. would explain what a cab driver was to do with a dollar fifteen on the clock after ten hours of hacking and with the day almost done.

Hack the rest of the night was, Max supposed, the answer to that last one, and, to begin with, go somewhere else for customers. The present idea wasn't, clearly, working out, although it had seemed a good one two hours ago. He had wondered why none of the other hackers had

1

thought of parking here, at the last stop of a bus line on which buses ran infrequently and where hot men and women might be expected to pay the difference for a quick ride to the nearest subway. He didn't wonder any longer; the answer was "no men and women," or at least none with cab fare. He had better, he decided, get along back to the subway station where there was, at the least, animation. Max stood up and walked, without enthusiasm, around his cab. There was now a pedestrian coming down the sunny sidewalk and Max felt a faint rising of hope. He stood by his cab and tried to make everything look very inviting.

Max tried to look inviting himself by standing a little straighter than he felt like standing and by smiling like a good salesman. He tried to keep the heat and weariness out of his voice as he said, "Cab, lady?" He put his right hand on the door handle and began to open the door in welcome.

The lady didn't seem to see him and Max's hopes descended. But, jeez, he had to get a fare sometime.

"Taxicab, miss?" he insisted. "It's pretty hot for walking, isn't it?"

That sounded like a young man who had been two years at C.C.N.Y. and might have been a professional man if things had worked out that way. At any rate, Max hoped it did. And, sure enough, the lady hesitated and looked at Max. Max smiled again like a good salesman. Under other circumstances, Max realized quickly, it would be easy to smile at her like—well, like Max Fineberg, whoever that was. Like the Max Fineberg who had been going to be— The girl interrupted Max's fleeting introspection by saying yes, she thought so, to the nearest subway station.

It was better than nothing, Max thought, holding the door open while she got in. He went around to his seat like a salesman giving good service and started the motor. He flipped the flag down and, looking back at her, asked if she wanted the top down.

"No," she said. "Don't bother. It doesn't make any difference."

She sounded almost the way he felt, Max decided, starting up. Not that she had any reason to—not with those clothes and—and everything. Max knew the way women's clothes ought to look. When he could he loitered his cab in front of the big shops on Fifth Avenue, scanning the sidewalks for fares, and the windows you couldn't miss.

This customer's clothes, now, came out of windows like that. You could tell the difference, particularly when you had been married a couple of years and had had somebody to point the difference out to you. You could tell by the way people stood, too, and by their skins and, particularly with women, by their hair. This customer's hair, now, had been done in a good place and done as often as it needed doing. This customer did not belong among those who get too tired and wonder how they're going to make next payments. This customer belonged among those who had got the breaks. If she wanted to, she could let him take her where she was going, even if it were halfway down Riverside, and never know the difference. She would eat just the same. He pulled up at a red light and thought about Rose in the hospital, and a dollar fifteen—make it a dollar fifty-five, with maybe a ten-cent tip—on the clock.

"I think," the lady said, "that I'll change my mind. I think I'll go all the way down, instead." She gave an address, and Max brightened. Make it maybe three dollars on the clock, and a quarter tip.

"Yes indeed, miss," he said. "It's pretty hot for subways." He paused, as if considering. "I tell you, miss," he said, "I could take you down the parkway. It's cooler that way; there's sort of a breeze off the river. Would that be all right, miss?"

"Any way," the customer said. "It doesn't matter. The parkway will do."

Max felt a lot better. Make it three-fifty on the clock, maybe. And he could roll fast enough to stir up some sort of a breeze, going down the parkway. It hadn't been such a bad stand after all, back there by the bus stop.

It was the thought of the subway which had made Lois Winston change her mind—the thought of the slow trip downtown, with the car filling until hot humanity swayed in a mass in front of her and alien knees pressed her own; the thought of the suffocating, packed ride on the shuttle at Forty-second and the stampeding rush at Grand Central; the thought of the ride uptown again and the dutiful walk in the heat across town from Lexington. Her rule about such matters was a good little rule in its place, she thought, smiling faintly to herself, but this was not its place. Not after this afternoon.

She glanced at the watch on her wrist and reassured herself that it was now too late to do anything more today. The puzzle she had carried down the hot street and into the cab—the cab, vague interest prompted her to discover from the license card displayed, of Max Fineberg—that puzzle would have to go over until tomorrow. She would put it out of her mind, she told herself firmly, and she would think of something else. She would not think about Buddy and his Madge, either, nor about—not, at any rate, for an hour or so about—Dave McIntosh, who looked so little like his name, and yet could at times act so—so McIntoshy. She would, she thought, not think about anything but getting home, and the coolness of a shower and lying for a while with the slatted blinds closed and the air-conditioner conditioning like mad. The trouble with the world today, she thought, is that there isn't enough air in it.

"Perhaps," she said, "you might open the top after all, driver."

"Sure thing, lady," Max said, and pushed a button. The rear half of the roof folded obediently back. Quite a cab, Max thought—if you could pay for it.

"It's quite a day, isn't it, lady?" Max said. "Ninety-six at four o'clock, the radio says. Would you like the radio on, miss?" Max almost forgot, as they stopped for the parkway and then turned on it, and as the meter clicked comfortingly, how much he disliked calling customers "lady" and "miss," and how irritatingly he resented the fact that he always did.

"No," the lady said. "It would probably be baseball."

"That's right, miss," Max said. "Baseball *or* war news. You can't get away from them. If it was good music, now, like you hear at the stadium."

"Yes," the lady said. She said it as if she were forgetting Max. But Max hadn't said anything to anybody for hours.

"Do you know, miss, you're the first fare I've had since eleven o'clock this morning?" he said. "That's a fact. What do they expect?"

What did they expect? Max wondered. What did they expect a guy to do, with a dollar fifteen on the clock and a wife in the hospital?

"I don't know, Mr. Fineberg," the lady said. I *don't* know, either, Lois Winston thought. What is Mr. Fineberg going to do?

Max was warmed by being called Mr. Fineberg. He was tired of being called "driver." It was seldom, now, that anybody called him Mr. Fineberg.

"It's pretty hard going, miss," Max said, over his shoulder. It was time he told somebody what hard going it was—somebody who didn't know about such things. "I'm a married man, miss, and what do they figure I'm going to do about it?"

Lois Winston looked at the narrow shoulders, slight with youth, and maybe with more than youth. There was a thin neck above the dirty collar of the blue shirt. Max's thin face, as he half turned it, speaking, was thin and clear, with delicate bones leaving shadows on the planes of the cheeks. He was very young, she saw, and very worried.

"I know," she said. She didn't know, perhaps. Things hadn't happened to her. But if you could get to know from what you saw, she could say that she knew. She saw enough of thin, worried young faces, male and female. "Heaven knows I do," she thought, tiredly.

Max paid no attention to what she said. Her words were merely an encouraging murmur.

"In the hospital," he said, "with a baby coming. That's where my wife is, miss." He stopped, and she could see his neck redden slightly. "I'm sorry, miss," Max said. "It's nothing to bother you with." You're a fool, Max told himself. What are you whining to her for? What the hell does she care; what's it to her?

"Oh," she said. "A baby. Another baby!"

"Listen, miss," Max said. "Forget it, see? I'm just a guy who hasn't talked to anybody all day, and I got talking. But it's not *another* baby. It's our first baby." She saw his shoulders stiffen defiantly. "Any reason why we shouldn't have a baby, miss?"

I could think of a thousand, she told herself. If you'd come down to our office some day, Mr. Fineberg, I could show you—

"No, Mr. Fineberg," she said. "There isn't any reason why you shouldn't have a baby. I was—I was thinking of something else."

"Sure, lady," Max said. "You'll have to excuse me, lady. I'm sorry I got started that way."

It was odd, Lois thought, as the pause after that lengthened until it was, to all appearances, permanent, how circumstances kept pushing the puzzle back into her mind. Now it was worrying her again—that odd thing she had discovered this afternoon, an hour or so before she encountered the discursive and self-centered, and oddly touching, Mr. Fineberg. If it meant anything, it meant something extremely unlikely; something darkly peculiar and out of the ordinary run. She was uncertain what to do, or whether to do anything. Already, perhaps, she had done too much; certainly, if there was anything to do she had done too much. There could be no doubt that, when the quite outlandish suspicion had crossed her mind, she had given herself away as completely as she well could. Perhaps that was because she was, for all her experience, an amateur; what they politely called a "volunteer." Professional workers, perhaps, came against queer things so often that they learned to hide any evidence of surprise. Maybe, in other words, Dave was right, and she would leave the work to those trained for it, and living by it. A professional had, it might be—and as Dave insisted—an attitude which no amateur could ever attain. Perhaps there was something about knowing you could, at any time and without inconvenience, merely walk out which kept you from ever, in the real sense, quite going in.

But the fact was, Lois thought as they turned down the ramp at Seventy-ninth Street, worked south and cut east through Seventy-second—the fact was that she was doing good work. Or had been, until today. Now she might be making a mountain of a molehill, or of the shadow of a molehill. The chances were, say, a hundred to one that she was ascribing importance to the patently coincidental.

"After all," she said to herself, "why? It wouldn't make sense. I must be imagining things, and that's all there is to it."

And if she were, she had certainly been silly enough before the interview ended. That sudden change from accustomed friendliness, which reached even to the exchange of inconsequential confidences, to stiff professionalism. That suggestion of further steps to be taken, so flatly in contradiction to everything which had gone before. The implication, so clear in everything she had said in those last five minutes, that something had gone wrong and new problems been raised. And if nothing had, if it turned out to be all fantasy in the mind of a tired young woman on a hot afternoon—

"Well," Lois thought, "I'll take some sort of a prize, certainly. But still, I'll have to tell Mary Crane."

It was consoling to think of telling Mary Crane, who would understand and make so little of it, and who would advise so gently that you would feel, afterward, as if you had thought the whole thing out for yourself. Tomorrow, since it was too late tonight, she would tell Mary Crane. Tomorrow would, in any case, do as well as today.

The cab turned down Park and then east through Sixty-fourth to circle the block and come west again in Sixty-third, while Max looked for numbers. All very swank, Max commented to himself, when he found the number and drew in. The doorman in summer uniform opened the cab door and stood, politely attentive, as Lois Winston paid the bill. She took the change, as Max's expressive face revealed bitterness. But when she dropped it into the coin purse in her bag, her slender fingers brought something out again and the doorman looked surprised.

"Listen, miss—" Max started. "I don't know—"

"You can buy something for the baby," Lois told him. "Or for the baby's mother. Goodbye, Mr. Fineberg." She smiled at him. "It was much cooler on the parkway," she said.

Max sat blinking at her, and then he blinked at the five-dollar bill in his hand. He regarded the doorman darkly, and the doorman regarded him with some suspicion. Then Max shrugged, and put the cab in gear. It was something to happen, all right. But she must be rolling in it, so probably it didn't mean a thing to her. He looked back at the apartment house, and at the back of the withdrawing doorman, solicitously conducting Miss—what was it he called her? Winstead?—through the dangers between curb and foyer. She was all right, but some people had all the luck. You couldn't get past that, Max told himself, as he turned up Park and trundled north again, with quick glances at the possible customers on the sidewalk. Some people had all the luck.

Next morning he remembered having thought that and remembered it with the awe of one who has been brushed, in passing, by the portentous. He remembered it while, sitting by a bed in the ward, he described the ride over and over to Rose, wringing it dry of drama. And Rose, who looked so pale and ill but was, the doctors said, going to be all right, looked up at him from the pillow and looked with admiration, as at one returned from adventure. Looking down at her Max fell silent after a moment, and then he took one of her hands. It was warm and sentient in his. He turned it over and let his thumb move gently along her wrist. He could feel her pulse there, going steadily. Thump, thump. It made him feel as if he had something very important to say.

"Rose," he said. "I tell you, Rose. It makes you think." He said it with a kind of wonder, as if it were really something very important to say.

# • 2 •

TUESDAY
5:30 P.M. TO 9:45 P.M.

It was a surprise to find Buddy at home. It was a surprise to find him even in town. He called from the living-room as she stepped into the foyer of the apartment on the roof.

"Lois?" he called, and when, as she nodded to Mary, who stood smiling attentively at the foot of the stairs to the second floor, she admitted her identity: "Come here a minute, will you, Sis?"

"I'll want Anna in a few minutes, Mary," Lois said. "After I speak to Mr. Ashley. Coming, Buddy."

Buddy could stand up at the entrance of a lady with all the nonchalance of one who was still sitting down. He did so now.

"We thought you might like a drink," he said. "After your services in the cause."

Buddy was, she had to agree as she looked at him, handsome enough, for a man who drank as much as he did at twenty-three. He was wiry and thin, although you would never confuse his sort of thinness with that of, say, her little taxi-driver. He also looked discontented, and his voice was heavily ironic on "services in the cause."

"Hello, Buddy," Lois said. "Madge." She paused, with a tentative

9

smile for the third person in the room, a relaxed and olive-skinned young woman in the very enticingly cut print, who reclined in a deep chair.

"Carol Halliday." Buddy was casual. "This is my sister Lois, Carol. My half-sister, to be exact. Lois Winston."

"Oh, yes," Carol said. Her voice was attractively husky. "How do you do, Miss Winston?"

"You all look very comfortable," Lois said. "And cool."

"Buddy has simply saved our lives, Lois. Literally." That was Madge.

Lois said she was so glad. Buddy said, "What'll it be, Sis?" He said it a little as if he expected a refusal. But she took a cocktail and, still standing near the door, sipped it slowly.

He brought me in to prove he can have Madge here when he likes, Lois thought. And her friends. He is sometimes unbelievably callow, Lois thought.

"What I really want," she said, "is a shower and something dry." She finished the cocktail; put down the glass. He can have a dozen Madges for all me, she thought. My foolish little brother. I'm not responsible for what he does. But she wished she could really convince herself of that. She shook her head as Buddy raised the shaker again.

"Not now," she said, as she smiled at them again and turned through the door. "Perhaps later." Perhaps, she thought, I really will; the coolness of the apartment, brought by motors which somewhere turned with untiring ease, lessened her weariness. It was good to be cool again, and at home. It was good to have space and quiet and service.

It's fine to have money, all right, she thought, thinking of little Max Fineberg. Money and no real worries—except a little about Buddy. And of course, she added to herself, a little about Dave. And a little about the afternoon's puzzle.

But after all, she thought, I'm only a volunteer. I can quit any time and just play. And I'm young and people don't mind looking at me and . . .

And, she thought a few minutes later, as she stood under the shower and looked approvingly down at herself, I'm not going to have a baby. Hurray, hurray! Not like poor little Mrs. Fineberg.

Anna was quietly efficient when Lois came out of the shower. The spread on the bed was turned back, the shades closed, everything as she had imagined it that long, hot distance ago when she was walking down the street toward Max Fineberg's cab, and trying to convince herself that she should stick to the rules and walk to the subway. There was, she told Anna, nothing more for—she picked up her watch from the bedside table—at least an hour. Anna said, "Yes, miss," and started out. Lois made a sudden decision.

"Oh, Anna," she said, "you might bring me a copy of the Encyclopædia. The H's."

"The Encyclopædia, miss?" Anna repeated. "The volume with the H's in it?"

"Yes, Anna, please," Lois said. "There's something I want to look up."

Anna brought the volume and Lois Winston, resting it uncomfortably on her abdomen, read. Then she said, "Um-m-m!" and lay for a while looking at the ceiling. "That's what I thought," she said, after a bit. "I'll have to talk to Mary Crane." Then, quite unexpectedly to herself, she went to sleep.

It was almost seven when Anna rapped restrainedly on the door. Lois awoke and said, "Come," and tried to remember the wild turmoil of dreams which was slipping away. It was something about— But she could not remember what it was about. Anna said it was almost seven and Lois lay quietly for a moment looking at her. Then Lois was wide awake and off the bed and telling Anna she thought the blue print and then she was looking at herself in the dressing-table mirror. She looked rested, she thought, and a little flushed.

"I hope you had a nice rest, miss," Anna assured her. Anna was calm and unhurried and began to arrange Lois's hair. Lois rubbed cream into her skin and rubbed it out again. She said it was a lovely rest. Somebody knocked at the door.

"Yes?" Lois said.

"I want to talk to you a minute, Sis." That was Buddy, with a demand in his voice.

"I'm dressing," Lois said. "And I've just time before Dave comes for me. You can talk to me tomorrow."

"It won't take me long to say what I want to say," Buddy insisted. "And I want to say it tonight." He spoke as if only what he wanted was important. Lois stirred impatiently under Anna's fingers and made a face at Anna in the mirror. Anna looked dispassionately sympathetic.

"No," Lois said. "Tomorrow will have to do, Buddy. And if it's about—"

"You know what it's about," Buddy broke in. He had half opened the door. "I just want to say—get Anna out of here, will you?"

Lois was on her feet, turning to face him.

"I told you no," she said. "I told you I was dressing. Get out of here, Randall. And stay out until I invite you in." She looked at him and he stared back. "All right," she said. "Get out."

She was stronger; she was always stronger when it was worth the trouble. She was always stronger when she called him Randall instead of "Buddy"; it made him feel, somehow, like a boy who has been reprimanded. It also made him sulky, and there was sullen anger in his gaze now as he stared at her a moment longer. Then he shrugged and closed the door behind him. Lois stood for a moment staring at the door and then she sat down at the mirror again. Anna's proper face showed sympathy and agreement.

"It will be about Madge again, of course," Lois said, only half to Anna. "If he'd only—only let it lie. Anyway until Mother comes back."

"Mrs. Ashley is coming back tomorrow, miss." Anna said. "For the day. For some shopping. She called Mary this afternoon, I think. I supposed Mary had told you."

"Oh," said Lois. "No—I only saw Mary a moment. I suppose she told my brother?"

"I think she told Mr. Ashley, miss." There was no comment in the tone. It hardly skirted a subject which was outside Anna's accepted sphere of comment.

"Yes," Lois said. "Of course. A little higher in front, Anna."

That would account for Buddy's insistence, Lois realized. "He wants to talk to me before I talk to Mother," she thought. "To find out what I'm going to say to Mother." She smiled to herself. "Poor Mother," she thought. "And after all, what do I care?" But somebody had to be—well, call it judicious. And it couldn't be Mrs. Ashley; it couldn't be Buddy. It had to be Lois and—she smiled to herself again—Madge. Being judicious in opposite directions. Because you couldn't, certainly, deny that Madge thought things out.

She heard quiet steps in the carpeted hall outside. That would be Mary, coming to report that Mr. David McIntosh was calling. She hoped that this was going to be an evening of the McIntoshy David, or at least the reasonably McIntoshy David. Not the one who sometimes seemed to be pulling and jerking at her; not the one who, once or twice, had grown so hard and bitter in jealousy and made so much of so little. She could do with the nice, comfortable David, or with the gay David, or even, and perhaps just now that would be best, with the reasonably McIntoshy David. But not with the one who glared.

She held up her arms while Anna lowered the blue print to her shoulders. It was a pretty dress, she thought, turning before the long mirror, watching its soft folds swing at her feet.

"And," she thought, smiling at the girl in the mirror, "there's nothing really wrong with the lady. Not with the lady who shows, anyway."

David was reasonably McIntoshy. He was quiet and gentle and said nice things about the way she looked.

"It makes me cooler just to look at you," he said.

"Well," she said, "I don't know whether that is quite the effect—"

He said she didn't need to worry about that. As she knew perfectly well. And that he thought the Ritz-Plaza roof, unless she had some place else in mind? The Crescent Club on the river?

"Oh," she said, "the roof, I think. And no lovely view of Welfare Island. I've had about enough welfare for one day." He started to speak.

"All right," she said. "I know how you feel. And you know how I feel. And let's talk about it again—oh, a month from Friday. Shall we?"

A taxicab came politely up to them at the curb. "The Ritz-Plaza," Dave said, and they waited for the lights to cross Park Avenue. The lights changed and they poked west through the still hot street, with the sun slanting in the driver's eyes. But there was a breeze with the top down.

There was a breeze, too, twenty stories above the street, with blinds cutting off the sun and higher buildings casting long shadows across the city. There was a cord stretched warningly between brass uprights at the entrance to the roof and several men and women standing disconsolately on the wrong side of it. But Nicholas smiled at them and beckoned.

"I have your table, Mr. McIntosh," he said. "Near the floor, yes?"

"Not too near," David said.

"But of course," Nicholas assured him. "Not too near, certainly." He led between tables, walking as if he were threading a needle. He whisked a "Reserved" sign from a table which was, as he promised, near the dance floor but not too near. He beamed approval on the table, and on Mr. McIntosh for receiving and himself for bestowing it. He seated Lois with delicacy; summoned waiters with the assurance of a magician whose effects have never failed.

"This be all right?" David asked, very McIntoshy and down to earth. Lois smiled at him.

"Perfect," she said. She waited until he was seated too, and smiled at him.

"What if I had said the Crescent Club, though?" she asked. David looked puzzled.

"Why?" he asked. "It wouldn't have mattered."

"Not after you'd reserved a table here?" she asked.

He looked puzzled still for a moment. Then he remembered.

"Oh," he said. "That. That was just Nick's little gag. Good customers and all that. There wasn't any reservation, really."

The waiters and the bus-boys hovered over them, filling glasses, procuring butter, offering menu cards. Frozen daiquiris came on summons and were cold and sour-sweet in the mouth, and relaxing. But Lois refused the second.

"I'm hungry," she said. "Believe it or not."

There aren't any worries worth worrying about, she thought, as they ate and talked idly; all the little things of the daytime vanished now, as lights went on here and there in buildings, as the city began its nightly transformation. How terrible blackouts must be, she thought, remembering London three years before and knowing that tonight there was a red glare over it. Both peace, as she had it then, and war seemed so tremendous, so overpoweringly important, that it was inconceivable that one could have time for little worries. They finished eating and sipped long glasses of iced coffee. Then, because it was so much cooler than she had thought, that afternoon, it could ever be again—so much cooler and more peaceful—they danced.

They sat and talked and danced again. Then Dave ordered drinks—brandy and soda for himself and, with a little grimace, a Cuba Libre for her—and they turned them lazily, letting the ice tingle against glass.

"It's lovely here," Lois said. "I don't ever want to go away."

Later, when the orchestra began again, Dave held out a hand to her and they danced again. "Lovely," she said, against his shoulder. "What's the use of anything?"

The floor was comfortably filled, this time, and after they had left the floor, couples brushed past their table as they returned to their own. The people made it seem warmer and the cold drink was refreshing. Lois, who had only sipped before, drank more deeply and then, as they talked, drank again.

"It's getting much warmer, isn't it?" she said, feeling a flush mounting in her cheeks.

David smiled at her.

"Dancing," he said, briefly. Then he looked again. "You do look rather warm," he said. "I hadn't noticed it."

She drank again, thirstily, her throat curiously dry. David looked at her and she felt him looking and smiled. Her skin felt hot and she could feel the flush in her face, and she drained her glass. But, although she let the ice caress her lips, they seemed to be growing hotter.

"It's imagination," she told herself. "I'm perfectly all right." She felt David looking at her, curiously. "Aren't I, David?" she said. She hardly realized she had said this aloud. But he was looking at her with concern.

"It's just the heat, of course," she said. "Like this afternoon with little Mr. Finestein and all we have to do is open the back and drive down the parkway. Isn't that right, David? Only not have a baby because maybe we couldn't keep it and then Madge and Buddy would have it. And you know Buddy, don't you, David?"

*I can't be saying this,* she thought. *I can't be saying any of this! Why does David keep looking at me like that? He looks as if he thought I was drunk. But you can't be drunk on what I've had. Something's happening to me,* she thought. *Something's happening dreadfully to me!*

It was hard to breathe, her lungs seemed to be snatching for breath and, while she strove to quiet it, she felt her breast rising and falling quickly, frantically. And all the time, even after she could no longer make out the words, she could hear herself talking—talking. David was standing across the table, his face anxious, and from a long way she could hear his voice.

"Lois!" he said. "What is it, Lois? Lois!"

She stood up, and now she was gasping for breath and it seemed that her skin was on fire. She could feel her heart pounding now and—

She was standing with a hand out toward David, but as he came around the table to her Lois slipped slowly to the floor and her voice, which had been breaking delirium into words, faltered and died away. Waiters were around David as he picked her up, and the maître d'hôtel, his face very worried, was coming hurriedly between tables. Nicholas's disapproval was evident at a range of twenty feet.

# • 3 •

## TUESDAY
### 9:30 P.M. TO 10:10 P.M.

None of the four in the Norths' living-room was speaking when the
telephone rang. Three of the four were looking at Mrs. North with
expressions which bordered on surprise, although there had been nothing essentially astonishing in Mrs. North's last remark. Mrs. North had
said, "Because it's election day, of course," and Mr. North had looked
at her with suddenly wide eyes and said, in gentle wonder, "My God."
William Weigand had looked at both of them with friendly pleasure and
then he had looked at Dorian Hunt and smiled with a kind of contentment. Dorian had blinked a moment and then all three of them had
looked at Mrs. North. It was then that the telephone rang.

Since dinner they had been sitting in the dimly lighted living-room.
The thick walls of the old house made it a little cooler than it was on
the street, and a silently turning fan stirred the air. They all had long
drinks and in silence ice tinkled against glass. They were comfortably
lethargic, filled with broiled chicken and wild rice and the peace which
descends on those who do not, for at least some hours, have to do anything whatever—which descends, particularly, on people who are,

momentarily, among those they like to be among and have no incentive to invent speech. Nobody had said anything for several minutes before Mrs. North spoke.

"You know," Mrs. North said, "sometimes I wonder how old I *really* am." She did not say it as might one who expected to start a conversation. Mrs. North merely laid the idea down and rested. Mr. North, who had been about to say something else, caught his own words and replaced them. Then he organized his mind carefully and spoke.

"What?" said Mr. North. Weigand and Dorian left it to him.

"How old I really am," Mrs. North said. "To the year, I mean. I know approximately, of course. But sometimes I get so I'd just like to know. Because of Louise."

"Louise?" Weigand had not meant to enter this. He had planned to leave it to Jerry North; to leave it between the Norths. But the irrelevance overcame him.

"Her younger sister," Mr. North explained. "That's Louise. Only I haven't the faintest idea where she comes in."

"Well," said Mrs. North, "she just started me wondering, that's all. Sometimes it occurs to me that I'm really younger than Louise, because it's only a year or so either way, and then it's very confusing." She looked at the others, and explained. "Because she's my *younger* sister, I mean," she said. "She always has been. Only it's just as likely that she's older than I am."

"Look," said Mr. North. "Look, Pam. She—" He paused, feeling the subject suddenly elusive in his mind. "I tell you," he said, "why don't you ask your mother? She'd know."

"Would she?" Pam said, as one who really wants to know. "I don't know whether she would, really. Father always used to call *me* Louise, you know."

Mr. North made a quick movement, as if he were clutching at something in the air.

"Look," he said. "That hasn't anything to do with it. He was just absent-minded and you know it."

"That absent-minded?" Dorian asked, suddenly. She looked at Pam

North with interest. "Really?" Pam nodded, and Jerry, who had known Pam's father, nodded too.

"When he met her on the street," Mr. North explained. "And after we were married he always called me Henry." He smiled, reminiscently. "Henry and Louise," he repeated. "He was always thinking of something else. But he was always very polite." Mr. North caught himself, quickly. "However," he said, "Louise was always younger than you, Pam—a year and some months younger."

Pam nodded and said that that was what she had always thought.

"But I never really *knew*," she said. "It was always just taken for granted. I knew when my birthday was, of course, but I don't remember that anybody ever told me what year. What year I was born, I mean."

"Well," said Mr. North, "I always thought it was 1907. So next December you'll be—" He calculated rapidly and was about to announce a result when Mrs. North intervened.

"That's just it," she said. "Nineteen hundred and seven was either me or Louise. And the other was 1909. But I can't remember that anybody ever said which." Mrs. North reflected a moment and then said, suddenly: "Teeth!"

Mr. North ran the fingers of one hand through his hair.

"Teeth?" he repeated, a little desperately. Weigand and Dorian looked at him with sympathy.

"Can't you tell by them?" Mrs. North asked. "Like horses?"

"Look!" Mr. North said. "Forget teeth. It's perfectly easy. We can just tie it to something. Say—say the other war. How old were you when it started? That would tell us. If you were—let's see—seven the next winter, then you were born in 1907. Or is that before you remember? Do you remember the start of the other war?"

He looked at her eagerly, hopefully.

"No," Mrs. North said. "But I remember when we went in. Papa told me."

"There!" Mr. North said. "How old were you then?"

"I don't know," Mrs. North said. "Eight or nine, I think. I was in either the second or third grade, but that wouldn't show, because I skipped a grade. So—"

Mr. North, his eyes bright with purpose, waved her to silence.

"That's it!" he said. "We can tell by when you were in school, making allowance for the grade you skipped. When did you start in school?"

"When I was five," Mrs. North said. "In kindergarten."

"Now we're getting it," Mr. North said. "If you were five when you started in kindergarten, and then went through seven grades, less the grade you skipped, we can work it out. How old were you when you got out of grade school?"

"Oh," Mrs. North said, "I remember that. I was thirteen." She looked confident a moment, and then her confidence clouded. "Only," she said, "did I really start in kindergarten, or right in the first grade? I don't seem to remember kindergarten, really."

"Try to," Mr. North asked her, eagerly. There was a kind of desperation in his eagerness. "Raffia," he suggested. "Making little rag rugs on a little loom." He cast around anxiously in his mind. "Blocks?" he begged. Mrs. North shook her head.

"Sometimes I think I do," she said. "And then sometimes I think it is just what somebody told me. I don't know really, Jerry." She looked at him. "I'm sorry," she said. "It really doesn't matter, Jerry."

"It's perfectly absurd," Mr. North said. "Of course we can find out how old you are. Just with a few facts and some logic. We—" He looked at Weigand. "Find out, Bill," he urged. "You're a detective."

Weigand shook his head, and said there were limits. Mrs. North made a face at him.

"Well," Weigand said, "how old were you when you graduated from high school, Pam? That might tell us."

"Seventeen," Pam said.

"And what was your class?" Weigand said. "You know, the dear old class of something or other. What was it?"

Everybody waited, anxiously. Including Pam. Then she shook her head.

"I don't know," she said. "I really don't." She looked at the others a little defensively. "I'm just not any good at dates," she said. "I mean—dates that are now. I was very good in history, though."

She looked at all of them, and said she was sorry.

"It doesn't really matter," she said. "I didn't mean to bring it up and worry everybody. I just wondered and—mentioned it. But there's no use trying to find out, because I'm just no good at dates." She paused and looked at Jerry. "I'll tell you, Jerry," she said. "I don't even remember the date we were married."

Mr. North started to tell her, but she broke through.

"Only the day of the month," she said. "I remember that. It was March 4."

Dorian and Bill Weigand looked at Mr. North, who nodded.

"It was, for a wonder," he said. He looked at his wife curiously.

"How do you come to remember that, Pam?" he asked.

"Because it's election day, of course," Mrs. North said.

They were still looking at her, in pleased astonishment, when the telephone rang. Mr. North was the nearer and scooped it up. He greeted it and said "yes" and, after a moment, "yes" again. Then he said "of course" and handed the telephone to Weigand. Weigand said "right" and listened. Knowing him as the others did, they could see him stiffen as he listened, and Dorian Hunt, whose gray-green eyes smiled as if by themselves when they looked at Weigand, said, "Oh, dear!" softly. After what seemed a rather long time, Bill Weigand said "right" again and put the telephone back in its cradle.

Weigand sat a moment, looking at the others, and then he smiled. It was rather a detached smile, as if its sponsor was thinking of other things.

"Trouble," he said. "And the police called in. So— I hate to break things up, Pam."

"Murder?" she said.

Weigand looked at her a moment.

"Well," he said, "it might be. That's where I come in, of course. Up on the Ritz-Plaza roof, a young woman." He looked from Pam to Dorian, thinking aloud. "It's an odd thing, apparently," he said. "She seems to have had too much to drink, and passed out. Only when she passed out, she was dead—just like that. Which worried the hotel doctor. And the ambulance surgeon, when he came. And that worried the precinct. Therefore—"

"Oh," Mrs. North said. "A young woman? Dancing?"

"I don't know, Pam," Weigand said. "She could dance there, couldn't she? They didn't say."

"It seems to—" Mrs. North said. She broke off for a moment. "Well," she said, "it won't be anybody we know, anyway. Not this time."

Weigand smiled.

"No," he said, "you and Jerry have had a bit more than your share. This isn't one that will bother you; no detecting for the Norths this time. We'll just find out who killed Miss Winston and let you know."

He stopped, partly because Mrs. North was staring at him.

"Winston!" she repeated. "Now, listen, Bill—not Lois Winston?"

The other three looked at her, but this time differently.

"Now don't tell me—" Weigand began. Mrs. North held up a hand.

"Was it a Lois Winston?" she demanded. They looked at Bill Weigand, who nodded slowly.

"Right," he said. "Lois Winston. Lives off Park Avenue somewhere. Money. Social Register. That's why the precinct—"

"Then," Mrs. North said, with a kind of detached resignation, "I do know her. Or know of her, anyway. She works for the Foundation."

"Works?" Weigand repeated. "She didn't sound like it. She sounded like money, and all that."

Mrs. North nodded.

"Yes," she said. "That part's all right. But just the same, she worked for the Foundation. A volunteer, I think—anyway, she—"

Weigand broke in.

"I've got to get along," he said. "But perhaps I'd better hear this. Do you want to ride up with me, Pam, and tell me the rest of it as we go?"

"Well—" Pam said, doubtfully—"I—oh, all right, Bill. Only I don't like it. Remember about Jerry's arm. And about my neck." She looked at him, rather darkly. "Remember, Bill?" she said. Bill nodded.

"Bring Jerry to look after you," he said. "Only you're not going to get into this one—nor is Jerry, nor are you, Dorian. It's just a chance to pick up some information without wasting time. Come on."

"All of us?" Dorian asked.

"Why not?" Weigand wanted to know. "I won't make you into a policewoman, Dor. Except maybe by—"

"All right, Bill," Dorian said. "Hold it, Loot."

"And," Mrs. North said, "remember how Dorian got almost—"

"Yes, Pam," Bill said. "I'm not forgetting. We'll be very careful of all of you. Are you coming?"

They went, of course. Weigand's Buick, with red lights blinking in front and with the siren speaking low at crossings, went north. Pam sat beside the driver, now very officially Lieutenant William Weigand, acting captain in the Homicide Bureau of the New York Police Department. It was also a somewhat different Mrs. North. Not for the first time, Weigand noted with underlying surprise how quickly cogent she could be when she wished.

She knew little about Lois Winston at first hand, it developed. She thought she had seen her once in the offices of the Foundation—the Placement Foundation, in West Twenty-ninth Street. "I'm on the committee," she said. "Names. Sometimes benefits. That sort of thing. Jerry sends a check now and then, too." In addition, Pam North was interested in the work itself. "They place children for adoption," she said. "Orphans, foundlings, children whose parents can't care for them and ask help—that sort of thing." As a result of her interest, she had got to know Mary Crane, who was the secretary.

"She's a professional," Pam explained. "Only don't think of social workers in tweed skirts and flat-heeled shoes, looking under the beds for dirt. This place isn't like that. And Mary Crane isn't."

"I know," Weigand said. "I've met them around. Go on."

Pam, she told him, had once thought of doing volunteer work herself, but abandoned the idea because— "Oh," she said, "because of a lot of things. They don't matter." She had asked Mary Crane about it and Miss Crane had been encouraging. They did, she had told Pam, now and then use volunteers; in rare instances, if the volunteers were exceptional and were willing to keep on through a long training period, and sometimes study in addition at the New York School of Social Work, they used volunteers for investigations and in other responsible capacities. Then Miss Crane had cited Lois Winston as an example—a girl who had been with them five years, who worked merely because she wanted to do something which would help people, who took the hours and the tasks of the professional workers but not the salary; who took, also, the routine and the supervision and the exacting personal responsibility which went with the job.

"She thinks—thought—a lot of Lois Winston," Mrs. North said. "You could tell by the way she spoke of her. Although it had raised problems, of course."

"What problems?" Weigand said, letting the siren snarl warning at a car which had injudiciously poked its nose from a side street. The nose withdrew precipitately.

"Well," Pam explained, "to most of the workers it's a job, of course. They are professionals—in that profession, usually, because they want to do something useful, but making their livings by it all the same. And when a volunteer comes in, they are inclined to resent it. Although, Miss Crane says, it merely means one more worker, usually; it doesn't put anybody out of a job."

"Then why—?" Weigand said.

Pam North said she didn't know, in detail. Naturally, Miss Crane had not told her in detail. She had merely let something drop. Pam added that there might, of course, be nothing to it; that, almost surely, there was nothing to it.

"I merely gathered," she said, "that about the time Lois Winston went on the staff—got to be a regular worker, that is—they had had to let a professional worker go. For some other reason. But apparently the girl they fired didn't believe what they said, and thought that Miss Winston had—well, done her out of a job."

"Well—" Weigand said, doubtfully.

"It's possible," Pam pointed out, "that I've—oh, built all this up; made a story out of it—out of something Miss Crane let drop. I do, you know."

She said it without apology, and not defensively. It was merely one of the things Pam North knew about Pam North, and expected others to know. Weigand nodded.

"It would have been five years ago, anyway," he said.

In the next block, outside the Ritz-Plaza, green and white patrol cars nudged against the curb. He swung the Buick in among them. Weigand got out, and the others, a little doubtfully, got out behind him. Weigand looked as if he didn't know what to do with them.

"Go ahead," Mr. North told him: "Forget us, if Pam's told you what you want to know. We may come up, though, and have a drink and look on. Now that we're here."

"Oh," said Pam. "Yes. On the murder roof."

The Norths looked at Dorian.

"The three of you," Dorian said, a little helplessly. Weigand looked at her, because it was fun to look at her. Even as she stood, not moving, she had that singular, poised grace which he had first noticed the autumn before when there was murder at Lone Lake and Dorian was in the thick of it, and he had abandoned a firm determination to continue a vacation. Weigand found, against all professional reasoning, that he hoped she would go with the Norths to the roof. He might get to see her again, for one thing. There really is a glint of red in her hair, Weigand decided, realizing that he should be thinking of Lois Winston.

"Oh, all right," he heard Dorian say, and there was a warm center of contentment inside Lieutenant Weigand, somewhere as he crossed the sidewalk to the lobby. It persisted across the lobby and to the express elevator, marked "Roof Only," at the end of a bank of elevators. A uniformed policeman was standing there, as if by accident. He saluted when Weigand came up and pressed a signal button. Weigand disappeared upward as the Norths and Dorian Hunt crossed the lobby. The policeman looked at them doubtfully. But he made no move to stop Mr. North when he, in turn, pressed the signal button. He merely looked at

them curiously when the three entered the express elevator and followed Weigand toward what Mrs. North called, and what she said the
newspapers would call in the morning, "the murder roof." (The newspapers, as it turned out, were more considerate of the Ritz-Plaza. They
merely called it the murder at the Club Plaza, which was obviously
more polite.)

# • 4 •

## TUESDAY
## 10:10 P.M. TO 10:50 P.M.

But when William Weigand reached the restaurant on the roof at a few minutes before ten o'clock that night, there was not yet admittedly a murder. It was a "suspicious death," and so entered on the blotter of the East Fifty-first Street police station and in the records of the Fourth Detective District. There was a girl in a blue flowered evening dress, caught with brilliants on each shoulder, and the girl was dead. The body lay on the bed where Lois Winston had died in the private suite of the roof's manager. The apartment, consisting of living-room and bedroom, opened off a corridor which led to the restaurant itself. When Weigand arrived, two doctors had looked at Lois Winston's body and a third was bending beside it.

There were several people in the living-room of the suite as Weigand passed through it to enter the bedroom. There were detectives from the district, and from the Homicide Bureau—these last waiting for Weigand's arrival—and several people Weigand had never seen before. He nodded to detectives and lifted his eyebrows at Detective-Sergeant Mullins, temporarily in charge of the Bureau detail. Mullins' face, which had been scarred by authority, relaxed. He said, "Hi-ya,

27

Loot?" Lieutenant Weigand nodded and went into the bedroom. Dr. Jerome Francis, assistant medical examiner, stood up.

"Well, Doctor?" Weigand said. The doctor spread his hands.

"Well," he said, "she's dead."

"And?" Weigand said. Dr. Francis shrugged. It could, he said, be several things, some of them quite innocent.

"Right," Weigand said. "But you don't think it is."

"I think," Dr. Francis said, "that she was poisoned. With one of the alkaloids. The hotel doctor—chap named Merton—thinks so, too. And he was here when she died."

Weigand looked down at the body and said she looked peaceful. Francis nodded. She might go that way, with some poisons, he said. According to Dr. Merton she had merely, quite quietly, stopped breathing. She was dead then, and dead on the arrival of the ambulance surgeon a few minutes later. The ambulance surgeon had talked with Merton, agreed with him, and added "suspicious death" to his "dead on arrival." Then the wheels had started.

"Right," Weigand said. "How soon will you know, definitely?"

Dr. Francis' shoulders were communicative. But they could hurry it up. If Lieutenant Weigand insisted, they might know something within a couple of hours.

"Depends on what we find when we get in," Dr. Francis reported, matter-of-factly.

"Meanwhile," he said, "and without quoting me, take it as poison. Belladonna, for a guess." Dr. Francis snapped his bag. He asked whether Weigand wanted the body where it was, for any purpose.

"Why?" said Weigand, reasonably. "She wasn't killed here. She just died here. Pictures, of course, but what we want is the p.m. as soon as we can get it."

Dr. Francis nodded. Leaving, he encountered Mullins at the door and said, "Uh!" Mullins, looking very official, said, "Telephone, Lieutenant." Weigand raised his eyebrows and Mullins said, sadly, "Yeh. The Inspector." Weigand picked up an extension telephone by the bed and found Deputy Chief Inspector Artemus O'Malley at the other end of it. Weigand said, "Yes, sir."

"So you finally got there," Inspector O'Malley told him, unpleasantly. Weigand said he had; that he had been having dinner with friends and that the Telegraph Bureau had found him there.

"Well," O'Malley said, "what does it look like? Anything in it?"

Weigand said that it looked like poison. O'Malley made sounds disapproving of poison, which he evidently regarded as unfair to policemen. Weigand spoke soothingly. Weigand admitted that it might be suicide. "Only," he said, "it would be an odd place to pick." Equally it might be murder.

"Well," said O'Malley, relapsing into friendliness, duty between superior and subordinate having been discharged, "get on with it, Lieutenant. We'll go over your report in the morning."

Weigand said, "Yes, sir," without animus. It was natural for inspectors to sleep of nights, while lieutenants, even when acting as captains, toiled. O'Malley vanished from the telephone and Weigand cradled it and stood for a moment looking down at the body. Then he turned to Mullins and said, "Well?"

"Well," Mullins said, "I had the boys get pix. D'you want them to print the joint?"

"Why?" said Weigand. Mullins looked around and said, yeh, that was right. Why?

"Right," Weigand said. "What's the setup?"

Mullins told him. The girl had been having dinner with a guy. One David McIntosh. "We got him here," Mullins said. They had sat at the table after dinner and had a drink or two. Then the girl had begun to act tight. She had stood and talked excitedly a moment, while those at other tables nearby looked at her in surprise, but knowingly. Then she had suddenly collapsed. McIntosh had carried her to the manager's apartment. "It looked like a pass-out," Mullins explained. The idea had been to handle an unfortunate emergency as unobtrusively as possible. But the girl's quietness had frightened them and they had called the hotel doctor.

"Then she just died, I guess," Mullins said. "Everybody was surprised, only the doc had said they'd oughta get a stomach pump."

Weigand nodded and considered.

"Right," he said. "Let's talk to McIntosh. We'll want the stenographer."

"O.K., Loot," Mullins said. He went to the door, nodded to the stenographer and said, "You!" to McIntosh.

McIntosh was a tall, broad, brown young man who looked like several good schools rolled into one. But his face was drained. Weigand was tall enough, but he had to look up at McIntosh. He did look up at him.

"I'm sorry," he said. "I'm Lieutenant Weigand, Homicide. Tell me about it."

David McIntosh's voice was heavy and lifeless. His description of Lois's collapse at the table followed that of Mullins, amplifying it with McIntosh's own surprise and consternation, which had given place to anxiety and fear.

"But at first it looked merely as if she had—well, had had too much to drink?" Weigand asked.

McIntosh nodded.

"She seemed excited and incoherent," he said. "Her face looked flushed. But she hadn't had anything to drink—not really."

"What?" Weigand wanted to know. McIntosh told him. A cocktail before dinner. Coffee afterward. Then a Cuba Libre.

"Nothing before you met her, do you think?" Weigand asked. McIntosh was sure she had not, or not more than one drink at the outside.

"She drank almost nothing," he said. "When she had a drink she usually showed it."

Weigand nodded.

"And you had water with dinner, I suppose?" he said. McIntosh agreed.

"Was it something in what she drank?" he wanted to know. Weigand told him they didn't know. But presumably it was something she had taken by mouth, in liquid or food. And liquid was more likely. It would, obviously, be more difficult to administer poison in solid food, without the opportunity for advance preparation.

"And I gather you ordered at the table?" he said. "You hadn't ordered in advance, before you came, I mean?"

McIntosh said they hadn't. Until they were actually in the taxicab, he said, they had not made up their minds where they would have dinner.

"Could she have been given something, or taken something, before I met her?" McIntosh asked.

"Frankly," Weigand said, "we don't know yet. This has to be merely a preliminary questioning, until we see where we are. Do you know of any reason why she should have taken her own life?"

McIntosh looked surprised.

"No," he said. "That's absurd. She never would have. And even if that isn't true, she would never have come here, with me, and then drunk poison. It's—inconceivable."

Weigand agreed it seemed unlikely. He said he gathered that McIntosh had known her a long time, and well.

"Yes," McIntosh said. "Since—oh, for a long time." He paused. "I wanted her to marry me," he said, simply.

"I'm sorry," Weigand said. "I know this is difficult. And she?"

"Sometimes, yes," McIntosh said. "But she was tied up, somehow. Her family—her half-brother, you know—and this job of hers. And some odd notion about being useful. I don't know. But I think she would have married me, eventually."

His voice was expressionless, strained. Weigand looked at him a moment. He felt compassion for McIntosh and his voice revealed it.

"All right," he said. "That's all for now. Give one of the detectives outside your address, will you?"

McIntosh nodded. He went out.

"It's tough on him," Mullins said, after McIntosh had closed the door. Weigand said it was. Very.

"Who else have we got out there?" he wanted to know. Mullins told him. The maître d'hôtel. A bloke who said he was Lois Winston's brother. Some dame with the brother. And—oh, yeh. A bus-boy.

"A bus-boy?" Weigand repeated.

Mullins nodded. He looked a little embarrassed and uncertain. He said it was this way. Not more than five minutes had elapsed between the time Lois Winston had collapsed at her table and the time she died in the manager's suite. By the time she died, the hotel physician suspected poison. He had suggested that the table at which she had been eating be left as it was until the police arrived, and Nicholas, the maître d'hôtel, had agreed. He had gone out to see to it and found the table already cleared and reset.

"He said it was just routine," Mullins said. "Seemed to think it was pretty smart of the bus-boy who did it. But I noticed when I got here that there were several tables around there that hadn't been cleared and I just sorta wondered—could the boy be in on something? So I thought—"

"Right," Weigand assured him. "Probably it doesn't mean anything, but we'll have a talk with the boy. He does seem to have been pretty efficient."

Mullins looked relieved. He wanted to know who the Loot wanted. Weigand decided on Nicholas.

Nicholas had little to add to the detail of Lois Winston's collapse at the table. He knew Mr. McIntosh well, since he often came there, usually with Miss Winston. And he knew who Mr. McIntosh was, naturally.

"Did you?" said Weigand. "Who is he?"

Nicholas looked surprised and a little shocked.

"Mr. McIntosh is the son of Mr. James McIntosh," he said. "The Mr. James McIntosh."

"Oh," Weigand said. "So." He could see the point of Nicholas's attitude. It was important, and not only in Nicholas's realm, to be the son of the Mr. James McIntosh. Nicholas noted the expression on the lieutenant's face with approval.

"So naturally," Nicholas said, "when we got the reservation tonight we saw that Mr. McIntosh received just the table he asked for, down front, near the floor. Which made it all the more—obvious—when the young lady behaved so strangely. Whereas at their usual table . . . "

"Oh," Weigand said. "Mr. McIntosh had made a reservation. By telephone?"

Nicholas nodded. Lieutenant Weigand thought it over.

"Was it Mr. McIntosh himself who phoned?" he asked.

Nicholas did not know, but he could try to find out.

"Do that," Weigand instructed. "But what about this bus-boy?"

Nicholas looked perplexed. Then his face cleared. That would be young Frank Kensitt. The boy who cleared the table so quickly? Weigand nodded.

"But that was nothing," Nicholas insisted. "We train the boys to be efficient at the Club Plaza. In the natural course he would have cleared the table at once."

"Even," Weigand said, "when he had no reason to be sure Mr. McIntosh would not return? He didn't know it was anything serious, remember."

Nicholas pointed out that he had seen the young lady carried across the restaurant. He might naturally assume that something not entirely trivial was going on. Weigand nodded slowly. He said that Nicholas had better go back to his post.

"Oh," Weigand said, "some friends of mine are out there, I think. A man and two young women, one of them with sort of reddish hair. See that they're well taken care of, will you?"

Nicholas, eagerly, would. Weigand drummed on the desk beside which he was sitting for a moment after Nicholas left. His face was abstracted, and Mullins waited.

"Let's have the brother," Weigand directed. Mullins went to the door and said, "You!" at the brother. The brother was a dark, discontented, slight young man who looked more worried than grieved. He was Randall Ashley; Lois Winston was his sister.

"Half-sister, of course," he amplified, sitting nonchalantly where Weigand indicated. "Her father was Clarence Winston, the oil man. Mine was Kenneth Ashley." His tone was faintly supercilious.

"What kind of a man was he?" Weigand asked. Randall Ashley looked faintly surprised.

"What kind of—oh, copper," he said. "Mother married Father about two years after Mr. Winston died."

Then, Weigand discovered, Lois was about three years old. Randall had been born to Mr. and Mrs. Ashley a little over a year later. Lois was twenty-seven—had been twenty-seven. So Randall was twenty-three.

"Although you'd have thought, from the way Sis acted, that I was about thirteen," Ashley put in, rather sulkily. Weigand looked at him without favor.

"You weren't here with your sister, I gather," he said. "I mean, you had your own party."

"I was here with a friend," Ashley said. The word "friend" seemed faintly underlined.

"Were you?" Weigand said. "Who?"

"I don't see—" Ashley began. Weigand didn't either, exactly, but he felt like being stern.

"Who?" he repeated.

Young Ashley looked more sulky than ever. Then he submitted.

"Madge Ormond," he said. "She's a singer."

"Night club?" Weigand hazarded. Ashley frowned.

"Does that make any difference?" he wanted to know.

"No," Weigand said. "As far as I know it makes no difference at all. I just wondered."

"All right," Ashley said. "She is. So what?"

Weigand said he would ask the questions. Where, for example, were Ashley and Miss Ormond sitting in reference to his sister and Mr. McIntosh?

"Most of the dance floor was between us," Ashley said. He looked a little worried, Weigand thought, and was pleased to think. "Why?" Ashley added. Weigand said it was merely routine.

"Although," he added, "it seems probable that somebody passed your sister's table and put something in her drink."

"Listen!" Ashley said. He stood up. Weigand remained seated and looked at him. "If you're trying to—"

"Oh, go home, Mr. Ashley," Weigand said. "Go home to Mama. Or home to Miss Ormond. We'll find you when we want you."

Ashley hesitated a moment. Then he turned quickly to the door. Weigand nodded after his back and Mullins followed him into the living-room of the suite. Then, after a moment, Mullins came back.

"O.K.," Mullins said. "He's got a tail. Why him?"

"I don't know, Mullins," Weigand said. "I suppose merely because I don't like him."

Mullins looked at Weigand a moment. Then he grinned.

"O.K., Loot," he said. "*O.K.*"

He thought a moment.

"What are you going to do about those people out there, Loot?" he inquired, waving in the general direction of the restaurant. Weigand regarded him and asked what he would suggest.

"Get their names and addresses?" Mullins suggested, doubtfully.

"Why?" asked Weigand. "They've been coming and going for—[he looked at his watch]—more than an hour since the girl died. If there was a murderer, and he was on the roof, do you suppose he has waited?"

Mullins thought it over, and said he supposed not.

"But maybe somebody saw something?" he suggested.

Weigand said that if anybody had, the police probably would hear from them when the news came out. However—

"You might have some of the boys ask anybody who is still at a table near the McIntosh table," he said. "There's no harm in it, except to the hotel's feelings, and you might turn up something." He paused. "And," he said, "you'll find Mr. and Mrs. North and Miss Hunt out there. You might ask Mrs. North to come in."

Mullins' face brightened.

"Jeez," he said. "Is Pam and Jerry here? And Miss Hunt?" He beamed. "We've had some times," he said, hopefully. Then his face clouded. "Only they was always screwy ones," he remembered. "The cases, I mean."

Weigand agreed that they were.

"And this one," he added, "doesn't seem to be any too clear." He drummed on the table. "You might chase the boys out of the living-room—have them ask some questions of somebody, or go over the tablecloth or something. Is there anybody else left?"

"Only," Mullins said, "this bus-boy guy. Just a kid, he is."

Weigand said Mullins could send the kid in. The kid came in. He had red hair, clashing with the maroon of his uniform, and he looked at Weigand with round eyes.

"Say, mister," he said, "are you a detective?"

Weigand admitted it.

"An officer?" Frank Kensitt insisted. "One of the mucky-mucks?"

"What?" said Weigand. "Oh. Yes, in a way. Why?"

Frank looked around anxiously, with wide blue eyes. The eyes fell on the body, and the boy said, "Jeez." Then, unexpectedly, his eyes filled with tears. After a moment he spoke angrily through the tears.

"Listen, mister," he said, "Miss Winston was a swell lady. Did somebody bump her?"

Weigand nodded.

"Did you know her, Frank?" he asked. Frank nodded. He sure had known her, he said.

"She got me this job," he said. "And got me out of the farm school and everything. She was a swell lady."

Weigand probed. Frank was, it developed, a ward of the "office." Weigand puzzled it a moment. "The Placement Foundation?" he suggested. Frank nodded. He was too old for adoption when the "office" took him and, after several other places, he had gone to the farm. And Miss Winston had got him out and got him a job and if any guy thought—

"All right, kid," Weigand said. He would, he supposed, have to follow this up, or have it followed up. But he had better get it from—who was that, now?—Mary Crane, at the Foundation. "Why did you clear the table so fast, kid?"

Frank looked around the room.

"Is there anybody else here?" he asked, tensely. Weigand shook his head.

"All right," Frank said. "They're in my locker!"

"Who are in your locker?" Weigand inquired.

Frank looked annoyed, and his voice was impatient.

"The dishes," he said. "The things Miss Winston ate and drank out of. What did you think?"

"You mean," Weigand said, "that you cleared the table and put all the dishes in your locker? Why?"

Frank looked contemptuous.

"Fingerprints," he said. "And things like that. I knew it wasn't no pass-out, not no ordinary pass-out. Not with Miss Winston. So I saved the things."

"Well," Weigand said, "I'll be damned." He looked at Frank, who was regarding him intently. "Well, I'll be damned," Weigand said. "You're quite a kid."

"You want 'em, don't you?" Frank's voice was anxious. Weigand nodded.

"Yes," he said. "I'll send a man with you to get them." Suddenly he grinned at the boy. "Only why fingerprints, son?" he said. "Why not some poison left in a glass or on a plate?"

Frank stared harder.

"Jeez," he said. "Sure enough!"

# • 5 •

The body of Lois Winston went in a long basket, down a service elevator, to an ambulance marked "Department of Hospitals. Mortuary Division." Nicholas arrived in time to stand aside for it, looking a little ill, as it was carried through the door of the suite. He looked after it and shook his head gravely, paying tribute to death.

"Yes?" Weigand said. He was sitting in a lounge chair in the living-room, and his nervous fingers tapped a cigarette against the side of an ash-tray.

"About Mr. McIntosh's reservation," Nicholas said. "You asked me to check on it."

"Right," Weigand said. "And—?"

"He appears to have telephoned himself," Nicholas said. "At least my assistant who took the reservation says a man called. He specified a table near the floor, although usually he preferred one of the divans against the wall."

"Right," Weigand said. He stared through Nicholas for a moment. "Suppose," he said, "you give me a list of all reservations made for this evening. You can do that?"

38

There was, Nicholas admitted, a list. But the manager would have to approve. If—

"All I want is the list," Weigand said. His voice sounded tired. "I don't care who has to approve. The manager, Mr. Ritz or the whole waiters' union. Just get me the list."

"Yes, sir," Nicholas said. He moved to the door and opened it. He became, instantly, Nicholas of the Ritz-Plaza.

"But I am very sorry, ladies-sir," he said. "This is a private apartment and I regret—"

"Nonsense," Pam North said, briskly, appearing around Nicholas. "Tell him, Bill!"

Bill told him. Pam came in and Dorian behind her. Mr. North, looking rather worried, followed them.

"Well," Weigand said. "A delegation. Sit, friends. Join me in a little murder."

Pam looked doubtfully at the closed door to the bedroom.

"Is it?" she said, and nodded at the door.

Weigand told her it was.

"They just took it," he said. "It was Lois Winston, of East Sixty-third Street and the Placement Foundation, daughter of the late Clarence Winston, who was an oil man, and the present Mrs. Kenneth Ashley who—" Then he stopped and looked annoyed. He looked around for Mullins and sighed. He emerged from the chair and sought Mullins at the door and returned with Mullins, who beamed at the Norths and Dorian.

"Hello, Mrs. North," Mullins said, pleased. "And Mr. North. And Miss Hunt! Sorta like old times, ain't it?"

"Hello, Mr. Mullins," Pam said. "It's nice—" She stopped and looked at him more intently. "By the way," she said, "I've been meaning to ask. Have you got a first name? To call you by, I mean."

Mullins suddenly looked sheepish and looked hurriedly at Lieutenant Weigand. Weigand nodded, remorselessly.

"Tell her, sergeant," he ordered. Mullins swallowed.

"Aloysius," he said, his voice suddenly booming. "Aloysius Clarence."

He looked at the Norths and Dorian defiantly. Mrs. North looked rather blank.

"Oh!" she said. "Oh—all right, Mullins." She looked at him gently. "I'm sorry," she said.

"Thanks, Mrs. North," Mullins said, warmly. "The times I—"

Weigand broke in, told him to save it.

"Get on the phone," he instructed, "and find out if Kenneth Ashley—the father of the squirt who was just here—is alive. Or what."

"O.K., Loot," Mullins said. He looked around for a telephone book, mutely indicated its absence, and exited.

"Listen," Pam said, "we've got something." She turned to Mr. North. "Where is he?" she demanded. "I thought you were going to bring him."

"Look, Pam," Mr. North said, anxiously, "you're not going to get into this one, are you?" His voice was pleading, but not very hopeful. "He's outside. I left him with a detective. But I don't really think—"

"Who," Weigand wanted to know, "is outside with a detective?" He looked at Pam, and his expression oddly mirrored that of Mr. North. "Please, Pam," he urged. "After all, I'm working here."

Pam looked a little indignant, and then softened. She said all she wanted was a chance. She said it was a waiter who had seen something.

"We got to talking while we waited," Pam said, "and then we sort of talked to our waiter, because maybe he had seen things." She looked at Mr. North, who was shaking his head. "Well," she said, "anyway, I did. And Dorian did, too. And it turned out he had seen something at—at the murder table."

"Listen, Pam," Mr. North said, "have you got to be so tabloid?"

Nobody paid any attention to him. Weigand looked interested and went to the door. He returned with a waiter, who looked worried.

"The lady," the waiter said, doubtfully. "She thought I ought—"

"Right," Weigand said. "You saw something?"

The waiter, a No. 67 by the disk on his coat, had seen something. Nothing, he supposed, important. But he had been near the table at which McIntosh and Miss Winston were sitting and had been looking around idly, with nobody to serve at the moment and a waiter's glance for the tables. The man and the girl who, somebody said, was dead—well, they had got up to dance. And while they were dancing, a man had come to their table from another table some way off and bent over it.

"I thought he seemed to be sticking something, perhaps a note, under the lady's plate," the waiter explained.

"And would you know the man?" Weigand asked. His tone was quick with interest.

"Yes, sir," the waiter said. "I—but perhaps I should speak to the manager, sir." He looked for advice.

"Just speak to me," Weigand directed. "You knew him, I gather?"

No. 67 looked rather unhappy, and nodded. He was the young man who had been summoned, a little later, to the living-room by a detective. After the girl had collapsed and been carried there. He was a dark, rather good-looking young man, rather slight.

Weigand nodded.

"And that was all you saw?" he asked. No. 67 shook his head. There was, he said, something else.

"After the young lady was—was carried in here," he said, "the young man went back to the table. He—well, I assumed he picked up the note."

"Why do you assume that?" Weigand asked. No. 67 looked a little confused.

"I suppose you looked, and there wasn't any note?" Weigand said. The waiter nodded. "Touch anything?" Weigand wanted to know. The waiter shook his head.

"Right," Weigand said. "I'll see that the manager doesn't mind. And thanks."

The waiter went away, still looking worried.

"Is it something?" Mrs. North said eagerly. "Is it a clue, or something?"

Weigand nodded slowly.

"Anyway," he said, "it was Mr. Randall Ashley doing something at his sister's table." He thought it over. "I'm afraid," he said, "that I'm going to have to break in on Mr. Ashley's sleep."

He looked at his watch. It was a little after eleven. There was a knock at the door and a detective handed in a long sheet with names typed on it. Whoever needed to had approved the surrender to the police of a copy of the reservation list of the Club Plaza, on the roof of the Ritz-Plaza Hotel, for the evening of Tuesday, July 28.

Weigand looked at the Norths and Dorian without seeing them. Then he saw Dorian and smiled. It was warming to see a smile answer him.

"Bill," Dorian said, suddenly, "I hope you catch him."

It was surprising from Dorian, who so hated all pursuit, all "hunting," and who had such excellent reason for hating it. Weigand was conscious of delighted astonishment and for a moment was puzzled by it. Then he realized that, for the first time, Dorian had abandoned the separation she had always maintained between Weigand as Weigand, and Weigand as police lieutenant. She had, and quite consciously, come over to his side and he felt very contented about it. He looked at Dorian appreciatively, and it occurred to him that he was beaming at her even before Pam North spoke.

"Lieutenant Weigand," Pam said. "Remember there are Norths present." She paused until he looked at her. "And murderers to catch," she added.

Weigand looked back at Dorian and they shared contented laughter with a glance. Then Weigand sighed and returned to duty. He went to the door and called Mullins and Mullins came.

The boys, Mullins reported, were asking questions around, without getting much of anywhere that he could see. Mullins was pessimistic. The dishes from Lois Winston's place had been salvaged from Frank Kensitt's locker. Half an inch of liquid in the bottom of a glass which apparently had contained a Cuba Libre had been bottled and labeled, as had what remained in a water glass. The glass from which, according to McIntosh's account, she had drunk iced coffee apparently had been returned to the kitchen when the drinks were served, as had the plates on the table. The bottles had been dispatched to the city toxicologist at Bellevue for analysis. Weigand nodded, checking off.

"I think we're finished here," he said then. "For now, anyway. We'll leave the boys to go on with their questioning for a while. Tell them to report at the division later. You and I'll be moving, Mullins."

"What," Mrs. North wanted to know, "about us? Do you just throw us back?"

"Well," Mr. North said, "we could always go home and—play three-handed bridge."

Mrs. North looked at him coldly and said, "Bridge!

"Bridge after murder!" she said. "You do think of the dullest things sometimes, Jerry."

She looked hopefully at Weigand, who shook his head.

"No, Pam," he said. "I'm not taking the three of you. Or even one of you. You're big boys and girls; you'll just have to think of something."

"Well," Pam said, "I think we'll go out and have another drink. I want a Cuba—" She broke off. "Or," she said, "perhaps a very weak brandy and soda. Come on."

She went and Mr. North went after her. Mullins, after a glance, went after them. Bill Weigand and Dorian stood and looked at each other.

"Hello, Dorian," Bill said, softly. She smiled.

"Hello, Bill," she said.

"She was about my age, Bill, or just a little older," Dorian said. "Wasn't she?"

"Yes," Weigand said. "About that."

"She must have wanted to do so many things," Dorian said slowly. "She must have thought there was time for a lot of things."

Weigand merely nodded. There seemed to be nothing much to say. Lois Winston was probably two or three years older than Dorian, he thought, and he wondered whether, a few hours ago, she had stood and moved as Dorian did.

"Well," Dorian said, "it sounds funny from me, Bill, but—good hunting."

There wasn't anything to say to that, either. It was merely something which stretched back between them to a day when she had had a good deal to say about men who were, professionally, hunters. But there was nothing which needed to be said about it.

"Well," she said, and paused, "I must be in the way." She looked at him. "Take care of yourself," she said, only half lightly.

Then, moving with that singular, balanced grace of hers, she was gone from the room. Police Lieutenant Weigand replaced Bill Weigand. The lieutenant went to the door and said, crisply:

"Mullins!"

Mullins reappeared.

"He's dead," Mullins said. "Airplane crash."

"What?" said Weigand. "Who's dead?"

Mullins looked hurt.

"This guy Ashley," he said. "This guy Ashley's father. The guy you were asking about."

"Oh," said Weigand. "So Kenneth Ashley's dead, is he?" He wondered vaguely why he had wanted to know. Then he roused himself. "Right," he said. "Now we're going places."

Mullins said, "O.K., Loot."

# • 6 •

TUESDAY

11:25 P.M., TO WEDNESDAY, 1:40 A.M.

The Buick stopped outside the apartment house in East Sixty-third Street and a man sauntered over, looking vaguely as if he were going to give advice on parking and offer to wash her off. Weigand nodded to him.

"Upstairs," the man said, jerking his head toward the building. "He came right along, with the dame."

"Right," Weigand said. The detective drifted off, to loiter in low visibility. It was convenient that Randall Ashley had come home and brought the girl—something Ormond, Weigand recalled—with him. Weigand slid from behind the wheel and Mullins joined him on the sidewalk. They went in and up, ignoring an attendant who was disposed to announce them. A slight, blond maid in uniform answered their ring, and Weigand told her they had come to see Mr. Ashley. The girl, he thought, looked pale, and as if she had been crying.

Neither Ashley nor Madge Ormond appeared to have been crying. Both had glasses. They sat together on a sofa in the long living-room and had, Weigand felt, been talking intently when they were interrupted. Ashley twisted to face them, frowned and stood up.

"Well, Lieutenant?" he said, coldly and with a little too much dignity. Weigand nodded to him; to the girl, who was also blond, but neither pale nor weeping. She was the sort of girl for whom almost any man could imagine himself going. Weigand observed with dispassionate interest. She looked back at him, levelly.

"Sit down, Mr. Ashley," Weigand directed, as he and Mullins crossed the room toward them. Mullins looked around the room, taking in the size of the apartment. "Wow!" said Mullins softly. "Quite a joint!"

"I want to know—" Ashley began again.

"Sit down," Weigand instructed.

"Look, detective," the girl said. "You can't bully him."

"Can't I?" said Weigand. "Who told you that, sister? Sure I can bully him."

"Sure," said Mullins, approvingly. "Didn't you know that, sister?"

The girl looked at him.

"Flatfoot," she said, disparagingly. Mullins began to get red. Weigand looked at him and Mullins swallowed and said, "O.K., sister."

"Let's see that note," Weigand said.

Ashley appeared to be very astonished.

"Uh-huh," Weigand said. "The note you left for your sister. And took away again after she collapsed. Let's see it!"

"You don't have to show him anything, Buddy," the girl said. "You don't have to tell him anything."

Ashley turned on her.

"I'll handle it, Madge," he said. He turned to Weigand. "I haven't anything to tell you, Lieutenant," he said. "I don't know what note you're talking about."

"Right," Weigand said. "If you want to play it that way. I thought there was a chance the note didn't mean anything, in which case we wouldn't have to take you downtown. The way things are, of course—" He left the sentence unfinished, looking down at Ashley. "Don't be a sap, Ashley," he said.

Ashley returned Weigand's gaze for a moment. Then he looked away and hesitated.

"All right," he said. "It wasn't anything. Merely a note to tell her I wanted to talk with her tonight about something important, and to wait up for me if she came in first. When I saw that she was ill, I just picked up the note so that it wouldn't be lying around for anybody else to—" he faltered.

"Let's see it," Weigand said, holding out his hand. There wasn't, Weigand knew, any good reason why Ashley should have kept the note, or why he should hand it over. But it was worth trying. He was gratified to see Ashley's right hand move instinctively toward a pocket. The hand hesitated.

"Right," Weigand said. "Hand it over."

It was a small note, twice folded. It read:

*"I've got to see you before you talk to M. So wait up for me and don't think you can get out of it.—Bud."*

"You're 'Bud'?" Weigand inquired.

Ashley nodded, sullenly.

"That's what Lois called me," he said. "Lots of people do, as a matter of fact."

"And who is 'M'?" Weigand asked.

Ashley started rebellion and abandoned it.

"Mother," he said. "It hasn't anything to do with this."

It was easy enough, however, to get a story out of him. It was easier after Madge Ormond, hearing him start, looked at him with contempt, but with affection, and said that if he was going to spill everything he knew, she was going home. She looked at Weigand.

"If that's all right with you, Commissioner?" she said, heavily ironic.

Weigand said, without expression, that it was all right with him.

"Call me up, Buddy, after—after you've sung your song," she said. Ashley appeared about to say something, but didn't. He merely nodded. Mullins looked inquiringly at Weigand, who shook his head. The headshake implied that there was no reason, at the moment, to waste a man on Miss Ormond's footsteps.

Then Buddy sang a song. It was, as Weigand had supposed it would be, a song about money. It was also, as Weigand had likewise expected, rather inadequate, sounding as if several verses had been left out.

Weigand would, Buddy said, have to get the background. "My father's dead," Ashley explained. Weigand nodded. The elder Ashley had died about two years previously, leaving a considerable fortune, the bulk of it to Randall Ashley, but under certain provisions. It was clear that Kenneth Ashley had not thought highly of his son's discretion, particularly in certain matters. The money was to be held in trust until Randall was twenty-five, and paid to him then only in the event he was not married. If he was married, he was to receive only a stipulated income, the principal to be divided among his children, if any, only when the youngest of them had reached the age of twenty-five. It was, Randall said bitterly, a lousy setup.

"I'd got—well, got mixed up with a girl Dad didn't like," Randall explained. "That was a year or so before he died. So he fixed it so that I'd think twice."

"And," Weigand pointed out, "so that there would be no percentage in it for a gold-digger. In marrying you, I mean."

Randall Ashley nodded.

"Well?" Weigand prompted.

There was, however, a provision which modified this arrangement. Mrs. Ashley, so long as she lived or in the event of her death, Lois Winston, had power to set the restrictions aside. As things stood, Mrs. Ashley could, if she chose, give approval to any marriage her son might make. In the event she approved and in the event that the marriage did not occur before he was twenty-one, Randall would receive the principal at once.

"Um," Weigand said, thoughtfully. "Yes, I see. So?"

"Well," Randall said simply, "I want to get married."

"Miss Ormond?" Weigand asked. Randall nodded.

"And?" Weigand said, since Ashley seemed to be running down. "Does your mother oppose it?"

That, Randall said, was the point. There was no reason why she should oppose it. But Lois had.

"Why?" Weigand wanted to know.

"I don't know," Randall said. He didn't, Weigand thought, say it as if he really didn't know. Weigand waited.

"Well," Randall said, "you don't know Mother, of course. She will—that is, she always would—listen to anything Lois said. What I said was nothing, what Lois said was gospel." He reported this bitterly. "Mother has been on Long Island most of the summer and doesn't know about Madge. She's coming back tomorrow for a day or so, and I knew that Lois would go to her at once and prejudice her against Madge. So I wanted to see Lois before she talked to Mother. I tried this evening, but she was dressing and wouldn't talk to me. So I wanted to be sure to catch her tonight."

He looked at Weigand, and there seemed to the detective to be a kind of challenge in his look. Weigand decided not to meet it, at the moment.

"Right," Weigand said. "That explains the note, I guess." He smiled at Ashley. "Not so complicated when you explain it," he said. "You shouldn't have made such a fuss about it." He watched Ashley's face, expecting to see relaxation in it. He saw relaxation in it and what might be smug self-congratulation. If Weigand had any reservations about the story—as I have, Weigand thought—young Ashley didn't realize it. Young Ashley felt the story had gone over big. That, Weigand decided, was as it should be. He started to rise, seemed to think better of it.

"By the way," he said, "I wish you'd look over this list of names." He handed Randall the reservation list from the Ritz-Plaza. "See any you know on it?" he inquired. "Besides McIntosh, of course."

It was a long list and Randall plodded slowly down it. Weigand watched him. He was a good-looking young man, Weigand thought, but he obviously drank too much. There was a kind of querulous expression in the relaxed face. "He looks like a sulky kid," Weigand thought. "And like a selfish one." Weigand hadn't much doubt he was both. Randall finished the list.

"I know one or two," he said. "But there's nobody we knew well—I mean that Lois and I knew well, or Mother. There are a couple of men I've bumped into, and some I've heard about. That's all."

"Which?" Weigand said. Randall pointed, and Weigand checked them off. Several were names known to people who read society pages; one or two appeared now and then in gossip columns. But there were not many checked, and none which seemed to mean anything. Weigand said thanks, and that he guessed that was all, for now.

"I suppose, though," he added, "that I might have a look at your sister's room. Just as a matter of routine."

He got up and Mullins got up. Then, in no hurry, Ashley got up and led the way upstairs. Mullins was impressed by the stairs. "Some joint," he whispered to Weigand. "Duplex and everything. It musta set them back."

Weigand nodded. It certainly must have set somebody back. But he gathered Mrs. Ashley could stand it, married twice to men in commodities. It made him think of something.

"By the way," he said, "did your sister inherit money—from her father, that is? He had money, I suppose."

"Plenty," Randall said. "Yes. Lois got most of it, except for a trust fund for Mother. When Mother dies Lois gets—Lois would have gotten—that too. Why?"

"Well," said Weigand, "we just like to know about such things. Who gets it now?"

"I don't," Randall said, rather hotly. "If that's what you mean."

Weigand said he hadn't meant anything. He just wanted to know.

"Well," Randall said, "*I* don't know. Except that she had made a will. You can find out from that, I suppose."

Weigand said he supposed he could.

Randall led them down a short corridor on the second floor of the duplex and opened a door. Lois Winston's bedroom was large, with French windows opening on a small terrace. It was done in soft tones of yellow and gray. Weigand noticed with an odd feeling that the bed had been turned back. He noticed a silvered thermos on the table by the bed and crossed to it, lifting the top. It was filled with water. The room, he thought, looked as if it had been lived in happily, and as if it had nothing to tell of unhappiness and death. Then he noticed, on the table beside the thermos, a heavy book—a volume, a glance told him, of the Encyclopædia Britannica. He lifted it idly. It was Volume 11, Gunn to Hydrox. Into the light-hued room it brought an inappropriate suggestion of weighty contemplation.

"I wonder," he said aloud, "what she had been reading in that?"

Nobody answered. Weigand supposed to himself that it had nothing to do with him. But it was an anomaly, and faint curiosity still stirred.

"Did your sister have a personal maid?" he asked Randall Ashley.

"Yes," Randall said. "At least, she and Mother shared Anna. Why?"

"I'd like to see her," Weigand said. Ashley looked about for somebody to send. Neither Weigand nor Mullins moved. Ashley went into the hall and called, "Anna!" Then he came back. Weigand crossed to a desk and opened it, looking at papers in pigeon-holes. A drawer was crowded with papers and photographs. All this would have to be gone through, but not now.

"We'll take this along," he told Ashley. Randall Ashley nodded, indifferently. There was a knock at the half-open door and Weigand, turning, said "Yes?" to Anna. Anna was a tall, spare woman of forty, her face gray and drawn. But her voice was unshaking and quiet.

"Yes, sir?" She said it to Randall Ashley, but Weigand answered.

"I'm a police lieutenant, Anna," he said. "I want to ask you a question or two."

"Yes, sir." Anna's voice was still quiet.

"I want to know what Miss Winston did this afternoon and evening," he explained. "When she came home, what she did, anything you remember she said."

Anna told him. Miss Lois had come home a little before six, spoken to Mr. Randall and his friends in the living-room and gone to her own room, after telling Mary that she wanted Anna. Then she had bathed and rested for perhaps an hour and then Anna had helped her dress to go out with Mr. McIntosh, who came for her about half-past seven. She remembered nothing of importance.

"I wanted to talk to her, Anna, don't you remember?" Randall said. "And she was dressing or something?"

Yes, Anna remembered that. It was not, she indicated, of importance. And nothing else? She could think of nothing else. The last she had seen of Miss Lois was when the girl left the room to join Mr. McIntosh.

"I stayed and—turned down her bed," Anna said. Her voice hesitated for a moment as she spoke, but regained its soft steadiness.

"You were very fond of Miss Winston, weren't you, Anna?" Weigand said.

"Yes, sir," Anna said. She did not amplify, or need to.

"By the way," Weigand said, "this copy of the Encyclopædia. It wasn't usually kept here, I suppose? Did she read it today, do you know?"

Anna remembered and seemed surprised.

"Why, yes," she said. "She had me get it for her a few minutes after she came in. I had forgotten."

"Did she read it, do you know?"

Anna thought she must have. It was lying on the bed, open and face down, when she straightened up after Miss Winston had left. Anna had picked it up and closed it, and put it on the table. Weigand said, "Um-m-m.

"You didn't," he asked, "happen to notice what page it was opened to? Or what subject?"

Anna shook her head.

"It was open about the middle," she said. "I didn't notice exactly."

"No," Weigand said. "There was no reason why you should. Probably it doesn't matter."

He turned to Ashley.

"We'll be going, now," he said. "I'll send a man in for the papers in your sister's desk—he'll be right in. And I'll want to see your mother when she gets in tomorrow. You've got in touch with her, I suppose?"

Ashley had. He had persuaded her not to come in tonight, but to wait until morning. Weigand nodded, and led the way out of the bedroom. Downstairs, the maid who had admitted them waited in the foyer to show them out.

"A drink or something?" Ashley said. Mullins looked hopeful, but Weigand shook his head.

"No, thanks," he said.

Ashley turned into the living-room and the maid opened the door. But then she stepped through after them and closed it behind her, so that the latch just failed to catch. Weigand looked down at her. She was a slight, pretty thing, now pale and agitated.

"Yes?" he said.

She spoke rapidly, excitedly.

"I've got to tell you," she said. "You ought to know. They're married. I heard them tonight when they thought I wasn't around and they're married. He said, 'Now that we're married.'"

"Who is this?" Weigand said. "Mr. Ashley?"

"Him," she said. "Buddy. And that singer girl. They're married, only nobody is supposed to know."

She spoke breathlessly.

"I tell you they're married!" she said. "And all the time he was—"

She broke off and looked up at Weigand. She was obviously about to cry.

"All right," he said. "I'm glad you told me. But I wouldn't worry about it—" He paused. "What is your name?" he asked.

"Mary," the girl said. "Mary Holden. But it doesn't matter."

Then, while he still looked at her curiously, she was through the door and had closed it behind her.

"Well," Mullins said, "what d'y know?"

"That Randall and his girl friend have hurried things a bit," Weigand told him. "And that Randall stands to lose a lot of money if it comes out. And that there is a chance his sister knew about it. What do you know, Mullins?"

"That this girl Mary is crazy about our Buddy," Mullins told him. "Is, or was. Right?"

"Right," Weigand said.

It necessitated a change of plan, Weigand decided, riding down in the elevator. He had planned to send the detective who had been trailing Randall Ashley to get the papers in Lois's desk, and take them to Headquarters. But now he wasn't sure; he thought it might be worth while keeping an eye on Ashley. He looked speculatively at Mullins, and nodded to himself. Mullins caught the nod and interpreted it.

"Listen, Loot—" Mullins began. Weigand stopped him.

"You'd better go back and get those papers, Mullins," Weigand said. "Take them to Headquarters and sit on them. We'll keep Conroy on Buddy."

The elevator stopped at the ground floor. Weigand got out. Mullins looked resigned and stayed in, reascending. Outside, Weigand spoke a word to the loitering detective. Then Weigand, after a glance at his watch, found a telephone. He called Bellevue Hospital, asked for the Pathology Building and got it. He asked for Dr. Jerome Francis and, after a pause, got him.

"Well," said Weigand, "how're you coming?"

"Listen," Dr. Francis said. His voice sounded tired. "Did you ever do an autopsy?"

Weigand asked him what he thought.

"Well," Dr. Francis said, "did anybody ever tell you it takes time? Or that analysis takes time? Call me tomorrow afternoon. Or Thursday morning. Maybe I'll have something."

"No," said Weigand, "I can't wait that long. What have you got now?"

"She's dead," Dr. Francis said, with heavy sarcasm. "I cut her up and she was dead. Thirty minutes for the autopsy, which is damned fast going, if you want to know." He paused. "Except for the head, of course," he added, honestly.

"What killed her?" Weigand wanted to know.

"I'm telling you I don't know yet." Dr. Francis' voice tried patience. "She didn't die naturally, so far as I can tell. The organs are perfectly normal. Her pupils were dilated. So I think she got a parasympathetic poison—probably belladonna or atropine. But that's what I told you before."

"I want to know definitely what killed her," Weigand said. "Isn't there any way you can tell? How long will a chemical analysis take?"

"About two days," Francis told him.

"Any other way of telling?" Weigand wanted to know. Dr. Francis hesitated.

"Well," he said, "I can run a biological test. It won't be decisive, but it will tell something. And I guess we can spare a guinea-pig. Call me in the morning."

"No," Weigand said. "I'll come down and see you. And the guinea-pig. And you can tell me what it means." He hung up. Francis would be there; grumbling but there. Weigand got the Buick and rolled downtown toward Bellevue. He was thinking. He tried to tell himself he was thinking about the case, and tried really to think about the case. But Dorian kept coming in.

At Bellevue he walked through the morgue, nodding to an attendant and not looking at the cupboards of the dead. In one of them, he supposed, was what remained of Lois Winston, who only a few hours ago must have been thinking of what she would do tomorrow. Francis was in the autopsy room. He was smoking a cigarette, gloomily. He wondered, audibly, if Weigand didn't know that even doctors sleep.

"So do detectives, when the chance arises," Weigand told him. "How's the test coming?"

"I was waiting for you," Francis told him. "Come along."

He led Weigand to the animal room but he ignored guinea-pigs, clustered softly in a cage. He went on, opened another cage and said, "Come on, kitty. Nice kitty." The nice kitty, a formidable gray bruiser with one devastated ear, hissed at him. Francis looked into the cage, doubtfully, and closed it.

"I think I'll get some gloves," he said. He got some gloves. "Andy doesn't like experiments," the doctor explained, opening the cage again. Andy emerged, well gripped and snarling.

"I thought you said a guinea-pig," Weigand said. "You can't fool me, Doc. That's a cat." Weigand looked at Andy, who sneered. "Quite a cat," Weigand said. "Do we have to kill a cat?"

"Who said anything about killing it?" Francis wanted to know. "And as for the guinea-pig—that was metaphor. Andy, here, is a metaphorical guinea-pig." He looked at Weigand, who regarded him questioningly. Francis seemed somewhat flustered. "Oh," he said, "all right. I did think of using a guinea-pig. They're always handy. But I checked up, and guinea-pigs won't do."

"Why?" Weigand wanted to know. "I thought guinea-pigs always did." Francis shook his head.

"Not for atropine," he explained. "Guinea-pigs eat it—thrive on it. In the wild state, anyway; we don't feed them atropine here. But they normally eat plants which have a large atropine content and don't turn a hair. They tolerate the poison so well, as a matter of fact, that it would take about as much atropine to kill a guinea-pig as it would to kill a man. And, of course, there's another difficulty."

"Is there?" Weigand's voice was mild.

Dr. Francis nodded.

"Human blood serum is almost as deadly to a guinea-pig as atropine is," he said. "If we injected enough blood to carry a normally lethal dose of atropine into the pig, the pig would die of the blood first. The atropine wouldn't make any difference. So I decided not to use a pig."

"I think you were very wise," Weigand assured the doctor, who looked at him suspiciously and then grinned.

"O.K.," he said. "O.K. I just looked it up. I don't carry everything in my head. Do you?"

"No," Weigand said. "How about the cat?"

Francis had been holding Andy, who was still annoyed, pressed against the top of a laboratory table. He looked down at Andy, who looked up at him, balefully, the black pupils of his eyes large and indignant in the normally lighted room. Francis, keeping both hands on the cat, nodded toward the cat's eyes.

"See the pupils," he directed. "It seems light enough in here to us, but the cat's eyes know better. Out in the sun, the pupils would be slits. Now—here, hold him a minute."

Weigand held Andy down on the table and scratched behind a pointed ear. Andy seemed a little placated. Francis wheeled a hooded lamp over and turned it on. Powerful white light beat down on Andy and Weigand's hands.

"Look at his eyes," Francis directed. Weigand looked. The pupils had narrowed to shut out the light.

"Now," Francis said, producing what appeared to be a medicine dropper, "I've got blood serum here, taken from Lois Winston's heart during the autopsy. I'll—hold that cat!"

Andy, taking advantage of Weigand's preoccupation, lurched under the detective's hands. Weigand's fingers closed, just in time, on departing hindquarters. Andy was rearranged.

"Hold his head up a little," Francis directed. Weigand got a finger under the cat's chin and lifted.

"Now," Francis said. "I'll put one drop of the serum in his right eye. Watch."

Francis, while Andy glared darkly at him, held the dropper over the cat's face. A drop came out. It hit the cat's nose, thanks to Andy's quick movement. Francis steadied the cat's head and dropped again. The second drop went into the right eye. Andy jumped under Weigand's hands, which this time were ready. Andy yowled.

"Watch the eye," Francis directed. Weigand watched. For a moment nothing happened. Then the pupil began to widen. The pupil of the left eye remained contracted against the light. Francis switched it off.

"No reason to blind the beast," he said. "You saw how they were. Now look at the right one."

The pupil of the right eye, now, was almost fully dilated. Even with the flood light off, the pupil of the left eye had dilated only a little. Andy looked oddly lopsided.

"O.K.," Francis said. "There's your test." He lifted Andy and put him back in his cage. "All right, boy," he told the cat. "It'll wear off after a while." He turned to Weigand.

"There you are," he said. "It was atropine, all right. There was enough atropine in the blood to dilate a cat's eyes—and enough to kill a girl. Probably administered in the form of atropine sulphate. Which dissolves in almost anything."

Weigand nodded.

"Good enough," he said. "Tell me about atropine sulphate."

Dr. Francis told him. Atropine sulphate was a drug used in medicine—in ophthalmology, for example; internally to check secretions; sometimes in cases of surgical shock to stimulate respiration and circulation. It acted by stimulating the higher nerve centers, while at the same time paralyzing the peripheral endings of the nerves of the autonomic system.

"Well, well," Weigand said. "Think of that. What does it look like?"

"It's a powder," Dr. Francis told him. "A white powder. No odor. No strong taste. At least, that's what they say. I never tasted it myself. The dose is very small, normally from one-two-hundredth to one-one-hundredth of a grain. A grain ought to kill a couple of people."

"How quickly?" Weigand wanted to know. Francis lifted his shoulders. It depended on the dose. Since it wasn't a custom to give lethal doses of atropine sulphate to humans, the data was incomplete. But from a few minutes to a couple of hours, depending on the size of dose, and other conditions.

"I'd say your subject got quite a dose," he added. "Probably about a grain."

It wasn't satisfactory, Weigand decided. Lois might have got the poison before she left home; she might have got it at the restaurant table shortly before she collapsed. But that wasn't, obviously, Dr. Francis' fault.

"How would you get it?" he asked. "I mean, just walk into a drugstore and say, 'I'd like some atropine sulphate, please. About enough to kill a guy!'"

"Well," Francis said, "*I'd* requisition it. But—no, I don't suppose you could get it at a retail store." He thought it over.

"I'll tell you," he said. "You could go to a drug supply house and say you were a manufacturer and wanted some atropine sulphate. If you looked all right, or went to the trouble of having letterheads printed or something, they'd sell it to you. There's no law against it."

"What would I be manufacturing?" Weigand wanted to know.

"What?" said Francis. "Oh—eyewash, of course. It's used, in minute quantities, in several commercial eyewashes. Makes the eye bright and glowing. See advertisements."

"Really?" said Weigand.

"Sure," said Francis. "Doesn't do any great harm, probably. Or much good, of course."

Weigand thought it over.

"How much is a grain?" he asked. "I mean, as to bulk. A table-spoonful?"

Francis looked at him in surprise.

"The things you people don't know!" he said, sadly. "You could pick it up on the tip-end of an after-dinner coffee spoon. You could hold it between your thumb and forefinger."

"So," said Weigand gently, "the medical profession naturally refers to it as a 'massive' dose. Very illuminating, Doctor."

But the doctor, he decided as he left the Pathology Building, had been illuminating enough. He thought it wearily and looked at his watch. It was after one o'clock. He thought of things he might do tonight and thought he might do them, also, in the morning. He telephoned Headquarters and conferred with Mullins. The detectives who had questioned customers at the roof had made reports but Mullins thought there was little in them. Mullins was sitting on the papers. The laboratory had not reported on the contents of the glasses taken by young Kensitt from Lois' table.

"Well," Weigand said, "call it a night. But get in early."

He turned from the telephone and drove across and uptown to his apartment in the West Fifties. The telephone was ringing. Weigand scooped it up and said, "Yes? Weigand speaking."

"Pam North speaking," she told him. "I couldn't sleep and neither could Jerry. What? No, of course I won't."

"Wait a minute, Pam," Weigand said. "What won't you?"

"Jerry says to tell you the only reason he can't sleep is that I keep talking," Pam said. "Only I won't, of course."

"No, Pam," Weigand said, "I wouldn't. What is it, Pam?"

"Well," said Pam, "have you found out who?"

"No, Pam."

"Or how?"

"Well," Weigand said, "as to that, yes. Somebody gave her something called atropine sulphate. A parasympathetic drug."

"Oh, yes," Pam said. "Paralyzes the nerve endings of the sympathetic system. How awful!"

Weigand restrained his gasp.

"How—" he began, and thought better of it. "Somebody gave it to her in a drink," he said. "It would only take about a grain, the M. E. says."

"Well," Pam said, "how would they carry it around in a restaurant?"

He had her there, Bill Weigand decided. He said he was afraid she didn't realize how small in bulk a grain of atropine sulphate would be. One could carry it, he told her, between thumb and forefinger.

"Oh," said Mrs. North. "I see. You mean a pinch."

"What?" Weigand said. He was too tired to keep up, he decided.

"A pinch," Mrs. North told him. "Like a pinch of salt. Only in this case, a pinch of poison."

# • 7 •

Routine awaited Lieutenant Weigand Wednesday morning at Headquarters. Mullins also waited, reading the morning newspapers. He held one up and shook it as Weigand entered.

"The Herald-Trib got your name wrong again, Loot," Mullins told him. "I before E."

"Well," said Weigand, who was grumpy and whose mouth tasted of coffee and last night's cigarettes. "Well, think of that." He spoke without pleasure. Mullins looked at him, and decided the point had better be waived.

"It's a very popular crime, Loot," he said. "Very popular. Except the war sorta gets in the way, of course."

"All right," Weigand said. He looked at his desk, which held papers in neat piles. "All right, sergeant. What's here?"

There was, Mullins told him, a lotta junk. There were reports from the detectives who had asked questions of late diners at the Ritz-Plaza roof after the murder. "Nothing in 'em," Mullins reported. There was the stenographer's transcript of the questions asked by Weigand himself. There was a copy of the formal, interim report, made by the

61

offices of the Medical Examiner. Weigand knew more than it contained.

"And then there's the Inspector," Mullins added, glumly. Weigand nodded. There was always the Inspector. He looked at his watch and decided the Inspector could wait, for a few minutes. He read the transcript of the questions he had asked McIntosh, Buddy Ashley, Nicholas and the rest. He read fast, knowing his way, but exactly, looking for things missed.

At one point he said, "Huh!" and made a note. Mullins, watching, made sounds of inquiry.

"Something we missed?" Mullins wanted to know.

"No," Weigand said. "I got it at the time. I was just checking to see whether I was right. As I was, Sergeant Mullins."

Weigand's voice was, Mullins decided, thawing.

"Yeh?" Mullins said.

"The reservation," Weigand told him. "At the roof. McIntosh says he didn't have one—at least, that seems clear from what he said. He didn't know where he was taking the girl until they got in the cab. But the headwaiter says there was a reservation for McIntosh and the list shows it was made at"—he consulted the list—"six-fifteen that evening."

"Screwy," Mullins said. He thought. "Say," he said, "this guy McIntosh ain't telling all he knows." He paused and looked at Weigand hopefully. "Maybe we ought to bring him in, Loot?" he said. "You know. Just ask him some questions, sort of?"

Weigand shook his head, and said they didn't know enough. It was, Weigand pointed out, merely something to keep in mind. There might be a perfectly harmless explanation. Mullins looked doubtful.

"Like what?" he said.

Weigand shook his head.

"You think of it, Mullins," he said. He went on through the transcript. It ran about as he remembered it. It was all clear enough, as far as it went—clear, at any rate, as to what people said had happened. But neither the people nor what they meant was entirely clear. Lois Winston was not entirely clear herself.

Weigand said, "Um-m-m," thoughtfully, and the telephone rang on his desk. He said, "Yes?" and then, quickly, "Right, Inspector." Mullins drew his face down dolefully and Weigand looked at him darkly. Then Weigand replaced the telephone, smiled.

"We've got to have them," he said. "It's regulation. Now—"

Mullins was to get things rolling. He was to hurry the office of the City Toxicologist, in so far as was politic, for a final report on the poison which had killed the girl. The police laboratories, less diplomatically, were to be hurried in their reports on the contents of the identified flasks which contained the dregs of Lois Winston's glasses at the roof. And, because there was not really much doubt as to the poison, Mullins was to get men working on that. Briefly, Weigand told Mullins of the assistant medical examiner's guess about atropine sulphate, and his speculation as to how it might have been obtained.

"So," Weigand said, "we'll have to cover all the wholesale drug houses. It may be a job. What we want is a list of atropine sulphate purchases in the past few days. Where a purchase was made by a man they didn't know, we want all the details we can get."

"O.K., Loot," Mullins said.

"And," said Weigand, "we want it this afternoon. So get them started."

"Listen, Loot," Mullins started, but stopped when the lieutenant looked at him. "O.K.," Mullins repeated, with emphasis. "You want me to go along? Personally?"

"Why not?" Weigand said. "Only check in, in case I want you."

Mullins went. Weigand summoned Detective Stein, who was a bright young man and came in looking it.

"I want you to get hold of the Encyclopædia Britannica," Weigand told him. Detective Stein gulped, but kept on looking bright. "Not all of it," Weigand reassured him, seeing the gulp. "Volume Gunn to Hydrox."

"Yes, sir," Detective Stein said, and waited.

"Start about a third through and make a list of general subjects," Weigand instructed. "I don't want names, or descriptions of cities or historical data. I want something that a young woman of twenty-seven or thereabouts, with plenty of money and O.K. socially but working as a volunteer for a social work agency, would be reading a few hours before she got poisoned."

Weigand looked at Stein, who looked rather baffled. Weigand smiled.

"I don't know what I want," he admitted. "I don't even know if it bears on what we're after—the guy who killed the Winston girl. But maybe it does. Work from about a third of the way through the volume to about two-thirds of the way through."

"Yes, sir," Stein said. "She was reading it, you say?" Weigand nodded. "And left it face down somewhere, opened about the middle?"

"Right," Weigand said. "So see what you can get me, Sherlock." But this tone was amiable and, Detective Stein decided, approving. Detective Stein, looking brighter than ever, went out after Gunn to Hydrox.

Weigand looked after him, reached for the telephone and let his hand drop, and went in to see Deputy Chief Inspector Artemus O'Malley. O'Malley looked as if he had had a long, comfortable sleep. He was all brisk alertness, and ready to hear all about everything. Weigand told him what he knew. O'Malley nodded.

"The brother," he said, all having been made plain. "He figured the girl was going to tell their mother about the marriage. So he would have lost the money. He was there; he went to the table; he tells a thin story about a note, producing a note he probably wrote while he was waiting for you to come around. What do you want?"

"Well," Weigand said mildly, "a little evidence wouldn't hurt. Like an identification of little brother buying poison."

O'Malley was impatient.

"Sure," he said, "we'll get that. We'll bring the kid in and ask him some questions and maybe he'll spill it. Then he'll tell us where he got the poison and we'll have the guy who sold it to him come around and identify." O'Malley looked at Weigand, who seemed doubtful. O'Malley glared at Weigand, and said that Weigand looked to him like turning out to be one of the bright boys.

"Making things complicated," he said. "Not seeing the noses on their faces."

Weigand was mollifying. Probably the Inspector was right. Nevertheless—

"I want to dig around a bit yet," he said. "I think there are some angles. Like McIntosh and the reservation he didn't make, for example. Buddy will keep; we're camping on him."

It took some time, but the Inspector mollified. He didn't, he admitted, want Weigand to work them into a jam. "This kid's got money, I suppose?" he said. "I mean his mama's got enough so they know people with money?" Weigand assured him that the kid knew such people. "Yeh," O'Malley said. "And they'd squawk." So, O'Malley admitted, they'd better sew it up first. As a matter of form.

"Only," he warned, "don't go losing sight of the kid. He's the guy we want, all right. We've just got to pin it on him."

Weigand agreed, watched for a pause, and said he had to see some people. O'Malley let him go. O'Malley called in the Headquarters men from the newspapers, told them that he, directing the case, had identified the poison as atropine sulphate and that he expected to make an arrest very soon.

"Within twenty-four hours," the man from the Sun helped him.

"Twelve," said O'Malley, firmly. "An arrest is imminent."

Weigand, thankful to get on with it, picked up the telephone when he was back in his own office. He got David McIntosh on the wire and told McIntosh what he thought McIntosh ought to know. Then he took up the reservation.

"No," David McIntosh said, decidedly. "I didn't make a reservation at the roof."

Weigand told him that, all the same, Nicholas had his name on the reservation list. McIntosh said he didn't know about that. Then he hesitated a moment.

"Come to think of it," he said, "there was something about a reservation. Oh, yes—when Lois and I got there, Nicholas said he had 'my table' and afterward Lois said I must have made a reservation. I told her that was merely Nicholas's way of getting good customers in ahead of outsiders who'd been waiting. But if there really was a reservation—well, I don't know."

"Don't you?" Weigand said. "All right, Mr. McIntosh."

It wasn't so all right, however, he thought as he hung up. There was something fishy about it. He drummed on the desk, filed the fishiness for reference, and picked up the telephone again. He called Mrs. Gerald North, and got Mr. Gerald North.

Mr. North said, "Hello, Bill."

"I wanted to get Pam," Weigand explained. "She knows the head woman—Miss Crane, isn't it?—at this place where the Winston girl worked. I thought she might call Miss Crane up and pass along the word I was coming around—sort of soften the old dame up. What do you think?"

"Pam," Mr. North said, "is out somewhere. I'm very much afraid she is out detecting, Bill. But if she comes in, I'll tell her."

"Right," Weigand said.

"Only she isn't an old dame," Mr. North said. "Or not very."

"Listen, Gerald," Weigand said. "You're getting to talk like Pam."

"My God," said Mr. North, prayerfully. "Thanks for telling me, Bill. Why?"

"Who isn't an old dame?" Weigand asked.

"Oh," Mr. North said. "You had me worried. That was perfectly clear—Mary Crane isn't an old dame. Very pleasant, really. And in her middle forties, I should think. How're you coming?"

Weigand was, he told Mr. North, still going, in several directions.

"How about coming around for dinner tonight?" Mr. North suggested. "Maybe we could get Dorian in. Pam will want to hear everything."

Weigand said it sounded swell. And that he'd try. He cradled the telephone, left word that he would be at the Placement Foundation for an hour or so, and left Headquarters. The relative coolness of the morning was gone, he discovered. His car, which had been parked in the sun, was like an oven as he settled behind the wheel. He opened everything and rolled. The breeze was pleasant and he decided on more of it. He touched the siren and rolled faster. On occasion, he thought, it was comfortable to be a cop.

*     *     *

Mrs. North seemed surprised and a little chagrined to see Weigand and said, "Oh!" Then she nodded.

"Of course you would," she said. "Only I got here first. She doesn't."

"What?" said Weigand. "Please, Pam."

"Know why anybody would kill Lois Winston," Mrs. North said. "Obviously. Isn't that why you're here?"

Weigand looked across the desk at the woman who lived at it and discovered that she was smiling, amusedly. His own eyebrows went up like the shrug of shoulders. Mary Crane, assuming this was Mary Crane, as the lettering on the door promised, apparently was well acquainted with Pamela North.

"This is Miss Crane, Bill," Mrs. North said. "But I've already asked her, of course."

Lieutenant Weigand said, "How do you do, Miss Crane." And Miss Crane said, "Hello, Lieutenant. Mrs. North's been speaking of you."

Weigand saw why Mr. North had taken exception to the "old dame." Miss Crane was not, certainly, young. But she had no particular age. She was brown and built solidly and her brown eyes looked as if she had seen a great deal and was still interested in seeing more. She wore a black silk suit that carried its own crispness and a soft white blouse. She would not, Weigand guessed, be wearing flat-heeled shoes or a shapeless felt hat. He thought of cartoons of social workers and looked again.

"No," Miss Crane said. "You needn't be alarmed, Lieutenant. And sit down. Although there isn't much I can tell you, I'm afraid." Weigand sat and looked around the casual, rather dimly lighted office.

"Tell him about the Pickett," Pam North advised. She was looking unusually perky, Weigand thought, with a hat which wore a tiny red feather. The color of the feather identified as Mrs. North's the red straw bag lying on Mary Crane's desk.

"If he likes," Miss Crane agreed. "But it is obviously absurd. The Pickett, as Mrs. North says, is Ellen Pickett, a worker we had until about a year ago—Miss Winston took over some of her work."

"Oh yes," Weigand said. "The one who thought Miss Winston had taken her job. I doubt whether—"

"No," said Miss Crane, decidedly. "Miss Pickett was very upset and just before she left she made a very difficult scene. She felt that Lois was an amateur who didn't need a job and who was taking hers. But it was just—well, difficult disposition on Miss Pickett's part. It was the disposition, really, which made us decide to let her go, rather than anything Miss Winston did."

"Although," Weigand pointed out, "there was some truth in what she said. Miss Winston was an amateur, and didn't need the job and there are, I suppose, only a certain number of jobs?"

It didn't, Miss Crane told him, work out that way. There were, to be sure, only a certain number of paid jobs. "But there is all the work in the world," she said, and sighed faintly. "We could use twice as many workers as we have; when we find qualified volunteers it is—what shall I say?—so much velvet.

"Of which," she added after a moment, "there isn't too much here."

"And Miss Winston was qualified, I gather?" Weigand asked.

Miss Crane was succinct. "Very," she said. She had gone to the school of social work and had spent three years at the Foundation in a, more or less, probationary capacity. Then, because, and only because, she was a useful worker they would have been glad to employ, she joined the regular staff of investigators. She took assignments like the rest, worked more or less the same hours—"with, naturally, some latitude," Miss Crane added—and was in every sense a staff employee, except that she was unpaid. Her status was unusual but by no means unique, Miss Crane explained. Most large, well-run agencies had one or two such volunteers on their staffs.

Weigand nodded and decided to clean up as he went along. Had Miss Pickett got another job, he wondered.

She had, Miss Crane told him. In Detroit in an agency— She paused, and sought words. "Which has somewhat different standards from ours," she said.

"The movie one," Mrs. North explained. "The one you're always reading about. *They don't keep any records!*"

Mrs. North spoke as if this were a rather dreadful thing, which came, Weigand thought, oddly from Mrs. North. He thought of investigating, out of sheer personal curiosity, and pushed the thought away. He wondered whether Miss Crane could tell him how Miss Winston had spent the previous day; her last day.

"As far as her work here went, I mean," he explained.

Miss Crane nodded. She already had got out the assignment record, she said. Miss Winston had been on an investigation during the afternoon, talking with prospective foster parents. Earlier she had been making a routine checkup at the Municipal Building.

"Yes?" Weigand said. "How was that?"

It was, it seemed, simple enough. One of the Foundation's older wards—a girl of seventeen, who had not been adopted and was being partly supported by the agency—had made up her mind to get married to a boy of about her own age.

"We hoped she hadn't," Miss Crane said. "There were several reasons, none of which matter. We tried to reason her out of it."

They were not sure they had been successful and had suspected that the girl had got married anyway, falsifying her age. Miss Winston, with her own appointment several hours off, had volunteered to check at the Municipal Building on marriage licenses issued during the past week or two. That was what she had done Tuesday morning. Weigand, listening, said "Hm-m-m" with interest and the women looked at him.

"That hooks up with something," Mrs. North challenged. "When you sound that way, it always hooks up with something. Doesn't it?"

Weigand admitted that it might, but volunteered nothing. Mrs. North commanded with her eyes and he shook his head. "Later, maybe," he told her. He turned back to Mary Crane.

"In the afternoon," she said, "Lois seems to have gone to see some prospective foster parents—a Mr. and Mrs. Graham who live"—she consulted a card—"up in the Riverdale section of the Bronx."

"Where," Mrs. North wanted to know, "is that?"

It was, Weigand told her, the section the Henry Hudson Parkway ran through after it crossed the Harlem River. She looked puzzled.

"Ben Riley's," he explained.

She brightened, and then clouded suddenly.

"Isn't that still Manhattan?" she said. "I always thought so."

Weigand told her it was the Bronx, all right. But not the Bronx one usually thought of. He broke off, thinking.

"This investigation," he said. "This may sound foolish to you but—could there be anything dangerous in it? I mean, could she—or any worker—find out something that she shouldn't and—well, antagonize people?" He saw that Miss Crane was smiling, and smiled back, rather apologetically. "I suppose," he said, "I'm thinking of our kind of investigations—police investigations."

Miss Crane said he probably was. Investigations of possible foster homes would not, she said, be at all likely to lead the investigators into dangerous situations.

"It is a little difficult to explain to a layman," she said. "Particularly against all the background of misinformation which has been built up in the layman. Our 'investigations' don't include any prying. They are conversations, chiefly—the worker talks to the prospective foster parents and tries to get to know them; she looks over their house and gets an idea about their financial standing. She asks them questions which, when they first apply for children, they are told will have to be asked. She sees neighbors and friends and relatives whose names the foster parents supply for that purpose. You can see there are a good many things we have to know, before we trust a child with strangers."

Weigand nodded.

"It is all done for the child, essentially," she told him. "But in some measure for the foster parents, too. The more we know about them, the better chance we have of—well, fitting them with a child. If the foster parents have been through college, for example, they will be happiest with a child who may, some day, go through college, and they would be disappointed with a child whose mind wasn't fitted for formal education. And we try to fit races and temperaments and—well, you can see it is something of a job."

"And Miss Winston was a good worker?" Weigand said.

"Very," Miss Crane told him. "She—well, it has been a very great shock to all of us, Lieutenant."

Weigand nodded. Pam North broke in.

"Are the Grahams the people who are going to get Michael?" she said. Miss Crane nodded.

"Michael?" Weigand echoed.

"The little boy we are thinking of placing with Mr. and Mrs. Graham," Miss Crane told him. "A child of about three. The placement seems to be very suitable, although Miss Winston's death will delay matters. She was handling it, and much of the investigation may have to be done over. I won't know until I have read her recent reports."

"Oh," said Weigand. He thought it over. Michael, he decided, didn't come in. He might see the Grahams, because it sometimes helped to find out what a person who had been murdered was doing and saying in the hours before death. It would be, just possibly, worth a trip to Riverdale. Meanwhile— He stood up and started to thank Miss Crane. He was glad, at any rate, to know that Lois Winston had had an opportunity to go over the marriage license lists at the Municipal Building. It would be interesting to find out whether, in searching them, she had run across a name more familiar to her than that of the wayward ward of the Placement Foundation.

"Listen," Mrs. North said, firmly. "I think you ought to hear about Michael. It's a very strange story and—well, you never know."

Weigand started to shake his head, and again met command in Pam North's eyes. She was, for some reason, rather eager about this, he decided. He looked at his watch. Another half-hour wouldn't make much difference, one way or the other.

"What," he said, "about Michael?"

Mrs. North looked at Mary Crane and nodded. Miss Crane seemed puzzled. She said she couldn't see what bearing it could possibly have. She looked at Lieutenant Weigand and smiled questioningly and he nodded, just perceptibly.

"If it doesn't take too long," he said. "We want to keep Mrs. North happy."

It wouldn't, Miss Crane agreed, take long. It was, like all the Foundation's case histories, confidential. "Mrs. North is on the committee, of course," Miss Crane explained. She looked a little bewildered about that, Weigand noticed. He merely nodded, barricading a sympathetic grin. The nod accepted the forthcoming information as confidential.

Michael, Miss Crane explained, was a little boy of three with a rather unusual history. He had come to the organization some six weeks earlier, being brought under care by a man who said he was the child's father. Miss Crane herself had eventually interviewed the man—an odd, unshaven man who looked ill and, eventually, said he was ill. He wore dark glasses, she said, and even so sat with his back to the window because the light hurt his eyes. He wanted to surrender Michael, his son, for adoption. He had not brought the boy.

"He said he was Richard Osborne," Miss Crane said. Osborne said he had been a draftsman, but recently had been too ill to work. He had been taking care of Michael by himself since his wife had left him, when they were living in San Francisco. He had come to New York on an offer of a job and had got it, but held it only a few months. That had been during the winter before. While he still had the job, he had begun to feel weak and ill and had looked around for someone with whom he could board the child. Through a man who worked with him he had heard of a woman—a Mrs. Halstead—who sometimes boarded children. She— Miss Crane stopped. She had been summarizing from a sheaf of papers on her desk, now and then checking her memory against something written there. Now she looked up.

"Oh, yes," she said. "I remember, now. I should have started back a bit. Mrs. Halstead lives up in Riverdale too, you see. But it isn't merely coincidence."

"Well," Weigand said, "let's finish with the boy."

The boy's father, Miss Crane continued, had gone to see Mrs. Halstead, decided she would be suitable, and arranged to board the child there. He had done so until recently, paying seven dollars each week. For the past several weeks, however, he had been unable to pay.

That was because he had, recently, grown so ill that he could not continue to work. He had gone to a doctor and, on the doctor's advice, to the Veterans Bureau. A complete physical examination had followed.

"I'm a very sick man, Miss," he had told Miss Crane. From his description, he was indeed a very sick man. He had contracted tuberculosis and, in addition, had a serious heart condition. Those things were, he said grimly, in addition to an eye ailment he had had, off and on, for years. The upshot was that he had been accepted for care at a Veterans Hospital. Because of his lungs, they were sending him to Arizona. But they were not hopeful.

"I am going to die very soon," he said. He said it matter-of-factly, Miss Crane remembered. Before he died, he wanted to make provision for Michael. He could no longer pay board to Mrs. Halstead, but he believed she would keep the child in any case. She had, he said, grown attached to Michael. But she was an old woman and, he had recently decided, a difficult one. "Cantankerous," he said. "I've heard—"

He had, he explained, heard indirectly that Mrs. Halstead was severe with Michael and irritable. He was sure that this was only on the surface; that at bottom the woman was deeply attached to the little boy. But she was too old to take permanent charge of him as Osborne suspected she now wanted to do. What he hoped was that the Foundation could take the boy under care and arrange, eventually, for his adoption by a couple nearer the right age.

"I don't want him brought up by an old woman," Richard Osborne had insisted. "And I can't care for him. I'm not going to live long enough."

He had, he said, somebody in mind. When he had heard that Mrs. Halstead was irritable with the child, he had gone to a park in which he knew Michael and the boarding mother went for walks. He had watched, and seen Mrs. Halstead pull at the child's arm, and snap at him irritably. And he had seen Michael run to another, much younger woman, who called him by name. Michael had run to this woman and it had seemed to the man, watching, that there was a flow of affection between them which was what he wanted for his son.

It was that woman, or someone like her, he wanted for his child, he explained. Possibly that very woman, who had somehow got to know Michael in the park, and perhaps to care for him. He didn't know, of course, whether she would want to adopt the boy—so far as he knew she might have children of her own. But seeing her with his boy had made him realize more acutely than ever what the child should have. And it was that he wanted the Foundation to find for Michael. He wanted, he said, to surrender the child to the agency and have him cared for.

"I told him we could not accept a child without seeing him," Miss Crane explained. "We have to know whether children are suitable for adoption; sometimes, for various reasons, it is hopeless to try to find permanent, private homes for them. We told him that we would see the child and investigate conditions and let him know."

But he had insisted that that would not do. He was leaving for the hospital, he said, the next day; his transportation had already been arranged. He wanted things settled for the child before he went; doggedly, he kept insisting that he would die soon and that delay was impossible.

"It seemed to me a special case," Miss Crane said. "Finally I agreed on a compromise. Since he insisted, he could sign a release at once and authorize Mrs. Halstead to turn the child over to us. We would not be bound by it unless we found the child suitable for placement. If we did not, we would communicate with him and, if he could do nothing—I meant, really, if he was dead—we would have to turn the case over to the Department of Welfare. Finally he agreed to that and we let him sign the surrender, making us the guardians of the child."

It was interesting, Weigand found. It had nothing to do with him, but it was interesting—interesting and worrying to think of this gaunt, dying man sitting in that room, trying to provide in some way for a little boy.

"Now," Miss Crane went on, "we go back—and this is coincidence. Checking up, we found that that was not the first time we had heard of little Michael Osborne."

A couple of weeks before Osborne came with his story about the child, Miss Crane said, a woman in her early thirties had come to the agency and had asked to see Miss Crane. She had come about a little boy she had met with an old woman—a strange old woman, she said—in a park in Riverdale. She had met the two often and, because he was a charming little boy and she was childless, she had talked to him and petted him. "I've always wanted children," she said to Mary Crane, simply.

She had discovered, through talking to the woman, that the child was not related to the elderly woman; that she had been caring for him on a boarding basis, but had grown very fond of him and was beginning to think she might adopt him. It made the younger woman suddenly think that perhaps she might have the little boy for her own.

"The woman is too old to take care of him," the visitor had told Miss Crane. "She is cross with him—rough. I don't think he ought to be living there, in that dark old house."

The woman, who said she was Mrs. Graham, had gone home with the old woman and the little boy, once, and seen the house. "All run down," she said. "A strange, dark barn which must have been there on the hill for ages. Awful for a little boy."

Mrs. Graham wanted the agency to do something; to investigate and to take the child from the old woman and the strange, dark house. And then, if they thought it advisable, let her have the child. But that last was only if they thought best; in any case, the child must be got out of that house.

Miss Crane had told her, gently, that there was nothing they could do, directly. They might—or she might—take the matter up with the authorities, although it was not likely that the authorities would intervene. The Placement Foundation was a private charity and, although it worked closely with the Department of Public Welfare, had no official standing. So it could do nothing. Mrs. Graham had showed disappointment but had seemed to understand and had said she would think it over. Perhaps, if it finally seemed to her best, she might go to the authorities herself. Then, as she was going, she had stopped, suddenly, and asked whether the Foundation could get her a child.

"We told her, of course, that we were always glad to get applications from possible foster parents," Miss Crane said. "I had Miss Winston come in and she talked it over with Mrs. Graham and eventually took her application. It was on file when Michael's father came to us and wanted to surrender the child. Then—"

Miss Crane stopped suddenly, and looked at Mrs. North in a surprised way.

"You know, Mrs. North," she said, "perhaps you were right, all along. Perhaps there *is* a connection."

Miss Winston, Miss Crane said, had gone to see the child at Mrs. Halstead's and found conditions much as the child's father and Mrs. Graham had described them. The child's situation was not good, the environment, including Mrs. Halstead herself as part of it, definitely unsuitable. She had also reported that Michael was a nice, alert little boy, almost certainly suitable for adoption. As a result, the Foundation had decided to take the child from Mrs. Halstead's, acting on the strength of the father's surrender and his note to Mrs. Halstead. Miss Winston had gone alone first to get the child, and had run into a tirade of abuse from Mrs. Halstead, who refused to give him up. There had been nothing to do, then, but to bring the police in and in the end the child had to be removed almost forcibly.

"Mrs. Halstead was a strange old woman, apparently," Miss Crane said. "She was almost frantic. She railed at Miss Winston and threatened her and only calmed down when the police officer proposed to take her into magistrate's court with a view to having her committed to Bellevue for observation."

Weigand said "Hm-m-m" and then:

"What kind of threats, do you know?"

It might, Miss Crane said, be on Miss Winston's report. She turned back through the sheaf of papers, found a place and read:

"June 3. Agent went to Mrs. Halstead's to remove Michael, accompanied by a patrolman, since Mrs. Halstead had been abusive on a previous visit. She was again abusive, threatening agent violently and screaming, 'You're going to pay for this!' and other abuse. The child was removed and taken to boarding home in Queens."

Weigand said "Hm-m-m" again.

"Right," he said. "And the child is still in Queens?"

"Yes," Miss Crane said.

"No," Mrs. North said, at about the same time. She shook her head

at Miss Crane and added: "He's right here. Seeing the doctor or something. I saw him when I came in. Wait."

Nobody tried to stop her, which was as well. She went out and down
a corridor, leaving Weigand and Miss Crane to look at each other,
slightly baffled. Mrs. North returned with a small, blond boy who was
riding in her arms and trying to catch a watch, shaped like a little silver
ball, which dangled from her neck. He grabbed it and examined it carefully. He turned it over and beamed at it and made appreciative sounds.
At the back, a rounded crystal left the busy works visible.

"Wheels!" said Michael Osborne, quite clearly and in evident ecsta-
sy. He pulled at the watch as Mrs. North put him down.

"No, Michael," she said. "Break. You mustn't break my watch." She
cast an eye around. "Here," she said, dangling the red purse. "Pretty."

Michael looked and was not interested.

"He doesn't seem to like purses," Mrs. North said. She looked at the
purse. "Of course," she said, "he's perfectly right, really. There's nothing in it."

Michael was diverted, with some effort, by the offer of Weigand's
sturdier wrist-watch. He shook it briskly, said, "Ticks" with enjoyment,
and then suddenly put it down on the floor.

"Go, now," Michael said, and walked firmly to the door. There was
no diverting him this time. Convoyed by Mrs. North, Michael went.

Weigand and Miss Crane smiled after him. He was, they agreed, an
amiable child. One could see why he had instantly attracted Mrs. Graham and why she had wanted to get so much small sunniness out of a
dark house. Weigand was rising again as Mrs. North returned. Then he
remembered something and took from his pocket the reservation list
Nicholas had given him. Would Miss Crane, he asked, run down it and
see whether she recognized any names as connected with Miss Winston? She looked doubtful.

"There's always a chance," he said.

Miss Crane looked down the list, shaking her head. She was almost
at the bottom before she stopped and reread a name. Then she held it up
so that Weigand could see and pointed. Weigand read.

"Well," he said. "Now that *is* interesting."

"What?" said Mrs. North.

Weigand showed her the name well down on the list.

"Barton Halstead," she read.

She looked at Weigand, without surprise.

"Perhaps," said Mrs. North, gently, "this will teach you to pay some attention to what I tell you."

## • 8 •

### WEDNESDAY
### 11:30 A.M. TO 1:15 P.M.

Before he left Mary Crane's quiet office at the Foundation, Weigand sought a more precise description of Michael's father—always assuming, he thought, that the man who had introduced himself as Richard Osborne *was* the father of Michael. He did this on the theory of cleaning up, so far as possible, as he went along. He still could not believe, in spite of Mrs. North, that Michael would prove to have much to do with his problem. And even if Michael did, Weigand realized after Miss Crane had done her descriptive best, Michael's father was apt to remain nebulous.

When Osborne had complained of his eyes, Miss Crane said, she had had her secretary switch off the overhead lights, so that only a desk light and shadowy illumination from a window which opened on a court had remained. As a result, it had never been particularly clear what Osborne looked like. He was youngish, she thought, but his hair was beginning to show gray. His face was thin and shadowed; he hadn't shaved for a day or so, apparently. The dark glasses effectually hid his eyes, and with them those telltale lines which gather around eyes, telling of age and health and, often, of disposition. He was shabbily dressed, but it was hard to put a finger on the shabbiness—a blue suit, rather worn; run-down brown shoes; a tie which had been knotted too often. Miss Crane reviewed her description privately and said she was sorry.

"He looked ill and he looked thin," she said. "He might have been almost any age from the middle twenties to the middle thirties. I'm sorry; there was nothing about him that stood out, except that he was obviously ill. You could tell that from the way he moved."

"Or, of course," Weigand pointed out, "that he wanted you to think so. An uncertainty of movement could be assumed. Even a day's growth of beard makes any thin man look unhealthy."

"Yes," Miss Crane said. She was vexed with herself. "I should have observed more closely, but of course I expected further information. We are waiting for a report on him from the Veterans Hospital."

She had no reason, Weigand told her, to think it was particularly important. Probably, as a matter of fact, it would turn out not to be particularly important.

Pam North walked to the elevator with him and rode down. She said why didn't he come to dinner, and that they would have Dorian if they could.

"And Mullins," she said. "I miss Mullins."

Weigand said it would have to be left open, and that he would bring Mullins if possible.

"Don't forget Michael," Mrs. North said, and waved eagerly at a taxicab.

"What?" said Weigand.

"Important," Mrs. North told him, leaning from the window of the cab as it started up. "I think it's Michael—"

Mrs. North and the taxicab went around a truck and vanished. Weigand found a telephone and got Headquarters. Things were going along. Mullins was assisting, personally, in the search for a man who had bought atropine sulphate. A report on the contents of the glasses from which Lois Winston had drunk at the Ritz-Plaza roof had come in. One of the glasses had contained water. The contents of the other was more complicated. Headquarters read over the report to Weigand. It was detailed and confusing.

"Did they say what that meant?" he inquired.

They had. It meant rum, Coca-Cola and a little lime juice—in other words a Cuba Libre.

"No atropine?" Weigand insisted.

"It don't say so," Headquarters told him. Weigand said, "Damn!" Then he dictated a wire to be dispatched to a Veterans Hospital in Arizona, inquiring about one Richard Osborne. He left word that if Mullins came in, he was to be held. He hung up and stared at the telephone. Then he dialed another number and got David McIntosh. There was, he told McIntosh, one question. Was he certain that Lois had had only one Cuba Libre?

"Yes," McIntosh said. Then he paused. "Come to think of it," he said, "I'm not absolutely sure. What happened has put it out of my head. She may have had two—I'm not certain."

Weigand thanked him without enthusiasm and hung up. So young Frank Kensitt's carefully gathered evidence was worth precisely nothing. The drink left on the table was innocent, but there might have been an earlier one which was guilty—guilty, and removed when the second was served, and long since vanished. And now there was no evidence to show whether the poison had been administered at the roof or elsewhere. "Screwy," Weigand told himself, in the absence of Mullins. He looked up another number and dialed again, getting a voice at the Ashley apartment. Then he got Anna. He wanted Anna to remember something.

"After Miss Lois came home yesterday afternoon, did she drink anything?" he wanted to know. There was silence while Anna thought. Then there was guesswork. Miss Lois might have had a drink with Mr. Randall and his friends when she first came in. Afterward, in her room, she might have drunk water from the thermos on the table by her bed. Anna wouldn't know.

"The thermos was full when I was there," Weigand told her.

That, Anna told him, was natural. When Miss Lois had gone out, Anna had straightened up in the room. She had turned back the bed.

She had also emptied and refilled the thermos. Was it full when she emptied it? She hadn't noticed. She was sorry.

"There was no reason why you should," Weigand said. "Although I'm sorry too. Has Mrs. Ashley returned?"

Mrs. Ashley had. She was in her room, lying down. She had been almost hysterical earlier and a physician had been called to care for her. He had, Anna supposed, given her a sedative.

"If she's well enough, I'd like to talk to her later today," Weigand said. "Will you tell her, please?"

Anna would tell her. Weigand hung up again, feeling that he was hurrying on a treadmill. He telephoned Headquarters again and directed that a man be sent to check on recently issued marriage licenses and told what was to be looked for. He found that Mullins had returned and got him on the phone. Mullins said that things were moving and that here was a funny thing, Loot. It seemed, he said, like David McIntosh had been making reservations all over town.

"What?" asked Weigand.

The manager of the Crescent Club, on the East River, had telephoned in to volunteer information, after he had read of the case in the newspapers. David McIntosh had telephoned to the reservation office there a little after six the previous evening and engaged a table, stipulating that it be near the dance floor. He had never claimed the table.

"Screwy, ain't it?" Mullins said. Weigand said it was.

"Mr. McIntosh seems to have been a little confused," Weigand said. He considered. "Or," he said, "somebody has been making reservations for Mr. McIntosh; somebody who wanted the girl and him to sit near the dance floor."

"That don't make sense," Mullins told him, firmly. Weigand said it might.

"If a table is near the dance floor," Weigand explained, "a lot of people pass it, going from their tables to dance and coming back. Doesn't that mean anything, sergeant?"

Mullins digested it and said, "Say!

"For dropping things in drinks," he said, "it would be about perfect, Loot."

"Right," said Weigand, "Stay there and handle anything that comes in," he instructed. "I'll keep calling. I'll probably be in during the afternoon. You're invited to the Norths' for dinner, by the way."

"O.K., Loot," Mullins said. "That'll be swell."

"If," Weigand told him, "you get to go. The chances are you'll be working, sergeant."

He hung up while Mullins was getting a protest phrased and left the telephone. He retrieved his car and worked west, suffering traffic lights patiently. He drove under the express highway for some blocks and then climbed a ramp to it. He rolled north along the highway, then along the Henry Hudson Parkway, and might have been anybody driving out of town. But in the Riverdale section he turned off, looped and crossed the Parkway on an overhead. He worked through quiet streets beyond the row of new apartment buildings fronting the Parkway, dipped over the hill and went downgrade toward the river. The old houses there were older; it was a backwater in New York.

Mrs. Eva Halstead's house was, Weigand decided, probably the oldest of them all. It was a big, square house of damp-looking brick, set far back in a garden of weeds. An uneven brick path ran to a porch which was massive but tottering. Boards bent under Weigand's feet as he crossed to the door. He pressed on a bell and nothing happened. He knocked and then knocked more loudly. A dog barked shrilly somewhere inside and Weigand waited. The heavy door opened a crack and a smell of dust and cabbage emerged. A voice, harsh and forbidding, followed.

"Well, young man?" the voice said. "I don't want anything."

"Mrs. Halstead?" Weigand said. "I'm not selling anything."

"Then go away," the voice told him, and the door's crack narrowed. For the first time in years, Weigand put a foot in a door. His voice became authoritative.

"This is the police, Mrs. Halstead," he said. "Police Lieutenant Weigand. I want to talk to you about Miss Lois Winston."

"Killed," Mrs. Halstead said. "And none too good for her. Stealing children." But the pressure against Weigand's toe relaxed. The door opened reluctantly and revealed Mrs. Halstead. It also revealed a rather dirty and very fat white dog and a thin, very clean gray cat. The cat emerged and rubbed against Weigand's legs.

"Come here, Toby," Mrs. Halstead said, sternly in a harsh, cracking voice. The cat turned and went in, leaving Weigand impressed. He thought of the Norths' cat, Pete, and his inscrutable ignoring of all commands, and was more than ever impressed. He looked at Mrs. Halstead.

She was in all respects formidable. She was heavy and tall and an old, wrinkled face met the world implacably. Her lips were a slit above a jutting chin, and a heavy nose hooked over them. She was dressed stiffly in black silk and a boned net collar guarded a wrinkled throat. Weigand tried to remember when last he had seen a boned net collar and Mrs. Halstead frowned.

"Well, young man?" she said. "Are you through staring at an old woman?"

"I have been instructed to talk to you," Weigand said, evenly and inaccurately. "I think we might both be more comfortable inside."

Mrs. Halstead withdrew stingily and permitted entrance. The hallway, which split the house down the center, was musty and damp, and the odor of cabbage was stronger. When Mrs. Halstead looked firmly at Weigand and he still did not go away, she led him to a door on the right and entered, leaving him to follow. Overpowering heat met him at the threshold. The room, with shades drawn over closed windows, was stifling. Mrs. Halstead sat in a dirty morris-chair and faced Weigand.

"She ought to have been killed," Mrs. Halstead said. "I ought to have done it myself."

"Did you?" Weigand asked. It seemed possible that if she had she would say so, and stare him down.

"No," she said. "You're a fool, young man." She seemed, however, slightly more tolerant.

The cat crossed the room and jumped on her lap. She let it stay. A heavy, veined hand stroked its back.

"But you were at the Ritz-Plaza roof," Weigand asserted. "With your son."

"My son was killed twenty years ago," she said. "In the war; the other war. Barton Halstead is my nephew."

"But you were at the roof with Barton Halstead," Weigand insisted.

"Certainly," she said. "Since he was kind enough to ask me." There was hard emphasis on the word "kind." "Barton occasionally remembers a duty to poor relations," she said. She studied Weigand's face and something like a smile broke against her chin and lapped its way to her lips. "Because I knew he'd hate it," she said. "He thought I wouldn't go. So I went. It was very trying for Barton."

She seemed to relish Barton's discomfiture, in retrospect. The smile ebbed.

"Very well," Weigand said. "You threatened Lois Winston, Mrs. Halstead. You were present on the roof when she was killed."

"She was poisoned," Mrs. Halstead said. "I suppose somebody put something in her glass?"

"You guess well, Mrs. Halstead," Weigand said, without expression.

"Don't be silly, young man," Mrs. Halstead said. "Can you see me sneaking over to a table, without anybody noticing?"

Weigand looked at her. He had to admit he couldn't. He kept the admission to himself, however. There might have been some other way.

"I swore at her when she stole Michael," Mrs. Halstead said. "Michael was all I had and I was good to him. There was no foolishness, but I was good to him. She and those damned social pryers stole him." She glared at Weigand. "And the police," she added, with rancor.

"I have nothing to do with that, Mrs. Halstead," Weigand said. "I don't want to argue about it. You did threaten Miss Winston. She is dead. You were around when she was killed.

"And," he added, "Michael wasn't yours. He had a father."

Mrs. Halstead sat up in the old morris-chair and stared at Weigand.

"So you know about that, do you, young man?" she said. "What do you know about that?"

Merely, Weigand told her, that Michael's father had asked that the child be removed from her care, since he could no longer pay board, and that the father was ill and in a hospital in the West.

"You know that, do you?" she said. There was a kind of cackle in her voice, and an odd emphasis on "know."

"That's the record," Weigand said. "What do you know about it?"

He felt that he was being led down a side-path, but curiosity pulled him along.

"What should *I* know about it, young man?" Mrs. Halstead said. "A man brought the boy here and arranged for me to board him. I did. The man sent a money order each Saturday and I got it on Monday. I spent the money on the boy."

"Precisely," Weigand said. "Then he stopped sending the money and sent somebody to get the boy. You wouldn't give the boy up and the police were called. You threatened Miss Winston."

"She stole him," Mrs. Halstead said. "He wasn't hers. He was mine, more than anybody's."

"More than his father's?" Weigand said. Mrs. Halstead stared at him.

"Who was his father, young man?" she demanded, her voice harsh. "Do you know that?"

"No," Weigand said. "I only know what a man said. What difference does it make?"

Mrs. Halstead stood up. The chair creaked as she left it and the floor as she joined it. The cat skidded to the floor.

"You'd better find out, young man," she said. "Before you start accusing old women. I'm an old woman, Lieutenant. Nobody helps *me*."

The last was cryptic. Mrs. Halstead was cryptic. The heat made Weigand faintly dizzy. He stood up, too.

"If you know anything, Mrs. Halstead, I would advise you to tell me what it is," he said. "Did you kill the girl?"

She seemed to think it a reasonable reiteration.

"No," she said. She said it almost pleasantly.

"Do you think you know who did?" Weigand asked.

"I could," she said. "And I couldn't."

There was an odd expression in her eyes, Weigand decided. She was an odd old woman, living in an odd old house. There was no telling what she meant.

She was vague about the time she had spent at the roof. She gave Barton Halstead's home and business addresses with evident pleasure, clearly hoping he would be annoyed. Barton Halstead's business affiliation gave Weigand occasion for thought. He was with the Larmey-Fencott Drug Corporation. Mrs. Halstead watched his face.

"They probably have plenty of poisons," she assured him. "Only I'm afraid Barton never met Miss Winston." She seemed unhappy about this. "But of course he could have got some poison and given it to me," she said. Her ancient eyes gleamed. "He'd love to give me poison," she said, and laughed. Her laugh was an oddly shocking titter. Weigand felt, and suppressed, sympathy with her nephew, Barton Halstead. He told Mrs. Halstead that he would see her again.

"When you know something," she said. "Do. Although probably I won't let you in. Now go away so I can eat my dinner."

Weigand thought of what was apparently a boiled dinner, at midday in the musty heat of the old house, and went gladly. He went across the creaking porch and down the worn brick path and knew, as surely as if he had seen her, that Mrs. Halstead was staring after him from behind the shade of one of the windows. He stopped at the nearest telephone and directed that a man be put on Mrs. Halstead. She would know it, of course. Any watch kept near enough to the old house to be of use would be plainly evident to the watched. He hoped it would give her something to think about.

He sat at the wheel of his car, turned into a patch of shade, and drummed against the horn rim with his fingers. Where, he wondered, am I?

Reasonably, he told himself, I am midway of a chase for wild geese. Inspector O'Malley probably was right; the case was fundamentally simple. It was Randall Ashley killing for money, a motive hallowed in fiction and, equally, in fact. For Ashley one had motive, opportunity and, if it were as easy to procure atropine sulphate as Dr. Francis said, means. He seemed merely a spoiled, sulky young man, but spoiled and sulky young men were not badly adapted for murder. They lacked consideration, for one thing, and a murderer must be ruthless of others for his own ends. Expecting things to come easily, they might well turn nasty when things didn't. Almost certainly, their man was young Ashley.

And so he, a police lieutenant who ought, from experience, to know that in police matters the most obvious is the most likely, was in a far corner of the Bronx pursuing the ghosts of notions—talking to strange, but probably harmless, old women in smelly old houses, wondering about the paternity of little boys. It was Mrs. North who had started him on this, Weigand realized; Mrs. North with her insistence that little Michael fitted in somewhere. And Mrs. North was nobody's guide in matters of detection. Or, on second thought, wasn't she? The trouble was, you couldn't tell.

"So, as long as I'm up here—" Weigand said to himself, but half aloud. He started the motor, swung the car and sought another address. The Graham house was large, too, when he found it. But it sat on a clipped lawn, with trees shading it, and Venetian blinds guarded open windows from the sun. The bell rang at the Grahams' and a small dark maid answered it, and would see whether Mrs. Graham was in to Lieutenant Weigand.

Mrs. Graham was a small woman with fluffy, blond hair and intense blue eyes. There was a kind of hurried eagerness in her movements as she crossed the cool living-room to Weigand and said, "Oh, Lieutenant . . . about poor Miss Winston?"

Weigand was, he said, sorry to bother her. It was a matter of routine.

"In these cases," he said, "we try to discover all we can about the victims' actions immediately preceding the crime. I understand Miss Winston visited you yesterday afternoon?" Mrs. Graham nodded, grave now.

It was, Weigand told her, hard to say what he wanted. Probably there was nothing, but he would like to hear anything she could tell him—anything about how Miss Winston seemed, what she said—anything at all that she, Mrs. Graham, thought pertinent in the light of what had happened. Mrs. Graham nodded and then, after a moment, shook her head.

"She was very normal," she said. "Just as I'd seen her several times before. She was cheerful and, after we had talked a little about Michael, we had iced tea and—just talked. My father joined us for a few minutes and we—oh, merely talked about New York and how hot it could get. My father lives in Hartford, you see, and just happened to be here. It was all—inconsequential."

"You had got to know Miss Winston rather well, I take it," Weigand said. Mrs. Graham said, "Yes," warmly.

"She had come to see me several times because of our application for a child from the Foundation," she said. "She came first after we applied and then to tell us about Michael and then once or twice later—to ask about references and things like that. They like to find out all they can about families, you know. To protect the children."

"So you had grown quite friendly," Weigand said. "Got to like each other?"

"I had got to like her very much," Mrs. Graham said. "I don't know how she felt—but yesterday she stayed longer than she needed to, just to talk, so I suppose—I was terribly shocked last night when I heard about it."

"Oh," Weigand said. "You heard last night? How was that?"

It was, Mrs. Graham said, simple. Her husband had read about it in the papers and when he came home told her, because he had recognized the name of the girl killed as that of the agent who was seeing them about Michael.

"We were both terribly worried," she said. "And sorry, too, of course. But worried about Michael—about getting him. Do you suppose that Miss Winston's death will, somehow, hold things up?" She looked at Weigand, her blue eyes darkly intense. "We both so want Michael," she said. "And already we've waited a long time."

About that, Weigand said, he had no idea. Speaking as an outsider he didn't see why the death of the agent handling a placement should more than temporarily delay the placement. He advised her to call Miss Crane and find out.

"Oh, I will," Mrs. Graham said. "That's what John said. John is my husband."

Weigand nodded.

"By the way," he said, "about what time was it that he told you of the murder? It must have been rather late, I suppose; there couldn't have been anything about it in the earliest editions of the tabloids." He tried to remember. The standard-size papers came out about 11:30; they might have had something, probably did. He waited for an answer. There was a moment of hesitation.

"Oh," she said, "John was very late last night—something at the office. It was almost one when he got in. Then we sat up talking until after two. About Miss Winston and Michael."

That fitted, Weigand decided. Assuming John Graham had been something of an owl on Tuesday night, or devoted to his work.

"By the way," he said. "We have to clutter the record with all sorts of facts, most of them of no importance. What is Mr. Graham's business connection?"

Mrs. Graham looked surprised. Weigand couldn't blame her.

"Why," she said, "he's office manager for a perfumery manufacturer. Henri et Paulette. It's an American firm, really, but the name—well, it just seemed to sound better, I guess."

Weigand made a note of it, without any great conviction that it was a note he would ever have cause to refer to.

"Going back to yesterday afternoon," he said. "I would appreciate it if you would make a special effort to remember Miss Winston—how she behaved and what she said. I mean, the smallest thing might have importance. Something she said—about people she was going to meet, or things she was going to do—the little things that people let drop—something like that might help us."

He waited. Mrs. Graham was dutiful in her concentration. After a few moments she shook her head.

"I can't think of anything at all," she said. "We talked about Michael, as I told you. We talked about the heat. She said she would be glad when evening came and it got cooler, and something about going to a restaurant where it would be cool. She said something—oh yes, she said, 'It will be nice not to be a working girl for a while.' I'd heard that she had a lot of money, really, and didn't need to work, and just did it for the children. And so once or twice we'd laughed about her being a 'working girl.'"

Weigand said he saw.

"I suppose," he said, "she didn't mention where she was going. I mean any specific place?"

There was, he thought, a momentary hesitation, as if Mrs. Graham were thinking before she answered. Then she said, "No." He waited an instant longer.

"No," Mrs. Graham said, "I'm quite sure she didn't. She just said some place where it would be cool. That might be any place, of course, with everything air-conditioned."

Weigand agreed. He was a little puzzled, momentarily, and for the first time wondered fleetingly whether Mrs. Graham had told all she knew. But there seemed to be no reason why she should boggle at telling him if Lois Winston had mentioned the Ritz-Plaza roof. He let the incident click into a suitably inconspicuous place in his memory and started to speak again. But there was a slight sound at the door and a man stepped in from the hall and stopped, smiling in the deprecatory way of one who interrupts.

He was a spare, tall man with a thin, pleasant face and he was, Weigand guessed, in his late fifties although he carried years well. Old for Mr. Graham, Weigand thought, and then Mrs. Graham looked up.

"Oh, hello, Dad," she said. "How's Father Graham? Lieutenant, this is my father, George Benoit. Dad, this is Lieutenant Weigand from Police Headquarters. He has been asking about Miss Winston—you remember I told you?"

"Yes," George Benoit said to her. His voice, like his face, was pleasant. "How do you do, Lieutenant? Your father-in-law is very wide awake today, Margie. He wants to know what the policeman wants."

"What?" said Mrs. Graham. Her voice was surprised. "Now, how on earth did he know there was a—a policeman here?"

"I don't know," her father told her. "He was sitting by the window and looking out and he said, all at once, 'Margaret is seeing a policeman. I want to know why.' So I came to find out."

"How on earth?" Margaret Graham inquired, looking at Weigand helplessly. He smiled.

"There's a police shield on the car," he explained. "I suppose your father-in-law saw it, and saw me come in."

"Well," Benoit said, "he wants to see you, Lieutenant. He said, 'Send that policeman up here.'"

"Oh, dear!" Margaret Graham said. "Now what?"

She looked at her father, ruefully, and he smiled.

"You know Cyrus, Margaret," he said. "If policemen are in his house he wants to see them. He's not going to let anything go on he's not in on. He wouldn't be Cyrus Graham if he did."

Margaret Graham sighed and looked inquiringly at the lieutenant.

"Would you?" she asked. "He'll wear us out afterward if you don't. You see he is—well, he has a strong will, and it has got all the stronger since he's been so sick."

Weigand looked at his watch. It was after one and he had had no lunch. Also he had things to do and people to see, among whom he saw little reason to include Cyrus Graham. But Cyrus, whatever else he might be, and however apparently far from any conceivable line of investigation, was clearly an observant gentleman.

"Well—" Weigand said, slowly standing.

"It needn't take but a few minutes," Mrs. Graham assured him. "And it would be very kind of you. He hates to be out of things so, and it is very bad for him to be excited. And he is always excited when he doesn't get his own way."

"I gather," Weigand said, "that your father-in-law can't get around?"

Leading him toward the door, Mrs. Graham nodded. She stopped for a moment in the hall and amplified. Cyrus Graham, John Graham's father, had been ill for several years—so ill that he could not leave his wheelchair and was not permitted the slightest exertion. "It's his heart, chiefly," she said. "He may collapse at any moment. And several years ago he had a stroke—everybody thought he was going to die then. But he just didn't, somehow—the doctor said it was almost a miracle. It's almost four years, now, and he doesn't get any better or any worse."

"He seems active enough mentally, anyway," Weigand said. She agreed to that.

"He always was," she said. "And his mind hasn't changed—or not much. He's crotchety and a little querulous, as it's perfectly natural he should be, and he was always—well, he always wanted his own way. But he sees things."

She led him up wide stairs to the second floor and along a long corridor. She knocked on a door near the end and a nurse opened it and smiled without giving anything away. Margaret said, "Good-afternoon, Miss Nelson. May we see your patient?"

Miss Nelson opened the door for them, still smiling from a distance. An old, thin voice said, "Come in! Come in!" Cyrus Graham was sitting in a wheelchair by a window which opened on the street. He was emaciated, so that it seemed that the light from the window might shine through him. There was a little fringe of white hair around his head and the skin on top of his head was almost bluish white. He had long fingers on the hand he raised shakingly and he pointed one of them at Weigand.

"You're a policeman, sir!" he said. "Don't tell me you aren't!"

"I wasn't going to, Mr. Graham," Weigand said. He spoke gently. "I am Lieutenant Weigand, of the Homicide Bureau. I just stopped to ask your daughter-in-law a few questions. It is nothing."

"Nothing?" said the old man. "Of course it's nothing! About that Winston girl, eh?"

"Yes," Weigand said.

"Margaret didn't do it!" the old man said, and then he laughed, a little, creaking laugh. Weigand smiled in response and said he hadn't thought so. It was merely, he explained, that Mrs. Graham was one of the last to see Miss Winston before her death, and that as a matter of routine—

"Routine!" the old man said. Everything he said seemed propelled from his lips by a tiny inward explosion. "Don't talk to me about routine! You sound like that damned nurse!"

"Well," said Weigand, rather lamely, "that was all it was. Just checking up."

"She was a nice little thing," Cyrus Graham said, irrelevantly. "She was up here once. Told me about things. They think I don't know about things, you know."

"I imagine," Weigand said, still gently, "that you find out."

The old man laughed his creaking little laugh.

"You're damn right, son!" he said. "You're damn right! They thought I didn't know about the kid."

He turned from Weigand to Mrs. Graham, who had dropped into a chair. He looked at her wickedly.

"Thought I didn't know," he said. "But I did!"

"Did you, Father?" she said. She seemed placid. Or, Weigand felt rather than saw, almost placid. There was an undercurrent of something. "What did you know? We didn't try to keep anything from you."

"No good if you had," the old man told her. "No damn good if you had. I find out."

"Of course you do, Father Graham," she said. "You mustn't get excited."

"Who's excited?" the old man demanded. He seemed to have forgotten Weigand, who wanted to get away.

"All right, Father Graham," Margaret Graham said. "Nobody's excited. But there aren't any secrets about Michael. You know that."

The old man stared at her and then nodded his head.

"No secrets," he said. "That's right. No secrets. They want to adopt this boy." The last was to Weigand again.

"Yes," Weigand said, "I know."

"Can't have any children, you see," Cyrus Graham explained. "Silly business."

This was puzzling. Weigand showed it to the shrewd old eyes, apparently.

"Adopting," Graham explained. "Anybody's brat. But it's all right with me. As long as they don't try to keep it from me."

"Of course," Weigand said. "Lots of people adopt children, you know."

"Silly business, just the same," the old man said. "Damn silly business. Women!"

"Women want them," Weigand translated, more or less for his own benefit. "It seems to be very natural."

Old Graham nodded his head.

"Ought to have their own, though!" he said.

"Really, Father," Mrs. Graham said, "that's an odd way for you to talk."

Graham looked at her, and his manner softened.

"Don't cry about it, Margaret," he said. The tone was kinder than the words. "Not your fault. Except marrying a Graham. Somebody should have told you."

"There wasn't anything to tell," she said. "It just isn't true. Everybody's told you that. The doctor told you that."

"People are fools," old Graham said. "Look at my father. Look at his father. Don't tell me it isn't so."

Mrs. Graham looked at Weigand appealingly.

"I'm sorry," she said. "I didn't know he would get off on this."

"Well—" Weigand began. But the old man broke in.

"May as well know," he said. "No secret about it." He pointed a long finger at Weigand. "Crazy," he said. "That's what it is. Crazy." He waggled the finger. "Not me," he said. "It skipped me. But all the rest of them. My father. His father. So I decided to stop it. What do you think of that?"

"I don't know," Weigand said. "I don't entirely understand you, Mr. Graham."

"Fool!" Graham said. "Perfectly simple. Insanity in the family. In all the Grahams. Except me, of course. Even John's a little off."

He looked at Margaret Graham as he said this.

"Father!" she said. The tone was shocked, protesting.

"Not bad, yet," the old man said. "Nobody sees it except me. You wait!"

Weigand wished he were out of this. But, nevertheless, it was interesting.

"Told them they couldn't have children," Graham said, this time to Weigand. "Not and get my money. My son's smart, whatever I say. Knows money is better than kids. Humors me."

He laughed again, wheezingly.

"Not going to pass it on," he said. "Or I don't pass the money on. Got him, eh?"

"Yes," Weigand said. "Only it isn't generally believed that insanity can be inherited, you know."

"Fools," Graham said, positively. "Think I don't know about that? And whose money is it?"

"Yours, I assume, Mr. Graham," Weigand said. "Will you feel the same about an adopted son?"

"Of course not!" the old man said. "Why should I? No taint. They can adopt a dozen! A hundred! Nothing to me, as long as they're not under foot."

"Well," Weigand said. This time he really moved to go. Mrs. Graham stood up. Old Graham looked at them.

"Hope you catch him," Graham said. "She was a nice girl, for nowadays. Catch him and hang him."

"Right," Weigand said. "We'll try, anyway. Goodbye, Mr. Graham."

The old man wasn't looking at them any more. He was staring out at the street. He seemed to have forgotten them. Neither spoke until they were outside again. Then Mrs. Graham said she was sorry.

"I didn't know he would be like this," she said. "He is unpredictable."

Weigand looked at her, feeling sympathy.

"I'm sorry," he said. "It must be difficult for you. That is true, I gather—what he said about children?"

"Oh yes," she said. Her voice sounded tired, and without spirit. "That's true enough. If we have children we don't get his money. And John feels we need it. That's why we are adopting Michael. And none of it is true, of course. His father wasn't insane, nor his grandfather. Just as he is—explosive and odd, but quite sane. We found out. Even if insanity is hereditary, there isn't any to be inherited. But what can we do?"

Weigand didn't know. He admitted he didn't know.

# · 9 ·

Downstairs, George Benoit was standing by a window, looking out at the hot street. The elder members of the family seemed to like looking out of windows. Benoit turned as his daughter and Weigand entered and smiled at Margaret Graham's helpless, half-amused shrug.

"Difficult, I see," Benoit said. "Poor old Cyrus." He seemed gently amused. "And now, my dear, I'm off," he said. "Since I can't see Craven until tomorrow, I may as well see Smith today." It sounded a little like a riddle to Weigand, but evidently not to Mrs. Graham. She said, "But it's so hot, Father. And that long ride in the subway. If you insist on not driving."

He would, Benoit told her, rather ride the subway than try to park on Forty-second Street.

"Wouldn't you, Lieutenant?" he said to Weigand, smiling. He was a pleasant man, Weigand decided. Then he remembered that Benoit had met Lois Winston the day before.

"I'm going downtown from here," he said. "I can give you a lift if you like."

It was very good of him, Benoit said. He'd appreciate it. He repeat-

97

ed his appreciation when he sat beside Weigand in the Buick. Weigand
U-turned and headed toward the Parkway.

"Good of you," Benoit said. "Beats the subway. But I don't know
anything, if you had that in mind."

He smiled at Weigand, wisely. Weigand smiled back.

"Right," Weigand said. "Always a cop. But it's nothing, really. I
wondered what you thought of the girl—the girl who was killed—
when you met her yesterday. I suspect you think about people."

"I liked her," Benoit said. "I was sorry to hear of what happened.
And it disturbed my daughter, of course—she thinks it will complicate
matters about the boy. I don't suppose it will?"

Weigand said he shouldn't think so.

"You didn't notice anything odd about her?" he pressed. "She didn't
seem under a strain? Anything like that?"

Benoit shrugged.

"I didn't notice anything," he said. "But I'd never seen her before. I
don't know how she was usually, of course. My daughter would be a
better person to ask."

Naturally, Weigand agreed. He had asked. Mrs. Graham had noticed
nothing.

"Nor did I," Benoit repeated. "I wasn't paying much attention, actually. I was—well, not in a settled frame of mind, particularly. I was
thinking of my own affairs and of a cop in Danbury. Or should I say
policeman?"

It didn't matter, Weigand told him. "Cop" was all right.

"Traffic, I suppose?" he said, not caring.

They were talking idly, wheeling toward the Parkway. Traffic, of
course, Benoit told him. And a three-hour delay, where it would do the
most harm, while he paid a five-dollar fine to a judge.

"I was driving down from Hartford," he said. "I live there, you
know. Going to Washington to see a man. And so I get held up in Danbury until it's too late to make it. I decided to stop in New York
overnight and go on to Washington by train this evening. I was feeling
annoyed about the whole business when I saw Miss Winston, so I
didn't notice much about her."

Weigand agreed it was annoying. Although, he added, anything which would keep a man out of Washington in weather like this wasn't an unmixed evil. Benoit smiled.

"It's hot enough here," he said. "It's hot in Hartford."

A fascinating discussion, Weigand told himself, broodingly. And probably as valuable for his purpose as any other he had had that day. He had, he suspected, merely given himself a few irrelevancies to think about; merely cluttered his mind. "The trouble with me as a cop," he told himself, "is that I get interested in people. People who are none of my business." He sighed, and drew up behind another car which had stopped for a red light. O'Malley was, after all, a better cop. He stuck to the main issue—he stuck to Randall Ashley which, nine chances in ten, was the place to stick.

"Light's changed," Benoit said, half to himself.

Weigand pulled the gear lever toward him into low and let his foot relax on the clutch. Then he pushed it down again and waited while the car ahead jumped the light.

"I've got to be legal," he told Benoit. "At least, when there's no hurry. Our friend in front doesn't have to be, he figures. So he goes while it is still red both ways, which would make the traffic detail a little annoyed if they saw it."

"Oh," Benoit said. "I didn't notice. We have a different system in Hartford."

What he would do after he dropped Benoit and checked at Headquarters, Weigand decided, was to get back on the Randall Ashley angle. It might, he decided, be worth while to talk to Ashley's girl friend—Miss Madge Ormond, who sang in night clubs. It would be interesting to see what she did when he called her Mrs. Ashley. He turned onto the Parkway and picked up speed. It was only fifteen minutes later that he wheeled off at Forty-fourth and delivered Benoit to city traffic.

"This will be fine," Benoit said. "No use dragging you across town. I'll get a taxicab."

He was, Weigand explained, going across town about here in any case. He went across town, patient of the lights. He dropped Benoit and found a telephone.

Mullins had reports of three unknowns who had purchased atropine sulphate during the past week, all to make eyewash. The eyewash business must be good, Mullins thought.

"It's all a lotta eyewash, Loot," he said, cheerfully.

It was hot in the booth.

"Is it?" Weigand said. "Did you plan to mean something, sergeant?"

His voice was not encouraging. Mullins remained tolerant.

"O.K., Loot," he said. "We got a wire from the Veterans Hospital in Arizona. They never heard of any Richard Osborne. Have we gotta be surprised?"

"No," Weigand said. "We don't have to be surprised. What else?"

Detective Stein had turned in a funny-looking list of words which he said the lieutenant wanted. Something about an encyclopædia?

"Right," Weigand said. "Hold it. I'll be down."

Mullins had had a check made on Madge Ormond, who was, unless somebody had slipped up, safely at home in her apartment in the Forties. She was in the money, it seemed like. In the field of night club singing, she rated.

"Zori's," Mullins said. "Only it's closed, now, for redecoration. And she's been in a coupla shows."

"Right," Weigand said. "And?"

A man was on his way to keep an eye on Mrs. Halstead. Randall Ashley had not left the apartment; a middle-aged woman, identified as Mrs. Ashley, had gone in. So had a man with a black bag. (The lounging detective apparently had made friends with an elevator operator, Weigand decided.) David McIntosh had gone to his office about ten, gone out to lunch about one. He was still out to lunch, and Detective Hildebrandt was practically sitting in his lap. Young Frank Kensitt was, as he had indicated, a ward of the Foundation. Lois Winston had taken special trouble with him, and got him his job at the Ritz-Plaza. He was now doing a little floor scrubbing at the Ritz-Plaza.

Weigand ticked off detail.

"Right," he said. "There's no use your taking root there. Get onto the Ashley lawyer, or whoever knows. Find out the precise conditions of the will."

"What will?" said Mullins.

It was, Weigand decided, a sound question.

"Both wills, come to think of it," he said. "The will under which young Ashley gets his money, if he does. Lois Winston's will. Any other wills you run across."

Mullins said that would be O.K. And then what?

"Come in," Weigand said. "We'll see what you've got. Then, if you've been a good boy, I may take you to the Norths'."

Mullins was cheerful.

"O.K., Loot," he said. "I'll dig around."

Weigand went to lunch. It was, he realized after he had thought of it, high time. He absorbed a Tom Collins which was only fair and some cold salmon which tasted of nothing. He returned to the car, circled the block and pulled up in front of an elderly building which had a window card saying "Vacancy." Inside the vestibule he pushed a bell marked Ormond and the door clicked. On the third floor a colored maid said that Miss Ormond was dressing.

"She isn't seeing nobody," the maid said.

"She wasn't seeing nobody," Weigand corrected. "Now she *is* seeing somebody."

He showed his badge and the maid's eyes enlarged.

"Yessir," she said. "I'll tell her."

She went, leaving the door open. Weigand followed her in.

It was a surprisingly pleasant living-room, he decided, with light walls and unobtrusively modern furniture. The maid went through a door at the side and after a little while Madge Ormond came out the same door. She was wearing a pale yellow negligée and was stimulating to look at. Her eyes were wary and her voice had no particular intonation. It was low and husky and she laid it out flat on the air.

"Yes, Lieutenant?" she said.

She had decided, Weigand observed, not to be the tough little girl that she had been at their first meeting. Her new manner seemed to fit better.

"How long have you and Randall Ashley been married?" Weigand said.

She looked at him without answering for a moment and, still looking, sat down. Weigand sat down opposite her. The negligée opened as she crossed her knees and Weigand observed that she had very nice legs.

"'Bout six weeks," she said. She didn't ask how he knew. She closed the small rift in the negligée, without making a point of it.

"You know," he said, "it means that Ashley doesn't get his money. Only the interest."

"Yes, Lieutenant," she said. "We both knew that."

"And so tried to keep it secret," Weigand said.

She wasn't rising.

"Naturally," she said. "Not being fools. Wouldn't you, if it came to that?"

"No," Weigand said. "I don't think so."

She looked at him and smiled.

"But you are so upright, Lieutenant," she said. "And I'm just a night club singer. That's why the lady is a tramp."

"Are you?" Weigand said. "I wouldn't know."

"And," she said, "you wouldn't believe me if I said I wasn't. If I said I didn't give a damn about the money."

"I don't know," Weigand said. "I might, Miss Ormond. About being a tramp, that is. Everybody gives a damn about money." He looked at her, and this time her eyes did not reject his look so blankly. "Suppose I say I wouldn't pick you for a tramp. Suppose you pretend I'm not trying to put anything over. Just to see how it works out."

She studied him, this time. Then she nodded slowly.

"You don't seem so tough," she admitted. "Maybe you really want to know things. I don't think I'm a tramp. Randall's money is swell— any money is swell. We'd like to have the money, all right. *We'd* like to have it. Not *I'd* like to have it." She looked at him hard, leaning forward a little and searching his face. "Is that too deep for you, Lieutenant?" she said.

Weigand was patient.

"I can touch bottom," he said. "I just want to know, Miss Ormond. You can see why—you're not missing things. What Randall might do if you were just digging some gold is one thing. What he might do if you and he were really together is another. You'll have to take my word for it that I just want to know."

He paused.

"Or," he said, "you don't have to take my word. Play it as you want to. I'll get along somehow."

"All right," Madge Ormond said. "I'll take a chance. I love the kid. So what does that make me?"

He looked at her thoughtfully. Sophistication can be very defensive when it is challenged.

"It makes it different," Weigand said. He studied her face and then saw that her eyes were wet. Her smile was neat and exact and her face was smooth and lovely, but her eyes were wet. "Your mascara will run," he warned her.

"Not it," she said. "Guaranteed." She said it as lightly as she could, but it wasn't very lightly. Slowly she began to nod her head and her lips trembled. "All right," she said. "I'm not so tough. I love the kid. He loves me. He wouldn't do anything to hurt us." She said it challengingly. "He's different underneath," she said. "He's not the way he acted at all."

"Isn't he?" Weigand said. He said it gently. He didn't, he found, think Madge Ormond had gone into her act.

"We both started out being tough," she said. "I'll give you that. He was money in the bank to me and I was—well, I'll give you one guess—to him. And then—then it got different. Not all at once, or anything. Just after awhile it was different. And then we decided to get married. But we still didn't see any reason why he shouldn't have his money; we wouldn't be cheating anybody else. So we kept it secret."

"Where did you get married?" he asked.

"Right here," she said. "Only—well, Madge Ormond is just the name I use. I'm—" she hesitated. "Oh, the hell with it," she said. "My name is Stella Ormk."

"What?" said Weigand.

She laughed, a little hysterically.

"Ormk," she said. "Believe it or not, Ormk."

"I've got to believe it," Weigand said, awed. "It would have to be true."

He thought a moment.

"It was only six weeks ago?" he said. "That might be important. Remember, I can look it up."

"Yes," she said, "six weeks." She didn't ask why it might be important.

"And," he said, "how long before that had you been—going together?"

"About two years."

"Not"—he figured quickly—"nearer four years?"

"Two years," she said. "Why?"

He shook his head at her. A theory was growing in his head as he shook it.

"Before that," he said, "did he see a lot of some girl—some girl his father found out about? Some girl, maybe, who really was a tramp?"

"I don't know," she said. "I suppose so. We didn't talk about it."

"Do you know," Weigand said, bluntly, "whether he and this other girl ever had a child?"

She stared at him, her eyes widening.

"I don't get it," she said. "He was just a kid—what do you mean?"

He wasn't, Weigand reminded her, so much of a kid as all that. Four years ago he was nineteen. Plenty old enough to get into trouble.

"Suppose that had happened," Weigand said. "And it came out. He wouldn't get his money, would he?"

It was a stab in the dark, and he couldn't tell what it hit. She stared at him.

"I don't know what you're talking about," she said. There was no animus he could detect. "It was just if he married, I think."

Weigand puzzled over it. He didn't know, either. But it was worth trying.

"Suppose," he said, "that there is something in the will which provides that Randall doesn't get his money if he is married before he is twenty-five *or* if he is seriously involved with a woman before he is twenty-five. And suppose somebody—his sister, maybe—stumbled by accident onto the fact that he had had a son when he was a kid of nine-teen." He watched her face. If she and Randall were really close, and there was anything in his theory, she might know—she might know a lot. He waited.

"It wasn't that way," she said. Her eyes were very wide in a pale face. "You can't do that to Buddy!"

"I'm not trying to do anything to Buddy," he told her. "I'm trying to find out what you know. Maybe it wasn't in the will. But maybe Lois did find out about the child and was going to use what she had found out to influence her mother, so that she wouldn't agree to Buddy's mar-riage with you—and wouldn't be reasonable if she found out that you were already married. How does that sound?"

"I tell you it wasn't that way," she said. "I don't know where you get all this stuff about a child. Buddy didn't do anything to his sister—he couldn't." There was terrible anxiety in her face. "You believed me a while ago," she said. "You've got to believe me now—he couldn't! We didn't want to hurt anybody; we wouldn't ever have hurt anybody. We just wanted to be together, and we didn't see why he couldn't have his money. And so he wanted to talk to Lois."

She spoke eagerly, with a kind of desperate intensity. She believes that, Weigand told himself. I'm almost sure she believes it.

"That's why he went to her table," the girl went on. There was no effort, now, to maintain a pose. She seemed younger and, Weigand thought, very frightened.

"He just went over to leave a note," she went on. "About talking to her later—he was going to tell her everything about us. The way it real-ly was. He said he could make her understand—he said she just didn't understand how it was, because she kept remembering how he had been when he was younger, but that he could make her see. 'She's all right, really, Sis is,' he said to me. 'She'll be for us when she gets the picture.'"

Her eyes were anxious as they sought his.

"Everything was going to be all right," she said. "We both believed it was—we were sure. Don't you see we wouldn't have gained if any-thing happened to Lois—that we just wanted to explain things to her, so she would tell her mother how Buddy and I really felt. Don't you see that?"

"I don't know," Weigand said. "I think you believe it, Miss Ormond. I wondered about that, but now I think you believe it. But I don't know, really."

Her arm went out along the arm of the chair, and her head dropped on it. It was a defeated, touching movement.

"I'm sorry," Weigand said. "But you'll see how it is yourself when you think it over. You're just going on what your husband told you. I can't promise anything."

The blond head turned on the arm.

"Leave me alone," she said. "Can't you leave me alone?"

Weigand turned away. Then he stopped.

"I'm not trying to get anything on anybody, Miss Ormond," he said. "Nothing that isn't already there. If Buddy's in the clear I can't hurt him. You know that."

"All right," she said, her voice muffled and dull. "I have to believe you. But I'm afraid. I'm so afraid!"

There wasn't anything to say. Weigand turned and walked toward the door. Behind him he heard Madge Ormond sobbing. It's a hell of a racket, Weigand told himself, gloomily. He was tired of seeing people. He would go down to Headquarters and look at some papers. Papers didn't stir you up. It was easy to be a cop when you could do it on paper.

# · 10 ·

He was rather relieved than otherwise when, getting a physician on the telephone at the Ashley apartment, he was informed flatly that Mrs. Ashley was still in no condition to be interviewed. He drove downtown through the heat. It would storm later, he thought. Looking down a side street as he drove south he could see heavy storm-heads banking up in the west. At Headquarters there was word to see Inspector O'Malley. O'Malley wanted action, he said.

"Where's this Ashley guy?" he wanted to know. Weigand told him. The Ashley guy had gone out early in the afternoon to see an undertaker. Now he was back at the apartment again, presumably holding his mother's hand. David McIntosh had gone back to the offices from which he administered his affairs—the McIntosh estate. Then he had gone to the Harvard Club. Not being a Harvard man, the detective associated with David McIntosh had loitered in Forty-fourth street.

"Ashley," O'Malley said, positively. "Ashley's the guy. What are we waiting for?"

They were waiting for evidence, Weigand told him, with all proper politeness. Meanwhile—

"Meanwhile," O'Malley said, "you waste time talking to a lot of people who don't figure." He banged his desk. "If I wasn't nailed down here I'd do it myself," he said. "You young guys—!"

Weigand waited until Inspector O'Malley blew over. He was not particularly alarmed by the chance that O'Malley might leave his desk. O'Malley liked a place to put his feet.

O'Malley blew over. Weigand went back to his desk and found reports awaiting him. Two of the three men who had recently purchased atropine sulphate to use in making eyewash were, it developed, busily making eyewash. The third had not been located. At the address he gave, nobody had ever heard of him. Weigand brooded over this.

"There's our guy, Loot," Mullins said. "All we have to do is round him up."

"Is it?" Weigand said. "That's nice, Mullins. What does he look like?"

"Well," Mullins said, "we had a little trouble there. He's a short, fat guy about five feet, ten inches and weighing around a hundred and sixty pounds, and he's either got black hair or he's bald. A couple or three guys saw him, which makes it tough."

"Well," Weigand said, "let me know when you round him up, won't you, Mullins?"

"Listen, Loot," Mullins said, aggrieved. Weigand smiled at him.

"Right," Weigand said. "No doubt he is our man. It will be a help to have these couple or three guys look him over—when we catch him. The D. A.'ll like that. But I think we're going to catch him from the other end."

Mullins pondered it and said, "Yeah."

"It's screwy again, ain't it, Loot?" he said. "You think it was this guy, Ashley?"

Weigand shrugged.

"Well," Mullins said, reasonably, "who else we got? This guy McIntosh?"

"Why not?" said Weigand. "On the other hand, why? He wanted to marry the girl, and the only quarrel he seems to have had was because she wouldn't marry him fast enough and wanted to keep on working. So he kills her? Why?"

Mullins said he wouldn't know. Still, this McIntosh guy was there.

Precisely, Weigand agreed. And if he had any reason, he was a good bet. There was, already, something screwy about the reservation angle. Mullins nodded, approvingly. He thought the Loot had something there, all right. On the other hand, there was Mrs. Halstead to be considered. She, alone among the people they had run into, admitted animus toward Lois Winston. And she was at the roof.

"Yeh?" Mullins said. "How come?"

Weigand told him. Mullins brightened. Then his face fell.

"She don't sound like the kind of dame who would be dancing much, Loot," he said. "So why pass the table?"

"Right," Weigand said. "Things seem to cancel out."

"How about Mrs. Graham?" Mullins said. "Does she fit in anywhere?"

Weigand shook his head. There was nothing to indicate it. She denied, by implication, having been at the roof; she professed to have liked Miss Winston, and the smooth progress of the placement proceedings supported her contention, so far as it applied. If she had any special interest, it was to keep Miss Winston alive until the placement was completed. Mullins nodded. The same, Weigand said, seemed to apply to Mrs. Graham's husband, except that they didn't know where he was that night.

"He was out," Weigand said. "A business conference—maybe."

Weigand sighed. Graham would have to be interviewed. He looked at Mullins speculatively, and an expression of cheer crossed his face.

"Listen, Loot," Mullins said, quickly.

"Yes," Weigand said. "That's what we'll do. You pop along and see what Mr. John Graham was doing last night. We might want to know some time."

"Listen, Loot," Mullins said. "He ain't even in it. And it's hot as—"

Gravely, as a lecturer on police practice, Weigand told Mullins about routine and thoroughness. One should, he pointed out, leave no stone unturned, and no grass growing under foot. One should take the stitch in time that saved nine and watch the pennies so that the pounds would take care of themselves. One should—

"O.K., Loot," Mullins said. "I'll go see Graham. You got me, Loot."

It was, Weigand thought after Mullins had gone, probably foolish to waste Mullins' time. But it might be useful to have everybody placed, even those on the outskirts. He got an assistant of the city toxicologist and listened. Knowing what to look for and being prodded, they had hurried. It was now official that Lois Winston had died of a heavy dose of atropine sulphate. Things were thus kept in order as they went along, Weigand told himself. He picked up two typewritten sheets, dictated by Detective Stein, who had found an encyclopædia.

"Subjoined," wrote Detective Stein, "is a partial list of subject headings from Volume 11 of the Encyclopædia Britannica, Pages 199 to 810. This is approximately the center one-half of the volume."

Detective Stein was thorough, Weigand decided. And he liked nice words. "Subjoined," Weigand read over, pleased. He went on with the list.

It began with "Hawkweed" which was a "troublesome weed" native to the British Isles and North America. It included Haworth, which was in Yorkshire and "hawser" which was a thick rope. Hawthorne, Nathaniel, was fully dealt with. Weigand read on:

> Hay. (Grass dried in the sun. Two and one half pages.)
>
> Haydn, Franz Joseph.
>
> Hay Fever.
>
> Head-dress.
>
> Health.
>
> Heat. (Thirty-one pages.)
>
> Hebrew. (Nineteen pages.)
>
> Heir.
>
>> (Weigand paused at this one and made a note. It might be worthwhile, eventually, to discover what the Encyclopædia had to say about heirs.)
>
> Heligoland Bight. (Two pages.)
>
> Helium. (Colorless and odorless gas for balloons. Two pages.)
>
> Henry—

(The Henrys ran on indefinitely, by number.)
Hepatoscopy. (Method of divining the future.)
   (Weigand appreciated Detective Stein's explanatory
   notes. Otherwise, he feared, curiosity would have
   driven him to looking up "hepatoscopy.")
Hepplewhite.
Heraldry.
Heredity. (Resemblance between an organism and its ancestors.)
Herring.
Hibernation. (The more or less comatose condition in which
   certain animals pass the winter in cold latitudes.)
Hieroglyphs.
Hindenburg.
Hindustani.
Histology. (Science of study of the tissues.)
Hittites.
Hockey.
Holland.
Hollywood.
Homicide. (The "general and neutral term for the killing of
   one human being by another.")
"Well," said Weigand. "Why neutral?"
There was nobody in the office to answer him and he read on.
Hormones. (Discussion of adrenalin under this heading.)
Houses.

Underneath, apparently after he had read over the transcription, Detective Stein had written in longhand:

"These looked most promising. Might be something in hormones, do you think?"

Weigand read the list over, slowly. Here and there he crossed out. If Lois Winston had been reading about Hittites or Hollywood the previous afternoon it was hard to see that it meant anything. Perhaps she had merely read herself to sleep in the encyclopædia; Weigand knew a man, he reminded himself, who read the encyclopædia whenever opportunity offered, purely as a relaxation. It was difficult to think of any circumstances under which Holland or hockey or Hindenburg might apply. He crossed them off, shortening the list. Hay and Haydn went. Finally he ended and looked at the words remaining:

"Health—heat—heir—helium—hepatoscopy—heredity—hibernation—hieroglyphs—histology—homicide—hormones."

He looked it over again and scratched off "hibernation." Then he wondered where he was, and couldn't decide. Chasing wild geese again, probably. He sighed. The chances were, he thought, wiping his forehead, that Miss Winston had merely been reading up on heat. That would have been appropriate, if tautological. He stuck Stein's report in his pocket and looked at his watch. It was, he was surprised to note, after five. The Norths had said "any time" and he could hope they meant it. About now, he decided, Mr. North would be crushing ice for cocktails, using that short wooden mallet at which they had all looked, once, with so much widening surprise. The thought of cocktails was pleasant. And perhaps Dorian would be early. Then he had another thought, and called Dorian's apartment.

It was fine to hear her voice; to hear, or imagine, a new note in it when she heard his. She was, she said, going to the Norths'—just dressing. And it would be nice if Bill would drive by for her—very nice. Cradling the telephone, Weigand felt much better. What he needed was a drink and some conversation, and then he could come back with his mind rested and put two and two together. A picture of Dorian rose unexpectedly in his mind and he smiled at it. Well, he thought, call it "a drink and some conversation," anyway.

He left word that Mullins, when he returned, was to come on to the Norths'. He went out into Centre Street. The clouds were halfway up the sky now; it was strange, and somehow forbidding, that the storm was taking so long to gather. There was an odd, disturbing light on the streets and buildings as he drove uptown for Dorian Hunt.

# • 11 •

The storm broke while they were finishing dinner at the Norths', and it was a great relief to everyone. The strange, coppery light had held for almost an hour and then it had grown dark, an hour and more before it was time to grow dark. For a long while then, they could hear thunder rumbling off across the Hudson and Mr. North, staring out of the window, had seemed nervous and irritable.

"For God's sake, get on with it," he instructed nature. But it was still a quarter of an hour before nature obliged. Then nature got on with it in a rather surprising fashion, hurling noise at the city, rolling thunder along the streets, splitting the false darkness with lightning. Then a wind raced through the apartment and rain rattled angrily against quickly closed windows.

"Well," Mrs. North told her husband, "you asked for it."

It was intermittently too noisy, then, for conversation. They were sitting around the room with coffee cups balanced before it was worth the trouble to talk of more than subjects which came conveniently in snatches. And then none of them said anything for a time, but presently

113

they were all looking at Weigand expectantly. He looked back at them, one by one.

"Does it ever occur to any of you good people that I am a public servant, sworn to secrecy?" he inquired.

Pam laughed openly at him, and the others smiled.

"That's a good one, Loot," Mullins said. "That's sure a good one."

Weigand looked at him darkly and then he shrugged.

"You can't keep us out of them, Bill," Mrs. North told him. "You ought to know that by this time. And we're all very confidential."

"And," said Weigand, "very confident. Too confident by half. But what do you want to know?"

"Why," Mrs. North said, "who did it, of course."

Weigand shook his head. So, he said, did he.

"It's in all the papers," Mrs. North pointed out. "About David McIntosh and the girl's brother and his girl and everything. Even about Michael and the Foundation. Everything. So there's no harm in telling us the rest.

"And," she added, "it will be clearer to you after you talk. It always is."

There was, Weigand admitted, that. He looked at Mullins speculatively.

"This isn't happening, Mullins," he said. "Not officially. Right?"

Mullins merely looked hurt.

"Right," Weigand said. "And, by the way, what about John Graham, for a starter?"

"O.K.," Mullins said. "I talked to him. Up where he works."

He was, Mullins said, office manager for some place where they made perfume. He got out a notebook. "Henry et Paulette," he said.

Mrs. North looked puzzled. Then her face cleared.

"Oh," she said. "I see. It sounded—like a cannibal, somehow."

Mullins was puzzled and waited, but she did not clarify.

"Well," he said, "he's got a pretty good job there, apparently. Sort of in charge of things." He had a private office and a secretary and Mullins had just caught him before he went home.

"He was worried," Mullins said. "Seems like there's a nurse out there and she had called up and said the missus wasn't feeling good—she'd been hysterical or something. So he was about to close up and go home."

"Hysterical?" Weigand said. "She seemed all right—" He let the words trail off. "That's interesting," he continued, after a pause. "All right, Mullins. How about last night?"

"Well, Loot," Mullins said. "This is a good one. He was at the Ritz-Plaza roof. With the girl in his office—the secretary. What do you think of that?"

A large silence developed. The Norths and Dorian looked at Mullins; then they looked at Weigand and waited.

"I think," Weigand said, at length, "that it was a good idea to send you up there, sergeant. And then?"

John Graham had, Mullins indicated, been frank about it. He was at the roof for dinner, with his secretary. They had been working late and both had to eat. He had planned at first to go to a restaurant nearby; had, in fact, sent Miss Hand, who was the secretary, along to the restaurant to wait. He had had to make a detour on the way, conferring with the advertising manager. "And," Mullins commented, "he probably thought there was no use in people seeing him and the girl going out together."

Graham had joined Miss Hand at the restaurant in, as it turned out, about half an hour. The conference had taken longer than he had expected. And he was tired and hot and discovered that the air-conditioning in the restaurant they had picked had broken down—or, at any rate, wasn't cooling the restaurant.

"'And so,'" Mullins read from his notes, "'I thought it would be good for both Miss Hand and myself to go to some really decent place, considering the weather and the work we had to do later and everything. So I suggested the roof.'

"That," Mullins said, "is what he says. Do we have to believe him, Loot? Or was he just showing the girl friend a good time?"

Weigand said he wouldn't know. What did the girl say?

"Just what he says," Mullins admitted. "So what?"

"Right," Weigand said. "Did you check it?"

Mullins had partly checked it, at any rate. Graham had conferred with the advertising manager. Miss Hand had gone first to a restaurant nearby, on her own story. There hadn't been time to verify at the restaurant. There had been time, however, to telephone and ask about the cooling system.

"It didn't break down," Mullins said. "On the other hand, the man said, when I sorta got tough, that maybe it hadn't been working as well as usual."

Weigand drummed with his fingers on the coffee table. It would all, he decided, be worth looking into. With an inquiring glance, which brought a nod from Mr. North, Weigand picked up the telephone. He got Detective Stein and sent him forth to look into things. He replaced the telephone and sat for a moment looking at it. He started as if to pick it up again and then apparently thought better of it.

"Well," he said, "that's the newest bit. Now—"

Rapidly, he sketched the case as it stood, amplifying little but suppressing nothing which seemed of importance. He told of Mrs. Halstead and her hints of knowledge not divulged; of Mrs. Graham and her odd father-in-law; of Madge Ormond—but not of the baptismal name which "Madge Ormond" overlay. He showed them the list he had made from Detective Stein's longer list from the encyclopædia, and of the apparent disappearance of Michael's father.

"That wasn't much of a surprise," he added. "I never fell particularly for the mysterious man. It looked like a dodge to get rid of the child, all along. Although I don't know what Miss Crane could have done, even if she had suspected."

Dorian read over the list and passed it to Mr. North, who looked at it and gave it to Pam. Mrs. North made sounds of discovery.

"Heir!" she said, triumphantly. "That's what she was looking up—heirs. Or—what's hepatoscopy?"

Weigand told her. She shook her head.

"Heirs almost certainly," she said. "Or—or heat, of course. Because she wanted to know why it was so."

"Was so?" Mr. North echoed.

"Hot, of course," Mrs. North told him. "Only in that case it doesn't fit in, does it? It must have been heirs, only that doesn't fit in with my theory. And I'm pretty sure about my theory."

Everybody looked at her in surprise, and she nodded firmly.

"I'm pretty sure," she said. "Ever since I knew it started with Michael."

"Which," Weigand told her, "you of course only think you know."

She shook her head. She was, she said, sure as anything that it was Michael.

"And," she said, "he was kidnaped, of course."

"What?" said Mr. North, anxiously. Weigand said, "What?" at almost the same time, and with almost the same tone. Mrs. North looked at them triumphantly.

"Of course," she said. "Don't tell me you missed that. By Mrs. Halstead, or by somebody Mrs. Halstead was—well, was in with. And the man who brought Michael to the agency was a Federal agent."

"A what?" Mr. North said. "A Federal agent? Listen, Pam, I don't think—"

Mrs. North waved a stop signal at him.

"He had *re*-kidnaped him," Mrs. North said. "But he didn't want to do it officially because they were still looking for the rest of the gang. So he pretended *not* to be a Federal agent and brought him to the Foundation. And—" She stopped suddenly, her eyes rounding. "Listen," she said, "I'll bet I know something else. *It's David McIntosh's son!*"

They all looked at her.

"My God, Pam!" Jerry North said, in slow awe. "How did you ever—I mean, how did you?"

"Well," Mrs. North said, "it's all clear—except maybe about McIntosh. I'm not awfully sure about that."

"No," Weigand said. "No, Pam, I can see you mightn't be." He ran a hand through his hair, thinking how often he had seen Jerry North make the same gesture. "Why kidnaping, Pam?"

It stood to reason, Mrs. North said. Here was a little boy and a woman who sounded just like a kidnaper. She paused.

"Kidnapess?" she said, doubtfully.

Her husband and Weigand and Dorian Hunt shook their heads slowly, unanimously.

"And, of course, Lois Winston found out," Mrs. North said. "Something happened when she was out there—maybe she really went to see Mrs. Halstead yesterday, as well as Mrs. Graham—that made her realize it was a kidnaping. And she gave herself away, somehow. So they followed her to the roof and killed her."

There was a pause.

"Well," Mr. North said, "what do you think of that, Bill?"

"Oddly enough," Bill Weigand began, and got a calculatedly hurt look from Mrs. North. "Oddly enough, we don't know it isn't so. Mrs. Halstead's place wouldn't make a bad hangout; we don't always hear at once about kidnapings—often not until the parents have tried to get the child back on their own. Wipe out the McIntosh angle—you just put that in to make it harder, Pam—and the Federal agent, and it's a theory."

Pam looked pleased.

"I can't say I believe it for a minute," Weigand added. "But it's a theory. Very pretty theory. And it washes out a lot of bothersome things, like Buddy Ashley."

"Well," Mr. North said, "that's the trouble, isn't it? Because of course it *is* Buddy Ashley. I hate to agree with O'Malley, but you can't get away from it. The rest is all—well, just put in to make it harder. Not put in *by* anybody, you understand—the rest is just irrelevant material which always crops up in murder investigations, when you cut across people's lives. You've said as much yourself, Bill."

Weigand nodded.

"So," Mr. North said, "wipe out Michael, and with him Mrs. Halstead and the Grahams. Just don't make it harder. Here's Buddy Ashley, who's afraid his sister is going to give things away to his mother; give away the marriage, which she found out about at the Municipal Building yesterday morning. If that happens, and if the sister makes a damaging story out of it—and he thinks she will—he doesn't get his money. Maybe he needs money. So he bumps her off. Either he puts poison in her glass at the roof, or he fills her thermos bottle at the apartment with it, figuring she'll drink it sooner or later. And one time or another she does drink it. And there's the setup."

It was a long speech for Mr. North. He drank the last of his coffee thirstily. Then he looked at Weigand with expectant confidence. Weigand nodded.

"That's always been the safest guess," he agreed. "I never denied it. But other things have kept coming up. And there are a couple of points in favor of Ashley. One of them, I'll have to admit, is Madge. I think she's on the level. There's a chance that Ashley feels about her as she seems to feel about him. In that case, if she isn't a digger, it's hard to see why he'd murder his half-sister for the money. Remember, he gets the income from it in any case; it is merely a question of the principal."

"Is he hard up?" Mr. North asked.

Weigand nodded. Investigation indicated that young Ashley was hard up.

"As people get hard up in his league," he added. "He owes a lot, some of it to guys I wouldn't want to owe. But he's still eating, obviously. And nobody's pressing him too hard, that we've discovered."

Mr. North said, "Um-m-m."

"You know what it's like?" Mrs. North said. The others paid attention.

"It's like coming in the middle of a picture," she said. "I mean a moving one. There are a lot of people doing things and you don't know why, or who you're in favor of and who against. And so you have to just work things out."

"Just to work things out," Mr. North said. "I know what you mean. I hate to come in in the middle—never makes sense."

Mrs. North shook her head.

"I think I prefer it," she said. "It makes things seem so interesting— so much more interesting than things really *are* in movies. You can just sit there and imagine, and think maybe it is going to be different. Even when it isn't, in the end, you've had the fun of thinking."

"Well," Weigand said, "all right, Pam. You think it was kidnaping; Jerry thinks it was Ashley. You think, also, that it was David McIntosh's son, and a Federal agent and like coming in in the middle of a movie. Right. What do you think, Dorian?"

"I'm afraid of what I think," she said. Her voice was low. "You see, I'm afraid it was the Grahams. I'm afraid Lois Winston was looking up heredity."

"Yes?" said Weigand.

"Suppose," Dorian said, "that the old man—old Cyrus Graham— really is insane, and that his insanity is really inheritable. Suppose Miss Winston found it out and was going to report it. They wouldn't place a child in a home where there was insanity, would they?"

The question was to Pam.

"No," Pam said. "Obviously they wouldn't, I should think."

"But," Dorian said, "suppose they're desperate to have the child— suppose Mrs. Graham is desperate and her husband is devoted to her and, in addition, not quite sane. Perhaps they think that if they kill Miss Winston the truth won't come out. Maybe they figure they can fool the next worker and get the child. So Mrs. Graham gives her something to drink with atropine in it at the house that afternoon, and it doesn't work until much later. Is that possible?"

"It might be," Weigand admitted. "The time the poison needs to take effect doesn't seem completely clear. A few minutes, or a few hours—depending on the dose, and the patient's susceptibility, which may vary. I suppose it isn't impossible."

He spoke doubtfully.

"I can't quite see it," he said. "The motive seems, even supposing that Graham is insane, altogether too weak. It would require that they were both insane, anyway—because on your theory, Mrs. Graham is in on it, even to the extent of being the actual killer. I'll admit they might both be a little off, but it seems like a lot of coincidence. Only—"

"Yes?" Dorian said.

"It would be simpler if we supposed that Graham administered the poison at the roof," he said. "He could have—anybody could have. Suppose that Mrs. Graham is entirely innocent. There's still a catch. So far as we know to the contrary, Graham merely went to the roof by accident. Suppose he did, and got an insane notion to kill Lois Winston so the insanity wouldn't come out. Does he just happen, accidentally, to be carrying poison around?"

Nobody said anything for a moment, and then Mrs. North spoke.

"There's another flaw in it," she said. "Apparently there's no secret about Cyrus Graham's *thinking* there is insanity in the family. He apparently tells anybody he sees, just as he told you, Bill. So where's the big secret they are murdering to keep?"

"I supposed that Cyrus really is insane," Dorian reminded her. "And that it is *really* hereditary insanity. Mrs. Graham pretends it isn't, but possibly Lois found out?"

"How?" said Mr. North. "I should think it would take a long period of observation, even for a qualified psychiatrist, to determine that. And, anyway, I don't think that insanity *can* be inherited."

"That," Weigand said, "would be worth knowing. I'll—"

But Mrs. North got up.

"What's good for the goose is good for the gander," she said. "No, that's wrong—sauce. Anyway, we've got an encyclopædia, too." She vanished, thumped from the hall, said, "Damn," and returned with a heavy book.

"Volume 12," she said. "'Hydroz to Jerem.' What's 'Jerem'?"

Nobody knew.

"Well—" Mrs. North said, and turned up a light. "Let's see—insanity. Instinct in man, insects, insectivora—here it is—insanity."

"Why," inquired Mr. North, "do you suppose she always backs into books? She backs into newspapers the same way."

Nobody answered, except Mrs. North, who made a shushing sound.

"Insanity," Mrs. North said. "U-m-m. Here we are. 'Predisposing cause. (1) Heredity. It has to be admitted that few scientific data are before us to establish on any firm basis our knowledge of the inheritance of mental instability.' They don't seem very sure of themselves, for an encyclopædia, do they? And so on and so on and so on. 'It seems that the absence of an hereditary taint makes the occurrence of insanity much less probable than the presence of it makes the occurrence probable.' What does that mean?"

"Read it again," Mr. North suggested. She read it again.

"I seem to get it," Mr. North said. "It seems to mean that if you haven't insanity in the family you stand a pretty good chance of not going nuts. Whereas if you have insanity in the family, you still stand a pretty good chance of not going nuts. You're a lot surer of staying sane if you have no family background of insanity than you are of going insane if you have."

"That sounds almost as bad," Mrs. North told him. "But I get it, I guess. Now—'in all studies there is lacking some method of determining what are the fundamental units that can be transmitted by heredity. It is probable that these will be found to be not actual diseases, or even definite predispositions to such, but factors that can develop into either insanity or other conditions (character anomalies, criminality, genius, etc.) according to the interaction of environmental influences.'"

"My God," said Mr. North. "Authors! We've got a man who writes just like that."

"Then," Weigand told him, "if you publish people like that you ought to be an authority on them. What does he mean?"

"I think he means that a certain potential instability may be inherited, but not insanity itself," Mr. North said. "He's very cagey."

"Yes," Weigand said. "That's what I gathered. He apparently doesn't think that there is much likelihood of direct inheritance of insanity. Very interesting. And where were we?"

"I should think that Lois would have had to be a lot surer than that before she said anything," Mrs. North said, practically. "Much surer than she could have been, if the authorities are so—upset about it. And anyway, from all I've heard, Mrs. Graham is a nice woman and terribly fond of children, so it's clear she didn't. Don't you think so yourself, Dor?"

"I'd rather," Dorian admitted. "I don't like my theory, really. But, of course, some very objectionable people are fond of children, Pam— some of them are even fond of dogs. Only I'll admit the motive seems pretty obscure, in this instance."

Weigand agreed.

"So?" he said.

"I gotta theory, Loot," Mullins said, unexpectedly. "It was this guy

McIntosh. Who had a better chance? Who lied about making reservations? Who didn't do anything until it was too late?"

Mullins' voice sounded pleased.

"Why?" Weigand asked him.

"Well," Mullins said, "I'll have to admit that ain't so good. But maybe he *did* kill her because she was standing him up—wouldn't marry him and just kept kidding him along. It wouldn't be the first time that happened, Loot."

"No," Weigand said. "That's quite true," he told the others. "There have been plenty of cases—rejected love, even in modern times. But usually the murderers weren't exactly McIntosh's type. They were usually little, injured men, so weak and insecure that they had to prove themselves in blood. Sometimes they go to their girls' homes and kill themselves on the doorstep, for revenge. But none of that sounds like McIntosh."

"Well," said Mullins, stubbornly, "you don't know, Loot. Maybe he's that kind of a guy, underneath. He's a rich guy, remember, and never had any knocks. Maybe the first one was too much for him."

Weigand nodded. He couldn't, he agreed, prove it wasn't so.

"At the moment," he said, "I frankly can't prove anything. And yet—"

Mrs. North took him up.

"You think it's all in?" she said. "That you, and now we, have had a chance to see everything there is to see and that—well, that we've been blind?"

"I wouldn't be surprised," Weigand said. "I have a vague sort of hunch that it's all spread out and—what did you say, Pam?"

"What?" said Pam. "Why, just what you just said. That we have had a chance to see everything and—"

"Oh, I remember," Weigand said, "'and that we've been blind.'"

He sat for a long minute and looked at her. Then he smiled slowly and looked from her to Dorian and then to Jerry North, still smiling faintly.

"No," he said, "I think you may be wrong, Pam. I think perhaps I see a light."

Pam sounded excited.

"Do you, Bill?" she said. "What does it show?"

Weigand smiled at her still, although the smile was fading. It had quite faded when he spoke.

"Oh?" he said. "The light? Why, it shows danger, Pam. It—"

The shrilling of the telephone bell tore his words.

# · 12 ·

It was strange to discover that, even on such an errand as this, discomfort still mattered. It was a wry and irrelevant fact, and obscurely unsettling. There should be a great and terrific dignity on such an errand, the murderer thought. Now you set yourself off, darkly, from other men and women; now you carried death in your hand. In the hand, gripped hard, was death, and in the mind was death and it was strange that when death moved with you all little things did not draw away, abashed by the dark, fearful majesty of the moment. "I am going out to kill," the murderer thought. And still there was discomfort, belittling the moment.

The murderer dragged feet through wet, tall grass in the darkness, finding a way with feet and with the hand which did not carry death. Wet bushes slapped and distracted with their small, impotent annoyance. Water sloshed through shoes and garments clung, cold and impeding, around legs. The world dragged at the murderer, as if to hold death back. But death could not be held back; once you have killed you must, if it is needed, kill again. And now it was needed. The murderer's mind fixed on the need and clung there.

Long ago, the murderer thought, I did all this before—long ago, when I was twelve or so, all this happened over. That night it rained and I was lost and after a while it was like this. Then the world was too big and all the walls fell back and there was nothing I could reach. And everything was unreal then, and I stood off and saw myself and I could not get back into myself for a long time, until somebody brought a light. It is that way now, the murderer thought, and for a moment the murderer stood still, in tall, wet grass. The murderer saw this other person standing there, clutching death. That is myself, the murderer thought.

It was only for a moment and then the murderer went on. It had been dark for a long time, but that was the false darkness of the storm. The clouds were rolling off now and there were wet stars left behind, but now it was really dark, with the darkness of night.

"I can't see my hand before my face," the murderer thought and held up the hand which clutched death. The murderer giggled softly because the thought was so irrelevant and inadequate and stale against the moment. "I can't see my hand before my face," the murderer thought. "My hand before my face. My hand before my face." The words became a rhythm and in the rhythm the murderer could forget the other little, futile things. The surface of the murderer's mind played with the words, over and over, and was occupied. The murderer forced through a low, uncared-for hedge and stopped. "My hand before my face, my hand before my face," the murderer's mind said over and over.

There was a light in the house. It was a pale, yellow light and the murderer watched it for a moment, not moving. The light was blotted out a moment and then reappeared, as if someone had moved between the window and a lamp. In the darkness the murderer moved forward slowly, carefully. The weedy grass was not so tall, here, but still the murderer's feet sank into it, sank to soft, yielding ground.

"Footprints!" the murderer thought, and stopped. "I'm leaving footprints," the murderer thought. Then, with a puzzled sigh, the murderer remembered that that thought had come before and been allowed for. The fear which had surged up for a moment, as if something vital had been forgotten until it was too late, ebbed away. "My hand before my face," the murderer thought. "My hand before my face."

The door of the house ought to be a little to the right of the window. They would be watching the house. For minutes the murderer had stood at the end of the street, in the darkness, and waited until there was dark movement near the house, just perceptible against the fading light in the sky to the west. That would be the watcher, the murderer had decided, and had moved backward cautiously in the shadow and gone down another street and then, very slowly and with a kind of desperate care, through a weed-grown lot. If they are smart, the murderer thought, they'll find out the way I came through the weeds. The murderer giggled, thinking how little good it would do them if they did.

It was, the murderer thought, moving with slow care toward the house, easier the other way. The white powder had looked so innocent in the little twist of paper; there was no terror in letting it slip from the paper into the glass. It was not like murder, the murderer thought—the mind would not accept a few grains of white powder in a glass as murder. You felt no particular responsibility for what happened; it was as if the white powder, in some fashion of its own, became the murderer. Between what you did, untwisting paper and letting powder spill, and the death which came afterward there was no connection that the emotions could compass. You knew you had killed, but you did not feel like a murderer. When you murdered you saw the other person's face near your own, and saw terror in it and then—you killed. You reached out a hand and there was death in it, and you killed.

It is real this way, the murderer thought, and there was a kind of savage eagerness in the thought. The other one who died had been an obstacle; you pressed a button and, at a great distance, the obstacle disappeared. But this one was an enemy and you would meet your enemy and see fear in the enemy's face and then your one hand would act. The murderer looked at the weapon. A knife would have been better; there was a kind of dreadful intimacy about killing with a knife. But it was too late to think of that, now.

Here was the door and the murderer raised a hand. It had come, now; now there was no waiting for it any longer. The murderer knocked.

A dog began barking shrilly inside. The murderer waited and the dog's bark died away.

"No!" the murderer thought. "She's got to be there!" The murderer knocked again.

There were slow, heavy steps moving toward the door. Then they stopped and the woman inside spoke.

"Who is it?" she said. "Go around to the front."

"No," the murderer said. "You know who it is. I've got to talk to you."

"Oh," the woman said. "So it's you. I wondered if you wouldn't come sneaking around. Wait a minute. You can talk to me, all right."

The murderer heard the metallic clatter, subdued and small, as the chain was lifted inside. Now, the murderer thought. Now it has come. The door opened a little way and the woman stood in it.

"Well," she said, "so it's you, all right, is it? I thought—"

There was no use letting her go on. It was now—now! The gun spoke three times.

It was not as the murderer had thought it would be. There had been no time for terror in the other face; it had merely been the old woman's face, with a kind of satisfaction in it, and then, in the instant before she fell, there had been nothing in the face at all—not even surprise. And then the woman was no longer standing at the door.

The murderer ran, now. Now the darkness was a friend, was safety. The wet grass and the wet bushes closed behind the murderer, like a concealing curtain; the murderer could feel the world thickening behind to protect. There was a kind of exultation in the murderer's mind. "I'm safe," the murderer thought. "Now I'm safe!"

# • 13 •

WEDNESDAY
9:20 P.M. TO 10:45 P.M.

When the telephone bell shrilled Weigand was nearest, and he scooped it up even as Mr. North nodded at him.

"Yes," Weigand said. There was a pause. "Yes? Right, Sullivan." There was another pause. Weigand's voice when he spoke again was not raised, but there was a new timbre in it. "Who got her?" He listened again. "No," he said. "I suppose you couldn't. Are you sure she's dead? Where are you?" Pause. "Well, get on to the precinct. Tell them to get some men around the block—around several blocks, if they've got enough. How long has it been?" He listened. "It won't do any good, probably," he said. "Tell the precinct it's our case and get them on it. Get the district squad on it. I'll be along. What?—Right!"

He was standing as he dropped the telephone back on its cradle.

"Mrs. Halstead has been shot," he said. "She's dead." He looked at the others; at Mullins, who was on his feet, too. "God knows I don't get it," Weigand said. "Unless—" He stared unseeingly at Mr. North for a moment. He pulled himself out of it. "All right, Mullins," he said. His voice was crisp and full of purpose. "We're going along."

"Do you suppose it's the same one?" Mr. North said. His voice sounded alarmed. Weigand looked at him and saw him.

"I wouldn't know," he said. "It looks like it, doesn't it?" He was reaching for the door when he spoke again. "I guess we'll have to wash out your kidnaping theory, Pam," he said. He was through the door and halfway down the stairs. Mullins, however, stopped a minute with his hand on the knob.

"Goodnight," Mullins said. "I'm—" He clutched for the correct words. "I'm sorry we have to bust off like this, Mrs. North. We had a swell time." Mullins took one last look at a tantalus which contained rye. "As far as it went," Mullins said, a little wistfully. Then he called, "O.K., Loot," in answer to a muffled sound from below, and went heavily, but rapidly, down the stairs.

"Well," Mrs. North said, looking after him. "That was sudden, wasn't it?"

"Very," Mr. North agreed. "There's nothing like a murder to break up a party."

Mrs. North said she was just thinking that.

"You know," she said, "do you suppose it could be something we do—something wrong, I mean?—*All* our dinners seem to end like this nowadays. With murders." Mrs. North looked perplexed. "Do you suppose," she said, "it could be something about us?"


The side street in Riverdale, so deserted an hour earlier—so distant, in its eddy, from the city of New York—was busy enough now. Weigand wheeled the Buick diagonally to the curb, so that its headlights joined others in sweeping the rough, weed-grown yard; in glaring harshly on the old brick of the house itself. Green-and-white radio cars stood by the curb. Behind the house, visible and audible as Weigand stepped from the car, men moved with lights. Somebody said, "Here. Look at this!" and lights converged in a knot.

A light swung into Weigand's face as he walked up the path with the car lights behind him. "All right, buddy," a heavily official voice started.

"Right," Weigand said. "Weigand. Homicide."

"Yes, sir," the voice said, still official, but less heavy. "They're waiting for you inside, Lieutenant."

He didn't need to be told that Mullins, moving in on the lieutenant's heels, was another cop. Even if Mullins had been alone, not sponsored by the Lieutenant, no other cop would ever have called him "buddy," in the tone reserved for interfering laymen. Mullins was policeman to his shoe-leather, and looked it every inch. "Hiya," he said to the uniformed man who had checked them. "Hiya," the patrolman responded, giving the password.

They were already rigging floodlights in the old house, augmenting the smaller glow from forty-watt bulbs in bargain basement lamps. The cold, inquiring glare of the floods was merciless to the old house—to old rugs on the uneven floors, to faded paper curling away from the walls of the hall, to the holes in the covers of heavy, ancient chairs.

"Right," Weigand said to a detective who told him, "right out there, Lieutenant." "Right," he said again, when another detective straightened up as he entered and said, "Weigand? Kenman. Bronx Homicide.

"Here she is," Lieutenant Kenman said, needlessly. "Three of them. Right through her."

Weigand knelt where Kenman had been kneeling. She had been a big, heavy woman, had Mrs. Halstead; a woman with an unrelenting face. The face had relented, now, but even in death it was formidable. She lay huddled, as if she had been half supported by something when she was shot, and had crumpled to the floor. Weigand swung a torch around, examining the old boards of the kitchen floor. Blood was dull on the boards. The beam of the torch swept under an old icebox, from which brown paint was flaking, and picked up two small, answering beams.

"What the hell?" said Weigand. He moved the light a little and, behind the tiny lights was a cowering cat. "Poor little devil," Weigand thought. "There ought to be a dog. Anybody seen it?"

"We've got it in another room," Kenman said. "It was a nuisance out there. It—it had been around after she was shot. Blood all over it."

"Right," Weigand said. "The M.E. been along?"

He hadn't, Kenman said. He had a ways to come. There wasn't, anyway, much they needed the M.E. to tell them.

"Somebody stood outside," Kenman said. "There are some marks out there—thin, dried mud. She opened the door. Somebody plugged her three times with a .38."

"So," Weigand said. "You got a bullet?"

They had found a bullet only partly embedded in the wall behind Mrs. Halstead. It had gone through her, missing bone. It came from a .38 and was in good enough shape for comparative analysis when they had a gun to check. Weigand nodded.

"That'll help, when we get the gun," he said. "Make your D.A. happy. Although I don't suppose he'll ever come in on it—New York County's got first crack, I should think. Right?"

It was, Kenman said, no skin off him. The district attorneys could fight it out.

"So you figure," he said, "that this hooks up with the Winston kill?"

"Well," Weigand said, "it wouldn't just happen that way, would it? I mean, it doesn't figure to. The people were hooked up, certainly. So one murderer probably does for both."

Kenman nodded. He'd figured it that way, of course.

"Right," Weigand said. "And where do we stand now? What's the precinct doing?"

The precinct had all the men it could spare on the job; so did the detective division which included the precinct. "They're cleaning up out back as well as they can in the dark," Kenman said. "They've found where the killer went through, going away. He wasn't waiting for anything. They've found where he stood on the porch—apparently he persuaded the old girl to open the door for him. Then he plugged her, and got going. He must have gone fast, or your man would have picked him up."

"Right," Weigand said. "Where is Sullivan?"

"Helping around somewhere," Kenman said. "You want him?"

Weigand did. Sullivan was yelled for by a man whose voice barked in the night. Sullivan appeared, not looking very happy.

"It's a hell of a note, Lieutenant," he said. "But what could I do?

There's no cover out front; unless I was going to go in and sit with the old dame, I had to hang out across the street. And how was I to cover the back door?"

"All right, Sullivan," Weigand said. "Nobody's blaming you. What happened?"

Sullivan had been, he said, standing across the street, where the shadow was deepest. He was standing so that he could look along the side of the house, and command a section of the back yard. There was only one light in the house—a dim one from one of the side windows, near the rear. He·was keeping an eye on it, and whatever else was going, when he heard the dog bark. He wondered about that and started across the street and stopped. The dog's barking was something to wonder about, but nothing to act on. It was about a minute—perhaps two minutes—later that he heard the sound of three shots, close together. Then he moved.

He ran along the side of the house, but couldn't run full out because of the roughness of the ground and an undergrowth of weeds and bushes. By the time he got around to the back door, he heard somebody running a good way off. But he looked for Mrs. Halstead, first, when he saw that the back door was partly open. He found her when he tried to open the door a little more; she was lying against it. He went around to the side and in through a window so as not to disturb the body.

"And I didn't know she was dead," he said. "I didn't want to push her around if she wasn't. It makes a difference, lots of times."

"Right," Weigand said. "I don't know what more you could have done. But by the time you found out about her, the murderer had got away. You didn't hear any more running?"

"That's it," Sullivan said. "But there's only one of me, Lieutenant."

Weigand nodded, abstractedly.

"What else do we know?" he asked Kenman. Kenman knelt again by the body. "Feel this," he said. "It isn't blood."

He directed Weigand's hand to the hem of the long, black skirt. It was wet. Moving his hand, Weigand found it was wet all along.

"Just water," Kenman said. "The shoes are wet, too. She'd been out somewhere just before—during the rain or just after it."

"Right," Weigand said. "How about a coat—a raincoat? Or an umbrella?"

The boys had been looking, Kenman said. He called to one of them.

"That's right," the detective said. "We just found it, hanging up in the bathroom. An umbrella, that is. No coat."

"Wet?" Weigand asked.

"Yeh," the detective said. "Pretty well soaked."

"Right," Weigand said. To Kenman he said, "Maybe it'll help, eventually. Anything else?"

"Well," Kenman said, "she'd eaten dinner before she went out. Stacked the dishes but not washed them. Had beans, apparently."

"Right," Weigand said. "We'll tell the M.E. Give him something to look for. And—"

There wasn't, Kenman said, much else yet. It was an odd house; about half of it apparently wasn't in use, and hadn't been for years. Mrs. Halstead seemed to have lived in a couple of rooms downstairs and the kitchen. There was another room upstairs which looked more habitable than the others, and more recently used. Nothing was very clean, including the clothes of Mrs. Halstead which filled a closet opening off the central hall. That was about all—

"Here's something, Lieutenant," a new voice said. A small, thickset detective appeared with it.

"You Lieutenant Weigand?" he said, addressing the Homicide Bureau man. Weigand nodded. "Then the old dame was writing you a letter," the thickset detective said. "Stuffed down by the cushion in that old chair of hers. We just dug it out."

He handed Weigand a sheet of paper. It was crumpled, and Weigand straightened it out. Kenman put the beam of his flashlight on it and Weigand read:

*"Lieutenant Weigand: I have been thinking things over since your intrusion today and have also made a discovery about Michael's father which I think will in—"*

The letter broke off.

"So then," Weigand said, "the murderer knocked at the door."

Kenman looked at him.

"Yeh," he said. "You make it sound like a book title, but that's probably the way it was."

"'In—'" Weigand quoted. "'Interest you,' probably." He stared at the letter. "Damn!" he said. "Just when she was going to spill it. This guy annoys me, Kenman."

"He is sort of annoying," Kenman admitted. "What's the routine?"

"Oh," Weigand said, "turn the boys loose, of course. I don't suppose the fingerprint boys will get much. Oh, by the way, they'll probably get mine—I was here today. Have them check at Headquarters before they start baying, will you?" He looked around the room. "The pictures will be pretty, won't they?" he said. "They ought to get the cat there, crouching by the body. The papers would love 'em."

"Sure," said Kenman. "They'd be pretty."

"We'll have to try to find out where she'd been," Weigand said. "It may not mean a thing—probably she was just out after a quarter-pound of tea, or something. And it may mean the hell of a lot."

"Yes," Kenman said. "I'll get the boys on it. Anything else special, since it's your case?"

Weigand thought and shook his head.

"Just the ordinary," he said. "We'll find out everything we can, and save the bullets and take the prints. I'd like reports downtown, of course. And if the boys in the back yard run across a murderer in the bushes they might bring him along."

"Yeh," Kenman said. "I'll remind them. You know who did it?"

Weigand looked at him.

"I wouldn't say know who, by a long shot," he said. "I've got a hunch, but I can't break it. I can guess why."

"She knew something," Kenman said. It was more statement than interrogation. Weigand nodded.

"Right," he said. "I'd say she knew something. And that she was going to spill it. And now where do you suppose Mullins is?"

They sought Mullins and found him in the back yard, looking gloomily at some footprints etched smudgily on a small expanse of weedless earth.

"Tennis shoes," Mullins said darkly, when they found him. "Old tennis shoes. No nice identifying marks or anything." He looked at the lieutenant, a little resentfully. "You and I sure get the screwy ones, Loot," he said. "And no breaks."

They left Kenman to carry on with the routine. There wasn't, Weigand told Mullins, anything more for them at the house, for the moment anyway. They swung away from the curb and headed toward the Parkway. They were about to enter it when Weigand stopped, sat for a moment with his hands resting idly on the wheel, and then backed the Buick away from the Parkway and swung it to face north again.

"While we're up here," he said, "we may as well look in on the Grahams. Find out how the lady is. That would be polite, wouldn't it, Mullins?"

"Listen, Loot—" Mullins said.

"She was all right this afternoon," Weigand told him. "A little nervous and strained, maybe, but all right. You know, Mullins, she didn't look to me like a woman who was getting ready to collapse. She didn't look that way at all."

The Graham house blazed with light; even the porch was flooded.

"Looks like a party," Mullins said as they drew up. "I thought she was sick."

So, Weigand said, had he. They parked and Weigand led the way to the door. He had barely touched the bell when the door swung open. The man who faced him was about medium height and thin, but it was, Weigand guessed, the thinness of the wiry. The man's light hair, graying at the temples, was disordered as if excited hands had been running through it. In the instant before he spoke, Weigand felt that eagerness drained out of the man.

"Oh," he said flatly. "Who are you? What do you want?"

Weigand identified himself.

"I came to ask about Mrs. Graham," he said. "I was up here, anyway. I was talking to her this afternoon and—"

"Were you?" the man said, bitterly. "So you were talking to her this afternoon, Lieutenant? And what did you say to her, I'd like to know?"

Weigand shook his head.

"I don't get it," he said. "I just asked her some routine questions. Why?"

"Because," the man said angrily, "she's gone! You scared her somehow and she's run away, or—or something's happened to her. Did you scare her about the boy?"

"No," said Weigand. "I didn't scare her about anything, Mr. Graham."

The man stared at him and appeared to accept the statement.

"Sorry," he said. "I'm—well, it's got me. She was all right this morning. This afternoon the nurse who takes care of my father called and said that Mrs. Graham was hysterical. I came home at once and she'd gone—just like that—gone. The nurse said she had seemed quieter after a few minutes and had been willing to lie down. The nurse had to go back to Father then, and didn't know anything more. But apparently Margaret just got up and—and went away. When I came home she wasn't here."

"Perhaps," Weigand suggested, "she's just gone to see a friend or—"

"And stayed away more than four hours?" Graham said. "When she knew the nurse had telephoned me and that I was coming home? You'll have to do better than that, Lieutenant." He stared at Weigand and Mullins. "Oh, come on in," he said. "I was going to call somebody anyway—get the police on it."

Weigand and Mullins went in.

"I thought maybe she'd gone to see somebody," Graham said. "I thought maybe she was nervous and upset about something and couldn't stand to stay here alone. And when she didn't come back I telephoned a lot of people. And then—well, it was crazy, but I'm pretty near crazy about it anyway—I went out and looked for her. I thought— God knows what I thought. That she had been going some place and that something had—happened to her. It's lonely up here. I—I looked in all the loneliest places."

He pressed his temples with the palms of his hands. *"Where is she?"* he demanded. *"What's happened to her?"* He seemed himself to be on the verge of hysterics.

"Take it easy," Weigand told him. "Probably—probably it's nothing. The chances are she's all right and—"

"Why are they?" Graham broke in. His tone seemed desperate. "*You* don't know what's happened to her, do you?"

"Why, no," Weigand said. "How should I know? But most people who disappear turn up all right, eventually. The chances are they will." He looked at Graham. "I can't promise anything, of course. But we have ways of finding people. Do you want to make a report about her?"

"I don't care what I do," Graham said. "I've got to find her."

"Right," Weigand said. "Just take it as easy as you can. I'll get on to the Missing Persons Bureau and start things moving. Now she was—let's see—about how old?"

Dully, Graham described his wife. She was thirty-two, he said, and weighed about a hundred and twenty pounds; she was blond and had blue eyes and probably was wearing a pale blue silk dress and a white linen hat. He, helped by the nurse, had looked through his wife's clothes, and those things seemed to be missing. Weigand, at the telephone, turned the particulars over to the Missing Persons Bureau.

"There may be a hookup of some sort with the Winston case," he told the lieutenant at the Bureau. "Give it what you've got, Paul."

"They'll do all they can," Weigand told Graham, turning back. "As fast as they can. There's nothing for you to do but sit tight and stay by the telephone. The chances are she'll call up. There's no sense in your wading around in vacant lots."

"I know," Graham said. He seemed calmer now. "There never was. But I had to do something."

Weigand said he could understand that. But now there would be good men working on it and—

"I'll tell you," he said. "Maybe we can do something else. Not that I think anything will come of it, but it will relieve your mind. I'll get the precinct to send a couple of men to look around the neighborhood just on the chance—well, that she might have fainted, or something. Right?"

Graham nodded.

"It might help," he said. "I wish you would."

Weigand called the precinct and listened to the desk sergeant. He agreed that it was too bad; that already the precinct was using a lot of men to look for things he wanted found; that the precinct wasn't made of men. He said it was tough, but there it was. It needed to be done. The sergeant lapsed into mere grumpiness; finally he agreed that it would have to be done. Weigand hung up and turned to Graham.

"They'll put a couple of men on it," he said. "It's their busy night." He looked at Graham thoughtfully. "Mrs. Halstead was killed tonight," he said. "You know who she is, don't you?"

"Halstead?" Graham repeated. "It seems to me—" He looked up suddenly, his interest appearing to quicken. "Wasn't she the woman who had Michael?" he asked.

Weigand nodded.

"Killed?" Graham said. "You mean, in an accident?"

"No," said Weigand, "she was murdered."

Graham looked at him, and his expression of worry and alarm deepened.

"What's happening, Lieutenant?" he said. "First Miss Winston and then Mrs. Halstead and—*Lieutenant, what about Margaret?*"

"Take it easy," Weigand said. "There's nothing to show any connection. I don't think anybody is after your wife, Mr. Graham. Unless—"

"Unless what?" Graham said. Weigand paused.

"Well," he said, at length, "I'm assuming that Mrs. Halstead was killed because she had some information which was dangerous to the person who killed Lois Winston. I don't know that's true, but I think it is. If Mrs. Graham had similar information she might be in similar danger. But apparently she hasn't."

He waited for Graham to say something. Graham merely looked at him.

"That's right, isn't it?" Weigand said. "She didn't know anything?"

"No," Graham said. "She didn't know anything. What could she know?"

Weigand shrugged.

"If I knew that—" he said, and let the sentence trail. "I suppose you don't know anything yourself, Mr. Graham, which might be—dangerous? To yourself or to your wife?"

Graham looked surprised.

"I?" he said. "What would I know?"

Again Weigand shrugged.

"Nothing, I suppose," he said. "Unless you saw something at the roof last night—something, perhaps, which didn't mean anything to you at the time, or even something you've forgotten. Something that might be dangerous to the murderer?"

Graham shook his head.

"No," he said. "I wasn't there long, as I told—as I told this man." He looked at Mullins.

"Mullins, Mr. Graham," Weigand said. "Sergeant Mullins."

"As I told Sergeant Mullins," Graham said.

"By the way," Weigand said, "when were you there?"

Graham thought it over.

"From about seven-thirty," he said. "At a guess. Until—oh, perhaps a quarter of nine. Then Miss Hand and I went back to the office and worked for about two hours, or perhaps longer. I didn't see Miss Winston."

He paused.

"Or," he said, "I didn't recognize her if I did. I'd only met her once, and not for very long and I don't remember people very well. And when they're all dressed up, in their war paint—well, I can recognize the paint more easily than the women."

Weigand thought a moment.

"Oh, yes," he said. "That's your business, isn't it? Something and Paulette, isn't it?"

"Henri et Paulette," Graham said. Mullins looked startled at the pronunciation. "Cosmetics and perfumes and the like. Why?"

"No reason," Weigand told him. "It just happened to come up."

Weigand spoke easily, offhandedly.

"It seems to be a good business," he said. "It keeps you working nights, apparently."

"Not often," Graham said. "But recently we've had quite a rush. That's one reason I took Miss Hand to the roof—thought she rated some sort of reward for the time she's been putting in."

He seemed, Weigand thought, rather unduly explanatory, as if having taken his secretary to the Ritz-Plaza were a little heavy on his conscience.

"I suppose," Weigand said, suddenly, "that Mrs. Graham understood—didn't get any false impressions, I mean. Because if she did it might explain—" He broke off, as if embarrassed. Graham looked puzzled for a moment, and then rather indignant.

"Oh," he said, "I see what you mean. I suppose I can't blame you for the notion. But there's nothing in it. I telephoned Margaret and told her why I couldn't get home last night, of course, and that I was taking Miss Hand to dinner."

"Oh," Weigand said. "I didn't really think—"

"If you want to know what Margaret said, I'll tell you," Graham said. "She said, 'Mind you take that poor girl to a nice place for dinner, making her work on a night like this.'"

"And," said Weigand, "you did. It's all very reasonable." He stood up.

"Try not to worry about your wife, Mr. Graham," Weigand said. "I think we'll find her, safe and sound." He looked at Graham, demanding his attention. "I really think we will, Mr. Graham," he said.

Graham stared at him, apparently attempting to find reassurance; apparently not finding it.

"It's easy to say that," he said. "It's damned easy to say that. But things don't seem very safe around here, do they?"

# · 14 ·

## WEDNESDAY
## 11:00 P.M. TO 11:50 P.M.

Back at Headquarters, Weigand stared at reports on his desk and spoke harshly of detectives. The reports had come by telephone from Hanlon and Smith and Healey, who had been set to dog the footsteps of, respectively, Randall Ashley, Madge Ormond and David McIntosh. All three detectives were very sorry and, Weigand suspected grimly, apprehensive. Hanlon and Smith, working together, had somehow managed to lose Ashley and the girl; Healey was beginning to have dark suspicions that he had lost McIntosh. All had good explanations and would, Weigand knew, have even better ones when they came on the carpet.

Healey's was the best; looking at it, Weigand was puzzled to think what he would have done in Healey's place, with McIntosh taking cover in the Harvard Club. Healey, a high school man himself, had waited outside in Forty-fourth Street. He had waited from the middle of the afternoon, when McIntosh left his office and went directly to the club, until almost ten o'clock, getting more nervous and perplexed by the moment. Inside the Harvard Club, protected from high school students and other tribesmen without the law, McIntosh had grimly stayed.

Or at least, Healey hoped he had stayed. There seemed to be very little Healey could do about proving it.

Finally he had asked the doorman whether Mr. McIntosh was in the club. The doorman had looked at him doubtfully and asked, in less direct words, what it was to him. He might, the doorman admitted, have Mr. McIntosh paged if—Mr. Healey—insisted. The doorman seemed to doubt whether either Mr. McIntosh, the club or Harvard University, which, the doorman's manner implied, had final jurisdiction, would approve. Still—Healey decided against having McIntosh paged. It would, eventually, have made an issue where there was no issue to stand on. He didn't want McIntosh for anything; he merely wanted to know where McIntosh was. It would be difficult to explain this to McIntosh, son of the James McIntosh and much more influential than any first-class detective, if McIntosh did appear.

So Healey had backed out and telephoned for instructions. Before he backed he had managed to find out that there was a service exit by which members could leave if they chose.

So, Weigand realized, they had no real way of knowing where McIntosh was during the period of Mrs. Halstead's murder; no way at all. He might in the end emerge harmlessly from the club, and again into Healey's ken, and still they wouldn't know. If they had occasion to ask him he might say that he had been there all the time, and they would be unable to prove anything either way. So—

Hanlon and Smith had less excuse, although even in their cases there was palliation. A little before six o'clock, Ashley had left his apartment and Hanlon had duly picked him up. Ashley had gone by cab to Madge Ormond's apartment, or at least to the house in which her apartment was. Hanlon had joined the watchful Smith on the sidewalk and compared notes. Both "subjects" seemed safely cooped. Smith had suggested that Hanlon hold on while he, Smith, went around the corner to grab a sandwich and Hanlon had agreed, stipulating that when Smith came back he, Hanlon, would be wanting a sandwich too. The sandwiches had occupied the better part of an hour, and it was not until then that it occurred to Hanlon that most houses have front and rear doors.

Hanlon had gone to the rear and verified his suspicion that this

house conformed to the general rule, and the two had watched both
doors industriously until almost nine. Then Hanlon, whose alertness, if
not sensational, seemed more acute than that of Smith, had begun to
wonder. Eventually, the two detectives had gone to Madge Ormond's
apartment and, when there was no answer to knocks, had let themselves in, illegally but understandably. Neither Ashley nor Miss
Ormond had waited.

Here was, at any rate, obvious intention to throw off surveillance,
Weigand thought. McIntosh might have eluded Healey quite uncon-
sciously—might not, in fact, have eluded him at all. But if Madge
Ormond and Randall Ashley had got away, as they had, they could
only have done it by plan. It was hardly likely that they made a habit of
leaving the building by the back door, going through another door in a
board fence, and emerging through the basement kitchen of a restaurant on the next street. Now, clearly they would have to be picked up.
He directed that they be picked up, as soon as they reappeared, and
brought in.

The telephone rang. It was Lieutenant Kenman, calling from
Riverdale with news. They had been lucky; with most stores and
restaurants in the vicinity closed, they had come on a drugstore which
Mrs. Halstead had visited—about, the clerk thought, eight o'clock or a
little before. The rain was just slackening. The clerk knew Mrs. Halstead and could be positive in his identification. She had wanted
aspirin and—this made Weigand blink—a package of Camels.

"And this is going to get you," Kenman went on. There was interest, close to excitement, in his voice. "She wanted to know about
atropine sulphate."

"Did she?" Weigand said. "I'll be damned!"

She had asked the clerk and, when he was a little vague about it,
had inquired whether they didn't have a book in which she could look
it up. Knowing her, the clerk had seen no objection to letting her see
the United States Dispensary. She had sat down on a bench and read
about atropine sulphate and now and then, the clerk said, nodded as
she read. Then she had asked how one could get it. The clerk had told
her that she couldn't get it in a retail store, but that with reason given, a

wholesale supply house probably would sell it. It wasn't a narcotic, he had told her, so that there was no law against its sale. She had nodded over that, and asked whether it was used for any commercial purpose—in addition, she explained she meant, to its stated medical uses. The clerk was vague, but thought it was. Somebody had told him that it was an ingredient in certain eyewashes. Mrs. Halstead, he said, had seemed interested and, curiously, pleased. Then she had gone out. There was still a little light, then, and he had seen her walk toward the corner she would turn on her way home.

Weigand thanked Kenman, hung up and drummed on the desk. Mullins watched him. Weigand gave him a summary.

"What's the matter, Loot?" Mullins said. "Don't it fit in?"

"I don't see it," Weigand admitted. "Except that if Mrs. Halstead had been the murderer, she wouldn't have needed to look up atropine at this date. But getting killed herself had pretty well cleared her, anyway." He drummed further. "Kenman says she looked satisfied at the end. I wonder what she found out?"

"Yeh," Mullins said, helpfully. "I wonder?"

Weigand called the Missing Persons Bureau and asked whether anything had been turned up about Mrs. Graham. The lieutenant in charge wanted to know what he thought they were? He said they hadn't found her in the neighborhood; that they were preparing a description to go out on the teletype and that since Weigand was so interested, they were going beyond the routine applicable to this stage of the hunt—they were carrying on interviews, checking up on taxicab calls and generally worrying people.

"Right, Paul," Weigand said. "Keep at it."

"I think," he said, after a moment, "that we'd better have a man on the Graham house; one of our own men. Have we got any who know the facts of life—about back doors and the like?"

"Well," Mullins said, "there's Stein, if he's still on duty. He's sorta bright, in some ways."

Stein was still on duty. He was sent up to Riverdale in a radio car. Weigand looked at his watch. It was close to midnight. It was foolish, he decided, to wait up the rest of the night on the chance that Ashley and Madge Ormond might return and become available for questioning. He thought they would return, and that he could pick them up tomorrow. It wasn't on the cards, he told himself, that they were really planning to hide out. Tomorrow would be another day. He could use another day, he thought, rubbing his eyes, stinging from weariness, with his finger-tips.

"*O.K.,* Loot," Mullins said, when Weigand told him they would knock off until tomorrow.

# · 15 ·

THURSDAY
9:20 A.M. TO 11:30 A.M.

"Right," Weigand said, "that's the way I thought it worked." He put the telephone receiver back on the hook in the booth. He looked rather pleased with himself, Mullins thought. Mullins was pleased too, although he didn't know precisely why. The Loot was working things out, Mullins guessed.

At Bellevue, Dr. Jerome Francis put his own receiver back. He looked puzzled. He shook his head, admitting he didn't see what Weigand was getting at.

"However," Dr. Francis said, dismissing it. He could read about it in the papers. Meanwhile he had some interesting brain sections to do. Dr. Francis drew on rubber gloves and prepared to do them.

"What've you got, Loot?" Mullins asked, curiously, as they got in the car. Weigand seemed in good humor.

"A hunch," Weigand told him, uninformatively. "Nothing you couldn't have on what we've got, Mullins, if you'd use your head." Weigand looked at Mullins' head. "I guess," Weigand said, with some doubt.

"Listen, Loot," Mullins said. Weigand grinned at him. They went across town to the Placement Foundation. They rode up to Miss Crane's office. Miss Crane was cheerful and a little hurried. "The committee's meeting," she told Weigand.

He wouldn't, Weigand said, keep her. He merely wanted to look over whatever data they might have on Michael.

"The placement record," Miss Crane told him. "It's supposed to be confidential, you know." She smiled. "But I've already told you most of it," she said. "So you may as well see it all." She turned to her secretary.

"Have them send in Michael's record," she said. "Michael Osborne. The lieutenant can read it here, if he likes, while I see the committee."

That would do admirably, Weigand told her. The record arrived—it consisted of loose sheets, bound in cardboard folders. Weigand skimmed it, reading the condensed record of Michael's first appearance; a summary of the conversation with "Richard Osborne" who now more than ever, Weigand decided, had life only in someone's imagination; records of the child's physical examination, which showed him a small boy evidently pleasing to doctors; a summary of his psychological test, with the psychologist's findings. Michael was doing well mentally, too. He had passed all the tests at the three-year level, most of those at the four and one or two at the five. He was superior; estimated I.Q. 120 plus.

He ought to get along all right when things settle down, Weigand thought. He turned back to the physical record and reread it. Very husky for three, apparently, and with no defects—or, perhaps, one. "Protanopia," the record noted, and passed on.

"So," Weigand said, half aloud. "I was pretty sure it would be."

He leaned back in his chair. It was a funny case, he thought; in some respects strangely intricate. He remembered the little things which had put him on the trail—always assuming he was on the trail—and smiled. They were such absurd little things. The engrossment of a child; the impatience of a man. And a hunch or two.

"But I'm still a long way from proving anything," Weigand told himself.

In the outer office, Mullins was striking up an acquaintance with Miss Crane's secretary, who was looking at him, Weigand feared, with rather amused eyes. Weigand collected Mullins and went on. He stopped in the Forties and pushed a bell marked "Ormond." The door clicked and Weigand went up. Madge Ormond looked around the edge of a door and said, "Oh, hello, Lieutenant."

"I want to talk to you," Weigand said. "Not here, however. I want to talk to you and your husband at the same time. Would you rather have us bring him here, or will you come along to his mother's apartment with me?"

"Oh—about last night?" Madge seemed a little amused. Weigand showed no amusement.

"About last night," he agreed. "And other things. Will you come along?"

"Of course," Madge said. "Everything's all right, now."

"Is it?" Weigand said. "I hope you're right, Miss Ormond. If we wait out here while you dress, will you stay away from the back door—and the fire-escape?"

"Of course," Madge said. "I won't be a minute."

She wasn't, to Weigand's surprise, much more than ten minutes. She came out in a blue dress which looked crisp and cool, and with a small blue hat pitching on the waves of her blond hair. "Real blond," Weigand thought, looking at her eyes. "Well, well."

She was willing to talk as Mullins drove them to the Ashley apartment, but Weigand was not. He would, he told her, rather go over it once, with Ashley present. Mullins parked the car, with a strong look at the doorman, in the reserved space before the apartment house in East Sixty-third. The two detectives and Madge Ormond rode up together.

Randall Ashley, his hands extended, started toward Madge when she preceded the two men through the living-room door. Then he saw Weigand and Mullins and stopped and said flatly, "Oh."

"Go ahead," Weigand said. "Kiss your wife, Mr. Ashley."

Ashley flushed darkly. Weigand watched as Madge's hand went out to his arm, pressing gently in caution. Ashley made an effort, and smiled.

"All right, Lieutenant," he said. "I'll hand it to you. Madge said you knew. How did you find out?"

That, Weigand told him, didn't matter. He wasn't, right now, interested in marriage, anyway. His voice was not friendly.

"Suppose," Weigand said, "you tell me about last night. And if you were planning to say it was all an accident, skip it."

Madge and Randall looked at each other. They smiled at each other and Madge nodded.

"He's got us," she said. "He always seems to get us." Ashley shrugged.

"All right, Lieutenant," he said. "We were pretty sure you were having us watched—at least I was sure you were having me watched. And Madge and I just wanted to get off by ourselves. That isn't strange, is it?"

"Isn't it?" said Weigand. "I wouldn't know."

Ashley flushed again, and again Madge's touch silenced him.

"Let me tell him," she said. "After all, he has to find things out." She turned to the lieutenant. "Only this time there isn't anything to find out," she said. "Not really. It's just as Buddy says—we wanted to be alone. We wanted to talk about some things without the chance that somebody—well, that anybody might be listening in. Is that unreasonable?"

"I still don't know," Weigand said. "What things?"

"What the hell business—" Ashley said, and again Madge stopped him. It was interesting, Weigand thought, to see how the sulky boy drained out of Ashley at her touch, leaving a much simpler, rather more attractive man.

"I'll tell him," Madge said. "It wasn't anything. I suggested we get away and talk things over. I wanted to persuade him to quit trying to make a secret of our marriage. I wanted him to go to his mother and tell her about it, and accept any decision she makes. I tried to persuade him that—that getting the money in a lump isn't really important."

She stopped and looked at Weigand. Weigand met her eyes.

"I thought," he said quietly, "that he was already convinced on that point—that it didn't matter whether he got the money all at once, or merely the income. I thought that, Mrs. Ashley, because that's what you told me."

She flushed, this time.

"It was really true," she said. "It was true when I told you that. It isn't *really* important to him, any more than it is to me—not important enough to *do* anything about—anything—"

"Like murder," Weigand finished for her. "I hope you're right, Mrs. Ashley." There was no particular expression in his voice.

"I *am* right," she said. She spoke eagerly, searching Weigand's face. "You see what I mean. Of course, he'd *rather* have the money all at once, but it isn't anything—anything *vital*. Not to either of us. And now he agrees that we should tell his mother, and not try to influence her, don't you, Buddy?"

Buddy hesitated a moment.

"Yes," he said, finally. "I suppose so. I still think the old man pulled a dirty trick on me. But I agree with Madge that it isn't very important."

"Right," Weigand said. "I'm glad you've got together." It sounded rather cryptic, which was all right with Weigand. "Now," he said, "where did you go?"

"Out to Ben Riley's," Madge said. "The Arrowhead Inn, you know."

She said it calmly. Weigand stared at her, examining her face. He turned to Ashley. He couldn't see anything in Ashley's face either.

"Out in Riverdale," he said. "Yes, I know Riley's. And that doesn't mean anything to either of you?"

They both looked at him. They seemed surprised.

"Mean anything?" Madge repeated. "Ben Riley's?"

"Or Riverdale," Weigand said.

Ashley said, "Oh! That's where Lois had been Tuesday afternoon," he said to Madge. "Don't you remember? Out seeing some people in Riverdale about a child?" He turned to Weigand. "Is that what you mean, Lieutenant? I can't see that it would mean anything."

"No?" said Weigand. "Does Mrs. Halstead mean anything?"

"Halstead?" Madge repeated. Her face was, so far as Weigand could determine, completely blank. So was Ashley's. He waited for more than a minute, and then spoke.

"Assuming you don't know," he said, "although it was in the newspapers—Mrs. Eva Halstead was killed last night. She was the woman who had, up to a few weeks ago, been taking care of Michael. Michael is the boy about whom your sister was seeing those people in Riverdale, Ashley. And Mrs. Halstead lived in Riverdale—lived about half a mile or so from Ben Riley's Arrowhead Inn. I'm trying to make it all very clear for you—for both of you."

They stared at him.

"But I don't see—" Madge began. Ashley cut in.

"There's no way you can mix us up in it, Lieutenant," he said. His voice was hot and hurried. "I'll grant you you might make out some sort of a motive—a damned bad motive—for my—doing something—to Lois. But this Mrs. Halstead! We never even heard of her!"

"No?" said Weigand. "I hope you didn't. I'd hate to find you lying to me, Ashley."

Ashley stared at him, then made a gesture of resignation. His voice was quieter when he answered.

"Well, Lieutenant," he said, "I can't make you believe us, if you've decided not to. If you think you can prove anything, go ahead and try it."

Weigand nodded. If Ashley wanted to take that attitude, he said, it would be perfectly understandable—also perfectly all right with him. But if Ashley thought there was no way of tying Mrs. Halstead into it—

"Well," Weigand said, "suppose I outline a case. You don't have to say anything, unless you want to. Suppose I say that you got very much entangled with the young woman who—preceded Miss Ormond. The one your father knew about when he made the will. Suppose that was around four years ago and that the entanglement had a result—Michael."

"No," Ashley said. He spoke without heat. "You're barking up a wrong tree, Lieutenant."

Weigand nodded.

"All right," he said. "We're just supposing. Suppose the girl died, or disappeared, and left you with the baby. Suppose you found various people to take care of him, ending up with Mrs. Halstead. Then suppose Miss Ormond came along, and you decided to get rid of an entanglement and, posing as Richard Osborne—he was about your height and weight, and dark glasses and a growth of beard would be all the disguise you'd need—you unloaded him on the Placement Foundation. What do you think of that theory, Ashley?"

"I think it's lousy," Ashley said. He still spoke without heat.

"Do you?" said Weigand, evenly. "Right. Now suppose your sister, through her connection with the Foundation, somehow stumbled on the fact that Michael was really your son. Suppose you knew that if she told your mother that, you would never get the principal of your money. Suppose when she was home Tuesday night she gave away what she had discovered and that she *was* going to tell her mother. And suppose you needed the money bad—suppose you were pretty deep in debt, for example."

Weigand watched Ashley narrowly. The last shot, anyway, told, he decided. Ashley's voice was less even.

"All right," he said, "you've apparently been snooping around. I owe a lot—that's why I want to get the money in a lump. But the rest of it—phooey! You're wasting your time. There was a girl, sure. There wasn't any child. The girl didn't die or disappear—I could find her for you any time."

Weigand nodded.

"Sure you could," he said. "For a price—say around five hundred—you could find a girl all right. I know lots of girls who would say they'd played around with you for five hundred. Including girls who had been seen enough with you to make it plausible. So what?"

"Well," Ashley said, "we'll see what you can prove if it comes to it. How's that, Lieutenant?"

Weigand agreed that that was all right.

"Meanwhile," he said, "I'll remember you deny the whole thing. And, of course, I could be wrong. As a matter of fact, I can give you another theory." Weigand looked at Madge Ormond. He didn't like this one very much, he thought.

"It's possible," he said, "that Miss Ormond was the girl." They both stared at him. "It's possible," he went on, "that Michael is your son,

Miss Ormond. Or Mrs. Ashley. You say you've only known Ashley for a couple of years but—well, that's just what you say. It doesn't have to be true."

"It is true," Madge said. "I swear it's true, Lieutenant."

Weigand nodded at her.

"Why not?" he said. "If I were in your place I'd swear it was true. If it is, sure you'd swear it. And if it isn't—sure you'd swear it. Who wouldn't?"

Madge was watching his face.

"You know, Lieutenant," she said, suddenly, "I don't think you believe any of this. You just think there's a—oh, a remote chance there's something in it, and you're trying us out. Isn't that what you're doing?"

"Is it, Miss Ormond?" Weigand said. His voice had no expression. "Anyway, you both deny both theories, I gather?"

"Yes," Ashley said, "we both deny both theories. And I don't give a damn whether you, personally, believe them or not. So what do you do now?"

Now, Weigand told them, he saw Ashley's mother, if she was able to see him. They'd let the rest slide, for the time being.

"Do you want to find out whether she can see me?" Weigand said to Ashley. Ashley hesitated. "Yes, Buddy," Madge said. "Do what he says." Ashley went out, slowly. He seemed to hate to leave Madge with the detectives.

"*Do* you believe it, Lieutenant?" Madge said quickly, when Buddy had left. "All those things you said—about Buddy and about me? Do you really believe them?"

He looked at her. He spoke mildly.

"I only said they could be true, Mrs. Ashley," he told her. "And I want you to answer one more question. Was there anything the matter with your father's eyes?"

Madge stared at him, out of very large blue eyes of her own.

"My father's eyes?" she repeated. "What on earth, Lieutenant?"

"Was there anything wrong with your father's eyes?" Weigand repeated. "Surely that's simple enough. Never mind why."

Madge seemed to think a moment.

"I don't know quite what you mean," she said. "He wore glasses. He was near-sighted, I think. I used to try to look through his glasses when I was a little girl, and everything blurred. But I don't think there was anything else." She smiled. "I just thought all grown-up people wore glasses," she said. "I didn't think about what it meant."

"Right," Weigand said. "I just wanted to know."

She seemed about to say something more, but Ashley came back into the room. He nodded to Weigand.

"All right," he said. "You can see her for a few minutes. Are you going to—?"

"Tell her?" Weigand asked. He shook his head. "Not right now, anyway," he said. "If you've been telling me the truth, you're going to tell her yourself. And if you're telling the truth, I don't want to mess things up for you."

He motioned to Mullins to remain in the foyer, and climbed the stairs behind Ashley. The senior Mrs. Ashley was lying on a chaise-longue, and she had been crying. She looked younger, in some ways, than the sixty-odd she presumably was—one would have guessed her age at sixty-odd, with the mental reservation that she did not look it. She had a light voice which would, Weigand suspected, twitter over conversations when she was herself. Now it was thin and drained.

She said, "How do you do, Lieutenant?" and Weigand said he was sorry to intrude. He waited until Ashley had gone out, and said he was very sorry about what had happened. Mrs. Ashley's pale blue eyes filled and she nodded. She wiped her eyes with a tiny, lacy handkerchief.

"It is dreadful," she said. "Dreadful. I can't understand why anyone should want to hurt Lois—she was always so—gentle and sweet to everybody."

Weigand waited.

"You don't suspect my silly boy, do you, Lieutenant?" she said. "That would be too absurd. Or his wife, that he thinks I don't know about?"

Weigand was startled, and showed it.

"Oh," she said, "you didn't know I knew? But I did, so you see if you thought that might be a motive for Randall, you were wrong. I've known it for weeks. A friend of mine found out, and told me."

She is shrewder than she looks, Weigand thought.

"Did your son and Miss Ormond know you knew?" he asked casually. "And do you approve?"

"No," she said. "I've been waiting for them to tell me. And yes, Lieutenant, I approve—at any rate, I don't disapprove. I would have preferred—but that doesn't matter. I think Miss Ormond is charming and that she is really in love with my son. I also think she is good for him, don't you?"

She is *much* shrewder than I thought, Weigand decided, looking at her. Her eyes challenged him.

"I think she quite possibly is good for him, Mrs. Ashley," he said. "But to go back—you don't really think that your knowledge eliminates the motive, do you?"

"But of course it does," she said. "The only reason he could have had for doing anything to Lois was because he was afraid that she was going to tell me about the marriage. Or about something else. But if I already knew—oh!"

Precisely, Weigand told her. It might be something of which she knew nothing. And it might still be the marriage.

"They didn't know you knew," he said. "They thought you didn't. And your son, if he acted, would have to act on the basis of his own belief, even if it was inaccurate. Of course you see that, Mrs. Ashley."

She nodded.

"I see what you mean," she admitted. "But you know it is perfectly absurd, Lieutenant. In your heart."

This seemed to be the day, Weigand thought, for women to explain to him what he really thought about things. He shook his head.

"I'm a policeman, Mrs. Ashley," he pointed out. "Policemen can't think with their hearts."

She looked at him closely.

"All right, Lieutenant, have it your own way," she said. She dismissed it, apparently. "What did you want to ask me?" she said.

"Whether there was anything wrong with your first husband's eyes, Mrs. Ashley?" he said.

She looked perplexed, as Madge Ormond had. Then she shook her head.

"No, Lieutenant," she said. "He had quite remarkable eyes. To the day of his death. Why?"

Weigand said it didn't matter. He thanked her and found his way out of the bedroom; then, collecting Mullins, out of the house. There was a new detective, looking almost too alert, on guard in the street. Weigand nodded to him and let Mullins drive the Buick. Weigand sat without saying anything after he had given instructions. The Loot, Mullins could see with the corner of an eye, was thinking. It was a spectacle cheering, as well as rather strange, to Mullins. The Loot was a funny sort of guy. He could just sit still and think. Mullins ran through a red light, touching the siren gently. Weigand said nothing. The Loot could sure think deep, Mullins told himself.

The interview with David McIntosh took only a few minutes. McIntosh received them in a very inner office, and was as bland as the expansive top of his irreproachable—and arrestingly unoccupied—desk. He raised no objection to telling where he had been the evening before. He had been at the Harvard Club for cocktails, dinner and finally for bridge. He did not ask why Weigand wanted to know.

"I gather you've heard of Mrs. Halstead's death," Weigand said. McIntosh remained bland.

"Certainly," he said. "I read it in the papers. I haven't the faintest idea why it arouses interest in my movements, but I'm perfectly willing to cooperate."

Weigand said it was good of him.

"By the way," McIntosh said, "didn't your man know where I was?" Weigand could be urbane also. He smiled.

"Naturally," he said, "they wouldn't let him in to nose around. He's not a member, you know. He thought you might have gone out some other way. The service entrance, perhaps. You see, he had no way of telling."

McIntosh nodded, approving the point. He said he saw.

"However," he said, "I stayed all evening at the club. I daresay it could be proved, if necessary."

"Right," Weigand said. "I'll let you know if we want it proved." He paused. "By the way," he said, "have you ever been married?"

McIntosh remained bland. He nodded.

"Once," he said. "It progressed from Southampton to Reno, at an accelerating tempo. Why?"

Weigand told him that he had just wondered.

"Any children?" he inquired. McIntosh allowed himself to look surprised, but remained polite.

"No," he said. "My wife and I didn't feel we'd be particularly good parents." His face sobered. "If Lois had lived—" he said, as if half to himself.

"Right," Weigand said. McIntosh seemed to feel his fiancée's death deeply, but to be putting a face on it.

"We should have been married months ago," McIntosh said suddenly, bitterly. "Then I could have taken care of her—then this wouldn't have happened. But she wouldn't have it—" He seemed to feel, still, hurt anger toward Lois; it was mingled, somehow, with his obvious sorrow at her death. He looked at Weigand. "Sorry," he said. "I break out now and then—forget it."

"Right," Weigand said. "I can guess how you feel."

He could, too, he thought—and thought of blue-gray eyes which now and then appeared to be green and which seemed alternately to advance and retreat. Weigand, thinking of Dorian, thought that Lois's apparent hesitation must have been very disturbing to McIntosh. Particularly if McIntosh, not trained to the patience which was stock in trade for a detective, was used to getting his own way with more than reasonable promptness.

Weigand remembered something else.

"By the way," he said, "you didn't make a reservation at the Ritz-Plaza. You're still sure of that?"

McIntosh looked annoyed.

"How many times—" he began. Weigand gestured.

"Right," he said. "You didn't make a reservation at the Ritz-Plaza. How about the Crescent Club?"

He watched McIntosh's face narrowly. He could see only surprise and bewilderment in it.

"The Crescent Club?" McIntosh repeated. "What the hell? I didn't even go to the Crescent Club. Why would I make a reservation there?"

"I don't know," Weigand said. "But you *had* a reservation there." He shook his head at the incredulity in McIntosh's eyes. "Oh, yes," Weigand said. "You had a very nice reservation there, the manager says. A table right near the dance floor. There's no doubt about that. But I suppose you say you didn't make it?"

"I don't get this," McIntosh said, slowly. "I don't get it. There's something—I don't get it. I didn't make any reservation anywhere. We didn't know where we were going." He stared at Weigand inquiringly, seeking explanation. Weigand's face offered none.

"Right," Weigand said. "That's all, I guess."

He was rising when Mullins, who had been sitting in a corner, suddenly spoke.

"Was there anything the matter with your father's eyes, Mr. McIntosh?" he said. McIntosh looked at Mullins, whom he had apparently forgotten, with evident surprise. Weigand looked with equal surprise, and then closed his lips on a grin.

"Oh, yes," he said. "I was forgetting—thanks, sergeant. Was there anything the matter with your father's eyes, Mr. McIntosh?"

"What the hell?" said McIntosh, wonderingly. He looked at Weigand, who apparently meant it.

"Why, yes," McIntosh said. "He had double cataract toward the end. Though what that has to do—"

Blandly, Weigand told him that it was of no consequence. "Just routine," he said, which left McIntosh looking more blank than ever. He was still looking blank when Weigand and Mullins were ushered out. In the building corridor, Mullins was evidently pleased.

"You pretty near forgot that one, Loot," he said. "Good thing I remembered." He paused, evidently in thought. "Listen, Loot," he said, "what do we want to know for?"

Weigand smiled at him.

"Routine, sergeant," he said. "Just routine."

# · 16 ·

## THURSDAY
### 11:30 A.M. TO 2:20 P.M.

Pam North was a little annoyed with herself that morning. She told her husband so, while he ate breakfast and puzzled over a two-column clarification of the war situation. It explained the Russian angle, but Mr. North couldn't seem to get it.

"It's annoying," Mrs. North said, when he was less than half through. "It isn't like me, at all. Usually I'm good at murders."

"Yes, dear," Mr. North said, absently. "That's nice."

Mrs. North said he wasn't listening.

"I'm *good* at murders," she said. "Don't you remember how good I was before? About our own murder in the bathtub and then about the one at camp? Wasn't I good about them?"

"Yes, dear," Mr. North said. "What?"

"Murders," Mrs. North said, rather more loudly. "Who guessed the first one? I did. Who guessed the second?"

"Bill," Mr. North said, coming out of it.

"Well," Mrs. North said, "I did too. At almost the same time. And now what?"

"What?" Mr. North said.

161

"I don't," she said. "It might as well be Greek. Except that Michael's in it, of course."

Mr. North drew his most reasonable tone out of its place of concealment. He told Pam to listen.

"After all," he said, "you don't have to. Bill will tell us, when he gets it worked out. It'll be just as good."

"Haven't you any pride?" Mrs. North said.

"No," Mr. North said. "Not about murders. And, anyway, I have got it worked out. It's Ashley. Bill's just getting—too complex." He looked at Mrs. North, speculatively. "Association, probably," he said. She said, "Jerry" and saw that he was smiling.

"All right," she said. "It isn't Ashley, of course, but all right. Because if it was—were?—Ashley, where would Michael come in?"

He wouldn't, Mr. North told her. Mrs. North looked triumphant.

"There!" she said. "That's the trouble with that one, of course. It doesn't bring in Michael. And then where are you?"

Mr. North looked at his watch.

"At the office," he said. "Where I should have been half an hour ago." He looked at her seriously; standing he took her chin in his hand, and shook her head gently.

"And you, kid, stay at home," he said. "Or go to the movies or—or anything. But leave the murder alone." He made her look at him. "I mean it," he said. "No more murders for the Norths. We get bunged up—you got bunged up and then I got bunged up. Next time—well—leave it to Bill, Pam. I mean it. I still think of you lying on the floor upstairs and—"

Pam wiggled a bit until her chin was loosed and then she kissed him.

"All right, Jerry," she promised. "I'll just look on. Spectator sports, sort of. All right?"

"All right," Jerry said. "See that you do." Jerry, after sticking his head out a window to see what the weather was like, and discovering that the storm hadn't done much for the temperature, went along to his office. Pam had another cup of coffee and read about the war. But she still was annoyed with herself, she discovered.

"Bill knows something," she said to nobody in particular, although Martha, cleaning up, said, politely, "Ma'am?" Mrs. North shook her head, abstractedly. "It hinges on Michael," she told herself. "There's something about him that I've missed." Then she thought that it would be perfectly all right with Jerry if she just went up to the Foundation and read Michael's record. She hesitated a moment, and then told herself that that wasn't really getting into it. Not really. It was interesting to have it settled, and she put on her hat with the red feather and tucked her red purse under her arm.

There wasn't any trouble about seeing the record. Miss Crane, who might have hesitated, was away somewhere, and Mrs. North pointed out, hardly firmly at all, that she was on the committee. She read the record carefully, with special attention to Richard Osborne's description and to his account of Michael's short, unsettled past. She shook her head, and read on. She found out, as Weigand had, that Michael was a smart little boy—"which I knew from the first!" she told herself—and was about to look up "protanopia" when it happened. Miss Crane's secretary got the message and said, in shocked tones, "No!"

Then she was talking very rapidly on the telephone, and asking hurried questions. There was such a stir in the air that Mrs. North stopped reading. Something exciting had happened.

The secretary cradled the telephone and immediately picked it up again.

"Get Miss Crane," she said, evidently talking to the operator. "Well, find her—it's vital. One of our children has been kidnaped."

"Michael!" Mrs. North said. She said it on a rising note of excitement. "Not Michael?"

The secretary nodded, holding a hand over the transmitter.

"This morning," she said. "Sometime in the last two hours. He was out playing and now—now he's nowhere!"

"Oh!" said Mrs. North. "Oh, no! Not Michael!"

She stood up and her red purse slipped from her hand and fell, spilling compact and lipstick and spraying oddments. Mrs. North stood for a moment with wide, frightened eyes.

"But he's just a little boy!" she said. "Nobody could!"

Possibly if Miss Crane had been there—if Pam could have had the feeling that something was being done, then, quickly—Pam might have remembered that she was to keep outside of things. She always insisted, afterward, to Jerry that it was because nobody seemed on hand to do anything that she had forgotten her promise. Jerry pointed out that the police could be notified at once; that, as a matter of fact, the police had been notified at once. But Mrs. North insisted that it wasn't, at that moment, enough to think of the police.

"I just thought of a little boy," she said. "And dreadful things happening, and the way he played with my watch. You'd have done the same thing, Jerry!"

"No," Jerry said. "Not I, Pam. But you—yes, that's different."

It had been different. Mrs. North had not waited, even for Miss Crane; even to be sure that news went to Lieutenant Weigand. She could trust Miss Crane for that. She merely tore at the record, riffling its pages excitedly, until she found the name and address of Michael's present boarding mother—Mrs. Konover, who lived in Queens Village. Then Mrs. North moved.

Caution of a sort did reassert itself as she went down on the elevator. On the ground floor, she almost ran toward a telephone booth. Why she telephoned Dorian Hunt instead of someone else—instead of, for example, Jerry himself—was always obscure to him. It was never obscure to Mrs. North.

"It was a little boy," she explained. "A child. So of course it had to be another woman! That's obvious!"

She telephoned Dorian Hunt and, luckily, got her at once. Her words tumbled as she told what had happened. "You've got to come with me, Dor," she said. "We've got to do something! Now! We can't wait!"

"Well—" said Dorian.

"Now!" said Pam, urgently. "Before something dreadful happens."

* * *

The police heard the news a few minutes after it came to Pam, but it was more than an hour before Weigand heard of it. For once he was out of reach, turning over odds and ends at the New York offices of Henri et Paulette. So, without his knowledge, the Missing Persons Bureau widened its net; the police at a Queens precinct went into action and O'Malley, fuming in his office, was snappish even with reporters and demanded that heaven and earth be moved to discover Lieutenant Weigand. Weigand, with Mullins beside him, turned over odds and ends patiently.

He talked, first, to Miss Hand—Miss Geraldine Hand, the secretary of John Graham. She had been at the roof, he told her, and they wanted to know everything that anyone at the roof that night could remember. Had she seen Lois Winston?

"Yes," Miss Hand said. "Although I didn't know who she was at the time. But I recognized the man she was with—Mr. McIntosh—from seeing his picture in the papers and then I looked at her just—well, just to see what kind of girl a man with all that money went around with. And then next day, when I read the papers, I realized who she was."

Weigand nodded. And, while she was watching them had she seen anything—well, anything suspicious? Anything which, looking back on the evening afterward, in the light of what had happened, seemed suspicious in retrospect?

She shook her head.

"By the way," Weigand said. "How long were you there? Do you remember?"

Miss Hand shook her head again, and said she was sorry. It was, she remembered, rather late—they had started late, because Mr. Graham had been detained. Then they had wasted more time going from the restaurant in which she had waited, and which Mr. Graham had object-ed to when he arrived, to the roof. So it was—oh, well after nine o'clock—when they finished dinner, and went back to the office.

"Right," Weigand said. "That's near enough. It's just routine, you understand." He paused, and consulted a note. "Although," he said, "I gathered from Mr. Graham that you had left rather earlier. However—

people don't always agree about the time, do they?"

Miss Hand agreed that they didn't. She might, she said quickly, very easily be wrong. Weigand nodded and studied her. He wondered, interestedly, what she would be like outside the office; what she had been like, for example, with John Graham at the roof.

"By the way," he said, "do you know Mrs. Graham? She's missing, you know."

He studied her. Her face assumed an expression of concern.

"Yes," she said. "Isn't it—dreadful? She always seemed such a—well, calm and even-tempered woman. Although, of course, I only met her a few times—she dropped in here now and then. Not often."

"It's very upsetting for Mr. Graham, certainly," Weigand said. "I suppose you didn't—but I can't ask you to betray any confidences." He paused, and she looked at once interested and appropriately noncommittal. "I suppose," he said, "that Mr. and Mrs. Graham got along all right? You know what I mean?"

Miss Hand's expression registered the question as indiscreet.

"Really, Lieutenant," she said, "if there were anything you wouldn't expect me—but, fortunately, there wasn't. So far as I know, at any rate. He never—well, said anything, or expressed anything, which would make me think different."

"Right," Weigand said. "I suppose he called her up when he was going to be late getting home—that sort of thing. He was considerate, I mean. When he was going to be delayed—as the other night—he would telephone and all that?"

Miss Hand nodded, and said, "Of course.

"As it happened," she said, "Mrs. Graham telephoned him Tuesday, and he told her then. But he was just going to call her—he'd told me to remind him."

"Right," Weigand said. His tone expressed conventional approval of marital consideration. Miss Hand, he could see, was thinking him rather stodgy—the substantial, middle-class policeman.

"By the way," he said. "Just what is Mr. Graham's position here. Office manager—something like that?"

Miss Hand nodded.

"And other things," she said. "He runs this end; our factory's in Long Island City, you know. He has something to say about everything except the actual manufacturing—sales, purchases, new lines—almost everything. Of course, the main office is at the factory, really, but a great deal clears through us."

"Quite an important position," Weigand said. His voice betrayed admiration of Mr. Graham's importance and, he trusted, a proper note of envy. "He must make a—well, a pretty good thing out of it."

Not, Miss Hand assured him, loyally, as much as he deserved to make.

"He has a great deal of ability," she said. "I sometimes feel that they don't appreciate him properly at the factory. He ought, really, to be a member of the firm, instead of just a salaried executive. But I suppose that needs capital, doesn't it?"

Weigand, with the air of a man out of his depth in commercial matters, but trying not to show it, agreed that it probably did. He thanked Miss Hand and collected Mullins. Outside, Mullins looked at him darkly.

"That was an act, Loot," he said. "Just an act."

"Was it, Mullins?" Weigand said. "Think of that!"

He shepherded Mullins to the Buick and drove downtown. He arrived between harried appearances of messengers in search of him, and had time for a telephone call before the storm broke. He made the telephone call to Danbury, and asked them to trace records. It was, he said, a routine item for the files—an item concerning a George Benoit, who had got a ticket there sometime Tuesday. The Danbury police checked while he held the line. The Danbury police reported.

"Yes," Weigand said. ". . . Yes . . . About what time? . . . How long did you hold him? . . . Um-m-m. . . . Did he have any explanation? . . . He did, eh? . . . What? . . . Yeh, that was a hot one, wasn't it? . . . And was he?" There was a longer pause. "Sure enough!" Weigand said. . . . "Yes . . . Yes, it must make it difficult. . . . Well, thanks, sergeant. Do as much for you some time."

He hung up and sat staring at Mullins.

"Well," he said, "that's that. The little pinch of corroboration, sergeant, that savors the best of hunches."

"What?" Mullins said. "I don't get it."

"Don't you, Mullins?" Weigand said, gently. "You should, you know. It's all been spread out for you. What you didn't see, I've told you."

Mullins stared at him.

"Listen, Loot—" he began.

Then the telephone on Weigand's desk rang harshly.

Deputy Chief Inspector Artemus O'Malley was beside himself. He had taken his feet off his desk when Lieutenant Weigand, summoned peremptorily, hurried to him. He pounded on the desk with his fist, which was a large fist. Small objects on the desk jumped affrighted. Inspector O'Malley wanted to know what was going on. He summed it up for Weigand.

"First the Winston girl," he said. "All right. What the hell could we do about that?" Weigand knew the question was rhetorical. "Right," O'Malley said. "That happened to us. And it stares us in the face— we've got everything—a guy nobody likes, to make it easy for the D.A.; motive, opportunity and, on top of that, he did it! That's what gripes me—a perfect setup, and *he did it!*"

O'Malley stared at Weigand, celebrating a perfect coincidence, rare in police annals. Not only could they pin it on a guy; it was the right guy.

"A natural!" O'Malley went on. "So what do you do? You get somebody else murdered—a Mrs.—what the hell's her name?"

"Halstead," Weigand said.

"I know it!" O'Malley said. "I know it. You don't have to tell me things, Lieutenant. I was on the force when you were wearing didies. Mrs. Halstead. So you get Mrs. Halstead murdered, because you won't see what's as plain as the nose on your face." Inspector O'Malley stared around his own nose at Weigand.

"I suppose you think that makes us look good?" O'Malley said.

Weigand shook his head.

"No, Inspector," he said. "Not so good."

"Look at the papers if you think it makes us look good!" O'Malley challenged. "And who gets it in the neck—*me!*"

Weigand doubted that, or doubted that it would be true for long. But he merely looked attentive.

"I get it in the neck," O'Malley said. "I tell 'em we'll crack it in twenty-four hours and what happens? Somebody else gets killed. And then somebody disappears. This Mrs.—Mrs.—"

"Graham," Weigand helped out. "Mrs. Graham disappears."

"Yeah!" O'Malley said. "So Mrs. Graham disappears. The first thing we know about her, she disappears. Is that a note?"

Weigand nodded. O'Malley glared at him.

"And now what happens?" he demanded. "Now we lose the kid! A kid that's tangled up in it somewhere. Now, along with everything else, we got a kidnaping. Don't you know what the papers do to a kidnaping? Don't you ever *read* the newspapers, Weigand?" O'Malley's anger seemed to be softening into grief. "Headlines," he said, gloomily, staring at the lieutenant. "Right across the page. 'Child in Winston Case Kidnaped.' How do you think that makes us look?"

"It's tough, Inspector," Weigand agreed. "Very tough."

"Tough!" O'Malley repeated. He addressed the universe. "He says it's tough!" O'Malley told the universe, hopelessly.

He turned back and glared at Weigand.

"Did you ever hear of Staten Island?" he said. "Did you ever hear of the Bronx, up around the Boston Post Road? Did you ever hear of Jamaica—way out on the edges? Did you ever hear of wise cops who went back in uniforms and sat at desks and nobody ever talked to them or heard about them?"

"Right," Weigand said. "Do you want me to say something, Inspector, or don't you?"

"You'd better say something!" O'Malley told him. "You'd sure better!"

"Right," Weigand said. "We're going to break it. You can tell the boys that. Say we'll break it in—well, say in twelve hours. Say that the police have a theory which explains everything that's happened; that the police are confident of finding both Mrs. Graham and Michael Osborne. If you feel like it, tell them the disclosures will be sensational."

"Yeah," O'Malley said. "And suppose we don't?"

Weigand looked at him, and half smiled.

"Well," he said, "you can always pin it on me, Inspector. And there's always Staten Island." He stared back at the Inspector. "What the hell?" he said. "You think I *like* Staten Island?"

"Twelve hours?" O'Malley repeated, after a moment's thought.

Weigand nodded. "Or less," he said. He said it confidently; he hoped he was right.

"Well," O'Malley said. "Get on with it, Weigand. You won't do it sitting here."

Weigand left like a man going somewhere, but he sat at his own desk and drummed his fingers on it. He telephoned Missing Persons and got Paul Durkin. He asked crisp questions.

"I think we've got a line," Durkin told him. "We rounded up a taxi-driver who picked Mrs. Graham up near her home last night—a guy named Fineberg—Max Fineberg. Funny thing, he drove Lois Winston downtown from there Tuesday afternoon. What do you think of that?"

"Well," Weigand said, "it's a fine time for him to be remembering it." He thought. "Although," he added, "I can't see it makes much difference. Where did he take Mrs. Graham?"

"To a hotel," Durkin said. "Or, anyway, to a hotel door—the Carney. It's a little place, very respectable, in the Murray Hill district. Naturally, she's not there now."

"Naturally," Weigand said. "That would be too easy. Did she ever go there? Or did she just wait until Max drove off and walk away?"

"I wouldn't know," Durkin said. "No Mrs. Graham registered there. A Mrs. Gebhart did, about the right time. The clerk's pretty old, and pretty short-sighted, but his description sounds as if Mrs. Gebhart and Mrs. Graham might be the same person. But he can't identify a picture—just shrugs and says, 'Maybe, maybe not.' You know the kind."

"Yes," Weigand said. "And what about Mrs. Gebhart?"

"Checked out," Durkin told him. "Took a cab this morning; the boy who brought her bags down also had a gander at Mrs. Graham's picture and says it looks like Mrs. Gebhart. He's not very sure, either; says he didn't look closely, and why should he? He put her in a cab. It's too bad he didn't pick one of the regulars that work the hotel, but he didn't. There are only a couple and both were gone. So he flagged a cruiser. A Paramount. We're checking, but it will take a while."

It might, Weigand realized, take hours, and with no vast certainty. If things didn't go as he anticipated, he might see Staten Island yet. Cab-drivers were supposed to make records of all their trips, showing where passengers were picked up and where set down. Usually the big company drivers did. Sometimes they didn't. It would take a while to look over the sheets; it would be several hours, at best, before all the sheets were available.

"How about the kid?" Weigand asked Durkin. Durkin said they had just started on that and that it was as much a precinct and reserve job as theirs. Some details had come along. Michael had been playing on the front stoop of the boarding home, which was a detached house with a neat little yard. Another boy who was under Mrs. Konover's care had gone to school; Mrs. Konover was busy with her housework. And Michael had merely vanished. The neighborhood was being searched and the precinct men, aided by a Missing Persons Bureau detail, were questioning people who might have seen something. So far—

"Wait a minute," Durkin said. "Let's see that, Mike." There was a pause. "Well," Durkin said, "here's something. There are a couple of women around inquiring, too. Or were during the morning. One of our men came on the track of them when he was asking some questions in the neighborhood. Any idea who they'd be?"

"No," Weigand said. "It's funny. What kind of women?"

"We don't get *anything* but lousy descriptions," Durkin complained. "Young women, apparently. They were around a while and then went off in a taxi-cab. Mean anything, do you think?"

"I hope not," Weigand said. "I suppose it's on the radio? Well, then, maybe a couple of helpful women who heard it on the radio and just wanted to poke around." He laughed, shortly. "Mrs. Konover better watch out," he said, "they'll be taking her yard along as a souvenir if she isn't careful."

"Yeah," Durkin said. "Ain't people wonderful?"

Weigand, disconnecting, drummed on his desk. He remembered something.

"You were going to find out about a couple of wills, Mullins," he said. "What did you find out?"

Mullins looked startled for a moment. Then remembered and hauled out a notebook.

"Ole man Ashley's," he said. "The money is left pretty much as Buddy says; all tied up. He gets the whole business when he's twenty-five if he isn't married. There's nothing about being mixed up with a woman any other way, like you thought maybe. Mama Ashley can say a marriage is O.K. if she wants to, and then sonny boy gets the jack. Like sonny boy said. O.K.?"

"Right," Weigand said. "How about the girl?"

Lois Winston, it developed, had left a considerable legacy to the Foundation. There were minor legacies to friends; a substantial one to the maid, Anna. The residue went to the college Lois had attended, with the stipulation that it be used for special research in the field of sociology.

"No motive there," Mullins said. "Unless maybe—say, Loot, how about Miss Crane? At the Foundation. Suppose she figures she can get her hands on the money that goes to the agency—"

He stopped, because Weigand was staring at him.

"Listen, Mullins," Weigand pleaded. "Don't think, huh? The Foundation, like all such agencies, is supervised by the state, and all their funds are audited regularly. I can't see Miss Crane killing anybody; she couldn't get the money if she did. Nobody at the Foundation could. And, if you were thinking of that, I don't think the president of the college killed Miss Winston, either." He looked at Mullins. "I don't like to discourage you, sergeant," he said. "How about Anna?"

Mullins shook his head.

"Huh-uh," he said. "She ain't the type." He looked at Weigand severely. "You got to know types, Loot," he instructed.

Weigand nodded, as admiringly as he could. He said he thought

Mullins had something there. Then the telephone rang. It was Durkin, and he was crisp.

"Got the kid, Weigand," he said. "For once a hotel dick kept his eyes open. A dick at the Fairmount, up on Forty-eighth. Just called in to say that the boy—he's pretty sure it's the right boy by the description—was brought in there two-three hours ago by a woman. Registered as Mrs. Anderson, the woman did. Got Room 1209. I'm sending—"

"Don't," Weigand said. "Don't send anybody. Put men on the doors; better have a couple on the twelfth floor, too. I want to pick the kid up myself." He broke off, thought. "No question about who found him, Paul," he added. "The break goes to the M. P. B., naturally. But I think it hooks in on the Winston killing, and I want to check it myself. Right?"

"Sure," Paul said. "I'll get the men out."

"Right," Weigand said. "I think you've broken it, Paul. Nice going. Be seeing you."

Mullins stood up, too. He responded to the change in Weigand's mood. They were going places, now. That was what Mullins liked; going places. His look at Weigand was hopeful, inquiring.

"Right, Mullins," Weigand said. "This is it, or close to it. Come on."

# • 17 •

The Hotel Fairmount towered without character over Forty-eighth Street; it was massive and nondescript—masonry with interstices into which beds and the occupants of beds could be fitted. The doorman's uniform was arresting; the doorman inside it pale and inconsequential. A few people sat in a grillroom which had windows on the street and pudgy waiters in noticeable uniforms looked out vacantly. Mullins pointed out that they hadn't had any lunch, and his step hesitated when, through the windows, he saw bottles on the bar. "Later," Weigand told him, curtly.

In the lobby the few people visible were without savor. Weigand's eyes flickered over the room. There were several men, waiting for nothing, who looked, if anything, more nondescript than the rest. There was one who didn't; who looked what he was. Bad work, that, Weigand thought. Cops who looked like cops had their jobs, but unsuspected observation was not among them. Precinct man, Weigand decided. One of the unnoticeable men turned from the cigar counter, vaguely, and brushed close to Weigand.

"Still there," he said, without moving his lips. Weigand nodded.

174

With Mullins beside him—and heads came up as Mullins passed, and one casual gentleman went, with studied indifference, toward the door—Weigand went to the elevators. The eyes of the black-haired young man at the controls of the waiting car slipped over Weigand without interest, but widened when Mullins followed. His eyes slid up and down Mullins.

"Twelve," Weigand told him. The young man looked at Weigand, leaving the car door open. Weigand looked back, without truculence. "Now," he said, almost gently. But there was no gentleness in the tone. "Get going."

The operator reached for the door. He kept his eyes on Weigand as he slammed it; groped for the control and moved it without shifting his gaze.

"You better look where you're going, son," Mullins told him. "You wouldn't want to run into nothing, would you?" Mullins turned to Weigand and beamed, falsely. "Sonny don't want to run into nothing," he told Weigand. Weigand smiled, fleetingly. This wasn't, he thought, the place he had expected to find Michael. But for anybody who wanted to keep under cover it wasn't a bad place. Only, if his theory was right—

He broke off as the car stopped.

"Twelve," the black-haired youth said. He said it indifferently. Mullins, following Weigand out, patted the boy's shoulder.

"Nice going, sonny," he said. "Didn't run into a thing."

The operator glared at Mullins and met a pleased smile. The door, clanging shut, nipped at Mullins' ankles.

"Temper," Mullins said, and sighed. A short fat man with a red face who had apparently been waiting for an elevator looked at Mullins. Weigand's eyes flickered over the short fat man.

"Homicide," Weigand said. "Lieutenant Weigand. You're the house man?"

"Yeah," the house man said, heavily. "I called Missing Persons. The kid's in twelve-nine. What is it? A snatch?"

"It could be," Weigand told him. "Which way's twelve-nine?"

The short man waved a short arm.

"Couple your guys around here, somewhere," he said. "You gonna do any shooting?"

"Why?" said Weigand. "Who'd we want to shoot?" He looked at the fat man. "Go look in some keyholes, brother," he advised. "Keep it clean."

"Listen—" the fat man started.

"Right," Weigand said. "You gave us a buzz. We've got it in the books. A nice gold star for Mr. Zepkin, house detective. The Police Department appreciates it. But we'll take it from here."

"Sure," Mr. Zepkin said. "Sure you will, Lieutenant. We don't want anything funny going on at the Fairmount."

"Sure you don't," Weigand said, cordially. "Not at a high-class house like the Fairmount." He paused a moment. "We'll be seeing you, I wouldn't wonder," he said. He started down the hall toward twelve-nine; stopped.

"Let's borrow your key," he said to Zepkin. "I'd just as soon not knock. I'll leave it at the desk."

Zepkin handed over his pass-key. He looked knowingly at Weigand, who returned the look blankly. Mr. Zepkin pressed the signal button on the elevator grill.

"It's a suite," he said. "Two rooms. Twelve-nine and twelve-ten."

"Right," Weigand said. They moved along the hall. At the end of the hall there was a window and a man was looking idly out it. He turned when he heard the steps of Weigand and Mullins. Weigand nodded to him.

"Keep an eye on twelve-ten," Weigand directed. "We wouldn't want anybody leaking out." He saw the man's hand move, instinctively, toward a holster. Weigand smiled. "You won't need it," he said. "Not if I'm right."

Quietly, Weigand slipped the pass-key into the keyhole of Room 1209. He waited for movement inside and heard none. He turned the key and pushed the door open. A small, pleased voice said, "Man!" Weigand stepped through the door. He looked at the woman and the little boy sitting by the window, the child in the woman's lap.

"Well," Weigand said, "I *will* be damned!"

"Oh, I don't know, Bill," Pam North said, over Michael Osborne's blond curls. "Not if you learn to knock at doors and say your prayers every night. How are you, Bill?"

"Well," said Mullins, looking over Weigand's shoulder. "What d'yuh know?"

"I thought," Pam said, "that you two would never get here. We—I, that is—I've been here hours. It doesn't seem to me that the police are very efficient."

Weigand looked at her darkly.

"So you were the women," he said. "Out in Queens, prowling around, asking questions, getting in policemen's way."

"Women?" Mrs. North repeated, wonderingly. "How could I be 'women,' Bill? Even if I was out in Queens, asking the other little boy—Andy—where Michael was. When he came home from school for lunch, because it's only around the block. I'm still not plural, Bill."

"Sometimes," Weigand said, "I wonder."

Mrs. North looked at him.

"Somehow," she said, "I'm not sure I like the way that sounds."

Bill Weigand smiled at her.

"Right, Pam," he said. "It was bright of you. And I suppose the other little boy—Andy—knew right away that Michael was at the Fairmount. All by himself, of course."

"I think," Pam said, "that there's something confusing about that sentence. Who all by himself?"

"Michael," Weigand said. "Michael, all by himself at the Fairmount. I suppose Michael just walked over here and registered and asked for a two-room suite? And so you just came over and looked at the register and telephoned up that you'd like to see him. And they let you come, even if they don't allow men to entertain women in their rooms." He waited.

"Sarcasm," Pam North said, sadly. "Just sarcasm. There was a woman, of course. The kidnaper. A large, dark woman with—with a wart. But she's gone, now."

"Pam," Weigand said. "Pam North." His voice sounded hopeless. "I—"

Then he turned, because he heard a door open. Dorian Hunt stood in the doorway.

"All right, Pam," Dorian said. "She won't go. She says she's going to stay where Michael is." Dorian looked at Weigand. "And anyway," she said, "there's probably a man outside the other door. You wouldn't slip up on that, would you, Bill?" Her voice was faintly scornful. Weigand wished it weren't, but his own tone was equable.

"No, Dor," he said. "I wouldn't slip up on a little thing like that. Tell Mrs. Graham to come out and—" He broke off. "No," he said, "wait a minute. Let's get this straight. You and Pam were the women over in Queens. Whose idea was that?"

"That was my idea," Pam said. "I didn't know, then. I thought—that is, I was afraid—something would happen to Michael. And I wanted to help. I thought Dor would want to help too, so I called her. And she did." She paused. Her voice was serious, now. "I was terribly frightened, Bill. About Michael—after all those awful things."

She looked at Michael, who was studying the dangling watch around her neck. Michael was having a really good look at the watch, now. He thought that if you picked at the back it might come open, so that you could feel the wheels. Pam, looking at him, thought he might be right.

"Look, Mike," she said. "How about the purse?" She reached the purse from the floor near her and dangled it before Michael. He looked at it, frowned slightly and returned to the watch. Pam shook her head.

"A phobia," she said, "that's what it is. A phobia against purses. He's going to be a socialist."

"Listen, Pam," Weigand said, "you thought Michael was in danger. So you got Dorian and went out to find him. You started in Queens. Then what?"

"Then," Pam said, "we found that Andy—he's the other little boy Mrs. Konover boards—had just come home from school. So we asked him where Michael was. You see, the detectives had asked Mrs. Konover everything they could think of, and gone away, and none of them thought of Andy. And Andy, just as he was going to school, had seen Michael go away in a taxicab with a 'pretty lady.' The taxicab came up where Michael was playing and the lady got out and called to him, and Michael ran to her and they both got in and the taxicab went away. And so we asked Andy if he heard the lady say anything and he did."

"What?" Weigand said.

"He said the lady was sort of crying and laughing and saying, 'Oh, baby! Oh, baby!' over and over. Andy said it was a lot of slush. And then, just as Andy came up to see what it was all about, the lady said something to the man who was driving the cab and they went off. Andy yelled after them, because he wanted to go for a ride, too, but they didn't stop. So we asked what the lady said to the man who was driving the cab. Andy said she said 'Fairmount' and something about a street, so we looked it up and came here. And here they were."

"Well," Weigand said, "that was simple."

"But I knew," Pam went on, "that you and Mullins would find the place, eventually, and I thought—well, I didn't want Mrs. Graham to get into trouble. So Dorian and I tried to persuade her to go home and promised to take care of Michael, but she wouldn't. Dorian was in the other room trying to persuade her, because we thought that if she was away from Michael it might be easier. But it wasn't."

Weigand looked at Dorian and then at Pam, and smiled.

"No," he said. "It wouldn't be. What did Mrs. Graham say—besides saying she wouldn't go?"

Pam started to speak, but Dorian stopped her.

"Bill," she said, "have you got anything against her? Against Mrs. Graham? Is she—the one you're hunting?"

The voice was very quiet. It seemed to come from a good way off. Weigand looked at her.

"What did she say, Dor?" he said. "What do you think from what she said?"

Dorian looked at him for almost a minute before she answered. When she spoke her voice was tired, uncertain.

"She can't be, Bill," she said. "She simply can't—wait until you talk to her. She's—she's almost hysterical. She thinks you're going to take the little boy away from her. She—oh, talk to her, Bill. Before you do anything!" There was emotion in Dorian's voice. "You can't do anything to her, Bill—you can't! She's so—so unhappy it breaks your heart!"

"I'm sorry, Dor," Bill said. "I'm sorry, God knows. But I didn't start it, Dor. You've got to remember that."

Dorian's answer was a helpless spreading of the hands. Then, quickly, she turned.

"Mrs. Graham!" she called. "Mrs. Graham!"

There was a pause and Mrs. Graham came to the door. Her face was pale and she had been crying; even now her lips were working and her eyes were dark and—yes, Weigand thought, frightened.

"Come in, Mrs. Graham," he said. He spoke gently. But she was not looking at him. She was staring, with a kind of frightened eagerness, at little Michael. The child looked up and stretched out his arms to her.

"Margie," he said. "Pick me up, Margie!"

Mrs. Graham was across the room, kneeling, with her arms around the child.

"You can't take him!" she said. "You can't!" Her voice was anguished. Her body half cut off the child from Lieutenant Weigand. "He's mine!" she said. "He's my boy—you can't take him away from me. It's been so long—so long!"

Her blond head went down against the little boy, while her arms held him. Michael's face puckered.

"Margie," he said. "Don't twy, Margie."

Dorian's gaze was on Weigand. He felt its demand before, slowly, he turned from Mrs. Graham and the little boy. He met the challenge in Dorian's eyes and his shoulders slowly lifted.

"Yes," he said. "Yes—but what can I do, Dor?" He paused. "How much have you guessed, Dor?" he said, more quietly.

Her eyes looked puzzled, for a second.

"Guessed?" she repeated. She seemed to think a moment. "That her heart's breaking for the little boy," she said. "That she's—hysterical with fear that he'll be taken away from her; that all this has spoiled everything, so that she can't have him. What is there to guess?"

Weigand nodded slowly, without answering. He motioned to Pam to give the child to Mrs. Graham and, when she had—when Michael sat on Margaret Graham's lap, with his arms around her, and when her arms had fastened around him as if they would never let go—Weigand drew Pam toward him with a motion of his head.

"And you, Pam?" he said. "How much have you guessed? What Dorian has—or, something else?"

Pam was very quiet, now, as she looked into Weigand's eyes—very quiet and thoughtful.

"I don't know, Bill," she said. "She—she didn't say anything more. Just about wanting the boy and being afraid he would be taken from her. But—"

"What did you guess, Pam?" Weigand insisted.

She shook her head.

"I don't know, Bill," she repeated. "It's all confused—but—" She paused again. "It hooks up somehow, doesn't it, Bill? So that you can't be sure about her—about her and Michael?"

Weigand nodded, slowly.

"I'm afraid it does, Pam—Dor," he said. "I'm afraid—" He broke off, hesitated a moment, and then crossed to Mrs. Graham. His touch on her shoulder roused her; her arms closed more desperately around the child.

"You hurt me, Margie," Michael said. He wriggled a little. "You hold me too hard, Margie," he explained.

"I'm going to have to take you home, Mrs. Graham," Weigand said, gently. She shook her head.

"Yes," Weigand said. "You'll have to come home, now." He hesitated. "We'll all go with you," he said. "It's almost over, Mrs. Graham."

She did not seem to understand what he said, or only a little of it.

"Michael?" she said. "Michael goes too?"

"Yes," Weigand said. "Michael goes too. For now, anyway." He looked down at her, trying to command her attention. "There are things to be worked out, Mrs. Graham," he said. "You know that, don't you?"

Her eyes grew wide. She was trembling.

"Michael?" she said, desperately.

"I don't know," Weigand said. "I can't tell you about that, Mrs. Graham. That's—that's outside anything I can control, Mrs. Graham."

He looked at her steadily, his eyes grave. He waited.

"All right," she said. "I'll go home. But I won't let Michael go! I'll never let Michael go!"

Weigand did not answer, directly. He motioned to Mrs. North, who took the little boy again and dangled the fascinating watch for him. Mrs. Graham stood up.

"I'll get my things," she said, dully. "I'll go with you."

Weigand nodded.

"There's one thing before we go, Mrs. Graham," he said. "One question. Is there something the matter with your father's eyes?"

Mrs. Graham stared at him, her own eyes opening.

"Oh!" she said. "How—how did you guess?"

He looked at her.

"Try not to be afraid, Mrs. Graham," he said. "And how did I guess? Oh, a light of course. It just had to be put together." He waited for her to say something, but her eyes were devouring Michael. "Was that the way Miss Winston found out, Mrs. Graham?" he said. His voice was still gentle, but the texture had somehow changed. She did not answer, but he thought she heard.

As he turned, as Mrs. Graham went to the other room for her things, he found Pam's eyes upon him. There was a question in them and, as he watched her, Pam's eyes went, involuntarily it seemed, to little Michael and to the purse on the floor and then back to Weigand. Pam's eyes widened and after a second she said, "Oh!" There was fear in the syllable.

# • 18 •

After the others were in the car, Weigand left them for a minute and found a telephone booth. Headquarters told him that all was under control; that the man he wanted was where he wanted him. Then, with Mullins at the wheel, they drove through Forty-eighth, swung back west and rolled uptown. Although Mullins was at the wheel, their movement was considered. Lights were observed; speed was no more excessive than convention allowed and motorcycle policemen tolerated. It was close to three-thirty when they swung to the curb in front of the Graham house in Riverdale.

Mrs. Graham, sitting by a window in the rear with Michael on her lap, had not moved or spoken. Her arms were around Michael; she stared out unseeingly over his tousled blond head. Pam North, between Margaret Graham and Dorian, had stared at the back of Mullins' neck and thought, not about the back of Mullins' neck. Dorian's eyes, fixed on nothing outside the window, saw, or seemed to see, no more than Mrs. Graham's. After the car stopped there was a little pause, and then Mrs. Graham stirred.

183

"Home," she said. She said it dully, with a kind of dull bitterness. Pam reached across her to open the door.

"No," Weigand said. "I want you three to wait here with Mullins for a few minutes. He'll tell you when to come in." Pam started to speak. "No," Weigand said, "I've got something to do, first."

A maid opened the door of the Graham house. Her eyes passed incuriously over the car.

"Mr. Graham," Weigand said. "Lieutenant Weigand, tell him. I have some news about Mrs. Graham."

Graham came to the living-room door as Weigand spoke.

"News?" he said. He spoke hurriedly, eagerly. "Is she all right?"

Weigand told him she was all right. He said it flatly, without expression and, watching Weigand's face, an odd expression came into Graham's.

"She's all right," Weigand repeated. "You'll be seeing her—soon. She's on her way here. But while we wait I've a few questions to ask."

"Questions?" Graham repeated. "What questions? Has something new happened?"

"No," Weigand said. "Nothing new. I just—well, say I want to check a few things. There seems to be a few discrepancies I'd like you to clear up. For example—I understood you to say that you telephoned your wife Tuesday afternoon?"

Graham seemed to be puzzled.

"Oh," he said, "that! What about that? Yes, I telephoned her."

Weigand's voice was mild. He said it was no doubt some mistake.

"However," he said, "Miss Hand says that Mrs. Graham telephoned you. She says that you had planned to telephone Mrs. Graham, but that she telephoned you first. Which is right?"

"Oh," Graham said. He seemed to be thinking. "I guess she is, as a matter of fact," he said. "Does it make any difference? I can't see—"

"Well," Weigand said, "it might, you know. Say your wife had something to tell you—then it might be interesting to know that she had called first. Did she have anything to tell you, particularly?"

"No," Graham said. "I don't recall that she had. I had said that I might be tied up that evening and she was going out and thought she might be away when I called and so she called me to make sure. Something like that." He looked bewildered. "I still don't see what difference it makes," he said. He looked hard at Weigand. "You're sure Margaret's all right?" he said.

Weigand nodded.

"She's quite all right," he said. "Now, to get back. Did she tell you anything about Miss Winston's visit when she telephoned? I'd like you to remember—did she, say, mention that Miss Winston had been here, or anything like that?"

"Well," Graham said, after a pause, "I think she did, just that Miss Winston had been here."

"She didn't," Weigand said, "say anything about Miss Winston's having met your father-in-law, Mr. Graham?"

Graham showed reflection.

"Come to think of it, she may have," he admitted. "She told me her father had dropped in, anyway—had some sort of trouble in Danbury when he was driving to Washington, and was delayed so that he decided to stop here. I may have gathered that he and Miss Winston met." His apparent puzzlement waxed to astonishment. "Don't tell me you think Benoit is mixed up in this," he said. The thought seemed to amuse him. "That's pretty absurd, Lieutenant," he said, with laughter in his voice.

"Is it?" Weigand said. His voice was unruffled, mild. "We have to check everything, you know, Mr. Graham. So I gather your wife did call you, instead of the other way around; that she told of Miss Winston's having been at the house, and of a meeting between Miss Winston and Benoit. Right?"

"Yes," Graham said. "This gets me, Lieutenant."

"Does it?" Weigand inquired, only interest in his voice. "I'm sorry, Mr. Graham. Now—did she say anything more about Miss Winston? Did she, for example, say where Miss Winston was going that evening?"

"What on earth," Graham wanted to know, "would I care where Miss Winston was going to dinner?"

"Right," Weigand said. "Why should you? Was anything said about it?"

"No," Graham said. "Of course not." He spoke emphatically, staring at Weigand.

"Right," Weigand said. "Now—did you tell Mrs. Graham where you were taking Miss Hand to dinner? No—wait a minute. You explained about that, didn't you? It was a last-minute decision—you'd planned to go somewhere else, but the other place was too hot or something. Wasn't that it?"

"Yes," Graham said. "That was it."

"Right," Weigand said. "We have to keep things straight, you know. Now—I gathered from Miss Hand that your position is a fairly important one at your office, Mr. Graham—that you're more than an office manager; that you're something of a sales manager, in addition, and that you occasionally act as a purchasing agent, too. Is that right?"

"Yes," Graham said. "Approximately."

"Yes," Weigand said. "You've made quite an impression on your secretary, Mr. Graham. Did you know that? She thinks the work you do is out of proportion to your position—and to your salary. She thinks you ought to be a member of the firm."

"Does she?" Graham did not seem much interested. "I'm doing all right."

"Of course," Weigand said. "But you would buy into the firm if—if you had the capital, wouldn't you, Mr. Graham? It would make quite a difference in your income, I suppose? And you wouldn't mind that, of course."

"Who would?" Graham said. "Listen, Weigand—I don't see—"

"Right," Weigand said. "You don't have to answer these questions, of course. But we like to get a clear picture. Now—I talked to your father and Mrs. Graham yesterday, and I gathered there is a rather queer situation about his money—something about your not having children, because of his belief that there is insanity in the family? I'd like your version of that, Mr. Graham."

"There's no version," Mr. Graham said. His voice was worn, irascible. "It's rot. He feels that way, but it doesn't mean a damn thing."

"Still," Weigand argued, "he could make it stick, couldn't he? If you did have a child, I mean? He could fix it so you didn't get any money, couldn't he?"

"The courts would have something to say about that," Graham said.

"Would they?" Weigand asked. "Even if your father *isn't* insane, Mr. Graham? And from what I saw of him, he isn't—not in any way that would invalidate a will. The courts are inclined to follow a testator's expressed wishes pretty closely, Mr. Graham—if he isn't insane, and the conditions aren't peculiar in any legal way. You know that, don't you?"

The last question came while Weigand was standing. As he spoke he moved toward the window and stood by it for a moment. Then he turned back to Graham.

"Your wife will be along any minute, now, Mr. Graham," he said. "Is there anything you want to tell me before she comes?"

"What the hell?" Graham said. His voice was hoarse, grating. "What would I have to—"

Weigand broke in. His voice now was level, and rather hard.

"Well," he said, "suppose you tell me this, Mr. Graham. What does your firm, Henri et Paulette, manufacture? Face creams? Scent? Face powder? Lipsticks? Things like that?"

"Yes," Graham said. "Things like that."

"And," Weigand said, "*eye-lotion*—something for women to put in their eyes before parties to make them bright and beautiful? How about eye-lotion, Mr. Graham?"

Graham stared at the Lieutenant, and his own eyes were bright and hard. Weigand waited a moment, but Graham merely stared.

"An eye-lotion, Mr. Graham?" Weigand repeated. "An eye-lotion—with atropine sulphate in it?"

He waited for Graham's gaze to falter. It seemed about to; then Graham was looking beyond Weigand to the door, where Mrs. Graham stood, holding Michael to her and with Pam North and Dorian behind her.

"Margaret!" Graham said. There was excited relief in his voice, and he started to cross toward her. "Margaret! You're all right?"

Margaret Graham did not move. She stood with the child, looking at her husband. When she spoke her voice held nothing.

"Yes, John," she said, "I'm all right."

Her tone seemed to stop John Graham. Then he turned, sharply, toward Weigand.

"What have you done to her, Weigand?" he demanded. His voice had a snarl in it. "What have you made her—"

Weigand shook his head, slowly.

"Why don't you say hello to your son, Graham?" he said. "Why aren't you glad to see Michael?"

The words had a harmless sound as Weigand spoke them. But they brought a strange change to John Graham's face; it grew hard and bitter, and a kind of blankness of fear spread over it. Graham stood motionless for an instant; then, with convulsive speed, he moved. Even as Weigand's hand reached toward his police automatic, it was too late. Graham was across the floor. His charging shoulder sent Mrs. Graham staggering to the side, clutching the child. His hand wrenched at Pam's arm, sending her against a chair. He had Dorian, who had stood behind Pam, in his arms for a moment; then, as she struggled, he was behind her, his left forearm against her throat, forcing her head up and back. And his right hand held a gun long enough for them to see it. Then the gun was pressing hard against Dorian's side.

Graham's voice was high, cracking, as he spoke. Across the few feet he seemed to be screaming at them.

"Don't any of you move!" he screamed. "She'll get it, if you do. Don't try to stop me!" His voice rose high, and broke. "*Any of you!*" he cried. "*Don't move!*"

He was backing into the hall, pulling Dorian in front of him. Weigand saw her eyes widening in a white face.

"Drop it!" Weigand said. "Drop the gun, Graham. You can't make it."

But Weigand's hand had dropped from the butt of his own gun. Fear was singing in Weigand's mind. "*He's crazy,*" Weigand thought. "*In a moment he'll break—and kill!*"

Graham was moving away from them still, into the hall. His eyes were bright, hysterical.

"*You won't burn—*" he was screaming. Then the scream went out in a choking sound, and there was a soft, muffled sound. Weigand was moving as Graham's right hand wavered, and the pistol began to spill from it. He was in time to catch Dorian as, released, she staggered away from Graham. Weigand seized her by the shoulders; he was shaking her and talking and he seemed to be very angry.

"You!" he said. "You—why can't you stay out of things?—Why do you have—" Then, suddenly, he stopped speaking, because she was looking at him and smiling faintly. He said nothing for a moment, and then drew her to him. She followed his eyes down to Graham, crumpled on the floor. Mullins was kneeling behind him, and fitting a blackjack into his hip pocket. Dorian's fingers closed on Bill Weigand's wrist.

"Is—is he dead?" she asked. The words came gaspingly.

Mullins stood up slowly. He was smiling, but the smile faded slowly. An expression of mild affront replaced it.

"Dead?" Mullins repeated, incredulously. "Dead, Miss Hunt?" He looked at her darkly. "Do you think I'm an amachoor, lady?" he inquired, with dignity. "Do you think I don't know how hard to hit a guy?" Mullins was a craftsman, insulted in his craft. It was clear that, for Mullins, the savor had departed, leaving ashes in the mouth. "*Dead!*" he repeated, dully. "Huh!"

But Graham was already stirring. Within five minutes, during which Pam sat with Margaret Graham and Michael at the end of the living-room, John Graham was conscious again; ready to be told that he was under arrest for the murders of Lois Winston and of Eva Halstead. He did not look at anybody when Weigand told him, but stared at the floor, dully. When Mullins clicked handcuffs about his wrists, he transferred his stare to them.

When Weigand told Graham, Margaret Graham's head dropped to her arms on a table beside the chair. Even when little Michael tugged at her arms and tried to see her face, she did not seem to know it.

# • 19 •

Mr. and Mrs. North were on hands and knees on the living-room carpet when Martha let in Dorian Hunt. Dorian looked at them with only moderate surprise, but she said, "What on earth?"

"Pete," Mrs. North told her. "Pete's back."

She and Mr. North regarded Pete. Pete, a black and white cat lying comfortably stretched out between them, regarded Pam distantly over his left shoulder.

"I tell you," Mrs. North said, "he does look shorter. Whatever you say, he's not as long as he used to be."

"I know he isn't," Mr. North said, argumentatively. "I never said he *was* as long as he used to be. I merely said that, for all practical purposes, he *looks* as long. Hello, Dor. Do you notice any difference?"

Dorian got down on her knees to look at Pete. Pete shifted his gaze to Dorian, putting his head flat down on the carpet and looking at her upside-down.

"You have to get to one side of him to see properly," Mrs. North said. "Perspective."

Dorian moved to one side of Pete. She looked at him carefully.

190

"I can't see any difference," she said. "He looks about the same to me." She looked up at Mrs. North. "Is he supposed to have shrunk?" she said.

"Oh," said Mrs. North. "Didn't we tell you? I suppose with the murder and everything. He lost some tail."

"With the murder?" Dorian said, lost. "I don't see how."

"Not *because* of the murder," Mrs. North said. "Because of the murder we didn't tell you. He lost his tail in the door up at camp. He was sitting in it."

"In the doorway," Mr. North explained. "The wind blew it." He regarded this statement darkly for a moment. "Blew the doors, I mean," he said. "French doors, you remember. It blew them together. And Pete's tail was in between."

"Oh," said Dorian. "How dreadful, Pete."

She looked at Pete sympathetically. Pete stretched out a paw, consolingly, and touched her hand.

"It was dreadful," Mrs. North agreed. "Poor kitty. At first he was just mad and hissed at the door and then he looked at his tail and began to yell. You know how cats can yell?"

"Yes," Dorian said. "Cats can yell."

"So," Pam said, "we took him to the vet's and had it bandaged, but the bandage came off and the tail itched or something and Pete went crazy. He ran all over, yelling and biting at his tail. So we had to take him to the vet's again and leave him until it was healed. That's where he's been. Now it's well, only he looks shorter, of course. Why wouldn't he?"

She directed this to Mr. North.

"It's a matter of proportion," Mr. North said. "He is shorter, of course. But he doesn't look shorter, that I can see. Have you heard from Bill?"

By common consent they got up as Mr. North said this. Pete, chagrined at this withdrawal of attention which he had approved as a cat's natural right, spoke unpleasantly about it. Mrs. North said, "Nice kitty," abstractedly.

"Yes," she said. "What about Bill? Is he coming to dinner?"

"Yes," Dorian said. "He'll be along. He telephoned me a little while ago. He said it was all over." Animation died from her face. "I keep thinking of poor Mrs. Graham," she said. "And wondering what it's all about and what will happen about her and Michael, don't you, Pam? I keep remembering how awful—how broken—she looked when they took Graham out, and how set her face was when Bill said they would have to take Michael back to the Foundation. Did you see Bill's face when he said it?"

"Yes," Pam said. "It—it must be tough to be a cop, sometimes."

"But he couldn't help it," Dorian told her. There was something like a challenge in the words. Pam's lips almost smiled, and then the smile withdrew.

"I know he couldn't, Dorian," she said. She let the smile show. "You don't have to defend him to me, Dor. I think he's swell, too."

Dorian and Pam looked at each other.

"All right," Mr. North said. "Break it up. Break it up. Especially you, Pam. Standing there mooning over Bill—" He grinned at them. "A heel if there ever was one," he added.

"Why—!" Pam began indignantly. Then she saw Jerry's face. "All right," she said. "You're just jealous, that's all. Isn't he, Dor?"

Dorian was saying "of course" when the doorbell rang and Martha crossed to click the downstairs door open. A moment later, Bill Weigand stood in the door of the living-room. His face was tired, but there was no strain in it. He answered the inquiries in the three faces.

"Yes," he said. "All over, including the shouting. Graham's spilled the whole business. A bullet fired from his gun matches one of the bullets that killed Mrs. Halstead. We've found the boy he sent out late Tuesday to get a package from a wholesale drug company—a package of atropine sulphate, to be sent along to the factory. The boy didn't know what it was; he just had a note. And the drug concern didn't report it when our men inquired, of course. It was a perfectly legitimate transaction. He's admitted making reservations for McIntosh at both the roof and the Crescent Club and—"

"Look," Mr. North said, "you're starting in the middle. The middle for me, anyway. Don't I count? All I know is that John Graham killed

Lois Winston and this Mrs. Halstead, and that Michael is really his own son. And his wife's?"

Weigand nodded.

"And his wife's," he said. "Born in legal wedlock, all on the up and up. That was the trouble, really."

"Listen, Bill," Mr. North said. He sounded a little exasperated. "Suppose you tell us about it. First, how did you find out?"

"Well," Weigand said, "to be honest I never did find out all of it—until Graham started talking, of course. I guessed part of it—the main part. As soon as I knew that Michael was really the Grahams' son I had it, of course. Just as Lois Winston had it, when she made the same guess for the same reason. The details filled in afterward."

"All right," Mr. North said. "If you will begin in the middle. How did you know Michael was really the Grahams' son?"

"Protanopia," Weigand said. Mrs. North nodded, contentedly. He smiled at her. "Got that, didn't you, Pam?" he said. "I thought you would."

"Michael is color blind," Mrs. North explained. "Red blind."

Weigand nodded. "Red blind" hardly said it, he told her, but it was close enough.

"And so," he added, "is Mrs. Graham's father, Benoit. I was tipped off to that when I was driving with him and he said the lights had changed, so we could go ahead. Actually, the lights we could see hadn't changed. The cross traffic lights had turned red, too, and the driver ahead jumped the gun, as most drivers will when the police aren't around. And, you see, color-blind drivers, when they're stopped by red lights—which don't show red to them—go by what other drivers do.

"That gave me a start on it. The rest, about Benoit, was confirmation—nice to have in court, but telling me nothing I hadn't guessed. Benoit was given a ticket in Danbury for passing a red light. You see, there weren't any other cars around to tip him off. They held him—they're strict there, just now—and when he claimed to be color blind they gave him a test. He was."

Mr. North looked puzzled.

"I don't see—" he began. Weigand's nod stopped him.

"I got the fact that Michael is color blind, too, from the record," Weigand said. "But again I only got something I expected. The hint had come earlier, when Michael wouldn't pay any attention to Pam's purse. Generally children go first for anything red; it used to be argued that red was the favorite color of all children. They think now, incidentally, that it is merely brightest to most children. But Michael wouldn't touch the purse. To him, probably, it was just sort of gray and uninteresting. He fastened on the watch, which was bright and fascinating."

Mr. North started to speak, but Weigand held up a hand.

"Wait a minute," he said. "I'm coming to it. Color blindness of this type is transmitted in a sex-linked inheritance pattern. That's what Lois was looking up in the encyclopædia, incidentally. Under 'Heredity,' of course. It's all there. It is transmitted like hæmophilia. Women don't show it. Mrs. Graham isn't color blind. But her father is, and some—not all—of her sons would be. Michael happens to be. I remembered something about that, and looked up the rest. I was following, incidentally, precisely the path Lois followed—to her death. Because she, already knowing that Michael was color blind, met George Benoit Tuesday afternoon. She wasn't supposed to; never would have, probably, if some traffic officer in Danbury hadn't stopped Benoit. It was chance—just one of those things."

"How did she find out?" Mr. North asked. Weigand shrugged.

"Graham wasn't there," he said. "We haven't questioned Mrs. Graham much, as yet. But it isn't hard to guess—Benoit told her. His mind was full of being held up in Danbury, because it was important to his plans, and he talked about it. He explained his color blindness, possibly. It was nothing to conceal, as far as he was concerned. And it is possible that, until Miss Winston showed what she knew—she may have said something about its being an odd coincidence, before she realized herself what it might mean—the Grahams didn't realize how this inherited vision defect was giving away their plot."

"Oh," said Dorian. Her voice was shocked. "She was in it, too? Mrs. Graham, I mean?"

Weigand nodded, slowly.

"In part of it, anyway," he said. He paused, thoughtfully. "I don't think she was in the murder, Dor," he said, gently. "Graham insists she wasn't, and I'm inclined to believe him. Technically, of course, she was an accessory after the fact. She knew—she guessed, even if he didn't blurt it out—what had happened." He looked at Dorian thoughtfully. "This isn't official," he said. "This is just among friends. I doubt if she will ever be tried for anything. With the motive she has—a natural longing to have her own child—it isn't the same as the motive her husband had—we'd probably never get a conviction. Even if we wanted to."

"Please," Mr. North said. "Please—*begin at the beginning!*"

"Right," Weigand said. "I know it sounds complicated. It isn't, really. It begins, of course, with old Cyrus Graham, and his belief that there is transmissible insanity in the Graham family. Whether there is or not—and after the way Graham acted this afternoon I'm not so sure there isn't—he made it clear that if the Grahams had a child, they didn't get his money. He has a lot of money; his son wanted it a lot, partly because he saw a chance to get ahead in Henri et Paulette if he had some capital. But—Mrs. Graham wanted a child a lot. She had that—oh, that basic craving for a child that some women have. Then, about four years ago, old Cyrus had a stroke and the doctors said he was going to die within a matter of weeks. And so—" He paused.

Pam nodded.

"Yes," she said. "I see. She decided not to wait any longer; to take a chance."

"Right," Weigand told her. "And by the time they knew that Cyrus might live for months, it was too late. Too late, anyhow, for anything Mrs. Graham would consent to. So there they were—the baby coming, old Cyrus—"

"Not going," Mrs. North said. "But the money going."

"Yes," Weigand said. "That was the way of it. So Graham made his plan, and his wife, because she was willing to do anything to keep the baby, and because she wanted to do what Graham wanted—and because there wasn't, she felt, anything really wrong in it—agreed. The plan was simple, at first. They would merely conceal the baby's birth— she went 'on a trip' when the time came—and arranged for boarding care until the old man died. But, again, the old man didn't die. It turned out to be not only months, but years—and all the time Margaret Graham was kept away from her baby around whom her whole life centered. After a while, she got desperate. She told Graham he had to fix things some way, she didn't care how, so she could have her son. But if he didn't fix them, she was going to have Michael anyway, whatever happened to the money. So he had to fix it."

Mr. North, motioning to Weigand to go ahead, spooned cracked ice from a thermos pail into a shaker, added gin and dry vermouth, and mixed. He poured martinis into glasses and twisted lemon peel over them. Weigand let the cool cocktail trickle down his throat.

Faced with his wife's ultimatum, Weigand told them, Graham had decided on a plan. They would adopt their own son—adopt him legally and by a method which would give the curious, alert old man in the wheelchair upstairs no faintest ground for suspicion. They would adopt the boy, not privately but from an agency publicly engaged in placing children. They would make it appear that only chance brought them Michael, instead of some other child. Then Cyrus could not possibly suspect the truth.

To accomplish this, Graham had first taken Michael from the boarding home he had been in—out of town, it was, for greater safety—and found some place for the child nearby. He had inquired around, carefully, and hit on Mrs. Halstead. Then he had posed as Richard Osborne, wearing dark glasses, letting his beard grow for a day or so, and pretending physical weakness, and arranged for Michael to be boarded with the old woman. They had waited for a time, then, to give Mrs. Graham a chance to meet Michael "accidentally" in the park. When that had been done, Mrs. Graham went to the Foundation and told about the little boy with the old woman, exaggerating conditions somewhat but not excessively. She arranged it so that, if the little boy did come under the Foundation's care, they would inevitably think of her as a suitable foster parent. She put in an application for a child—ostensibly for any suitable child. But, naturally, she would not have accepted any child but Michael.

"A little later," Weigand continued, holding out his glass for more,

"Graham got himself up again as Richard Osborne and visited the Foundation, telling his cock-and-bull story and arranging for the child to be taken under care. He knew enough—he'd gone to the trouble to find out enough—about the practices of such agencies to feel sure that, when a worker saw the conditions of Mrs. Halstead's, the Foundation would think it best for the child to act on his authorization and remove it."

"Don't," Mrs. North said, "call Michael 'it.'"

"What?" said Weigand. "Oh, all right. Where was I?"

They told him.

"Well," he said, "it all went according to plan, at first. The agency investigated and was about ready to place Michael, when Miss Winston's suspicions were aroused. And that meant, Graham instantly saw when his wife called up that afternoon and told him she was afraid Miss Winston suspected, that an investigation would be started. Now—any investigation would be almost sure to reveal the plan.

"The rest, he said, was obvious. When his wife telephoned Tuesday afternoon and told him what had happened, Graham made light of it—insisted that all he would need to do would be to talk Miss Winston out of it. He said, however, that he had better see her that evening, if he could. Fortunately for his plan, Miss Winston had spent some time merely chatting with Mrs. Graham and had given her a sketchy outline of her evening's plans—"

"As anyone might," Mrs. North said. "Talking about the heat, and how to get away from it, and about going to roof gardens."

"Right," Weigand said. "Miss Winston had actually mentioned the Ritz-Plaza roof and the Crescent Club to Mrs. Graham as likely places where she and McIntosh would go for the evening. Graham found this out from his wife. Then he telephoned to both places and reserved tables in McIntosh's name near the dance floors. He couldn't, you see, merely take a chance that Lois and McIntosh would happen to sit where he could pass their table without arousing suspicion; that was something he had to make sure of. He suspected, rightly as it turned out, that McIntosh wouldn't question a reservation—would just accept it as in the natural order of things.

"When he had made the reservations, Graham took enough of the atropine sulphate and twisted it in a cigarette paper and put it in his cigarette case. Then he told Miss Hand to go to the other restaurant, and promised to pick her up there after his conference."

Mr. North looked puzzled.

"Why bring Miss Hand into it at all?" he wanted to know.

Mrs. North looked at him sadly and shook her head.

"So he would have a dance partner, of course," she said. "So that—"

"Right," Weigand cut in. "And he had to park her some place while he found out whether Lois and McIntosh were going to the roof or over to the club on the East Side. So he went around to the apartment house where Lois lived and waited until the girl and McIntosh came out. He saw them get a cab and go straight across Park Avenue. Then he knew that, if they were following out their original plans—and he had to take a chance that they were—they were going to the roof. If they had been going to the Crescent Club, they would have turned north in Park Avenue and then turned back toward the East River. So, hoping he was right, he picked up Miss Hand, made his excuse about the cooling system in the other restaurant, and took her along to the roof. It must have been a relief to him to see McIntosh and the girl there, and at a table convenient for his purposes.

"The rest was fairly simple, as long as he kept his nerve and his wits. He did. He danced with Miss Hand—probably several times, until there was a time when McIntosh and Lois were on the floor, too. Then he maneuvered so that, as the music stopped, he and Miss Hand would be near the McIntosh table. Miss Hand went ahead, of course—he could, if he needed to, direct her so that she would pass the right table. He came along behind, took out a cigarette—and the paper of poison—and flipped the powder into Lois's drink. In the general movement and confusion—the music had ended, remember, and dancers were going back to their tables all over the room—there wasn't any real danger that he would be noticed. He wasn't noticed. Miss Hand, for example, was never even aware that he had hesitated.

"Graham and his secretary stayed at their table a little while and then went back to the office and did their work. He couldn't have been much interested in it—he'd already done his real work for the evening. He found out that he'd done it successfully when the early editions of the morning papers came out. He must have figured he was pretty safe when Buddy Ashley and Miss Ormond turned up as red herrings."

Weigand stopped and finished off his cocktail. He appeared to have finished.

"And Mrs. Halstead?" Dorian prompted.

"Just stumbled into it," Weigand said. "She saw Graham on the street and recognized him—maybe from the way he walked—as 'Osborne.' Tuesday evening, after I had seen her, she went around to the Graham house and accused him of being Osborne. He denied it, of course, but could see that she didn't believe him. Maybe she threatened to tell us. So he killed her. Actually seeing her die hit him hard, apparently—I think that murder, rather than Lois's, haunted him, and finally made him break after we had him."

"And Mrs. Graham—she knew all the time?" Pam was curious.

"Oh yes," Weigand said. "She knew. That's why she tried to kidnap Michael, finally. Miss Winston had let drop where the child was, I suppose. He was all that Mrs. Graham cared about by that time—she was distracted, and had only the one burning idea—*get Michael.* So she got him."

"And now?" Dorian said. Her voice was anxious. "Does she get him? To keep?"

Weigand shook his head, slowly.

"I wouldn't know," he said. "But, for what it's worth, I should think so. You see, he's her own child. She won't have to prove that; we'll prove it for her, when Graham goes to trial. And unless somebody presses the issue, and the court decides she isn't a fit parent—well, I should think the child would stay with her. Wouldn't you, Pam?"

Pam nodded.

"I don't see how it could be any other way," she said. "It's—it's something nice that has come out of it, anyway."

Nobody said anything. Martha finished setting the table. Mr. North stared at her, abstractedly. He was obviously thinking it over. Then he looked rather puzzled.

200                                    FRANCES & RICHARD LOCKRIDGE

"Listen," he said, "wasn't there a suspicious man who *had* bought atropine sulphate that day? What about him?"

Weigand shook his head.

"There," he said, "you've got me. We haven't found him; we don't figure to. For all I know, he may be another murderer, laying in his stock of poison. For all I know, he may be dropping it in a glass somewhere at this very—"

The telephone shrilled across his words. Everybody jumped and Mrs. North said anxiously, "Oh dear!" Mr. North picked the telephone up, after a second of looking at it with deep suspicion.

"Yes?" he said. "What? Who?" There was a little pause. "No," Mr. North said. He listened a moment longer, said "No" again and put the telephone back in its cradle.

"What was it?" Mrs. North inquired. There was excitement in her voice. Mr. North looked at her and smiled gently.

"A wrong number, Pam," he said. "Just a wrong number. Not another murder."

Pam said, "Oh," and sighed. It could be taken for a sigh of relief, of course. Mr. North decided he would take it for a sigh of relief. If it were anything else, there was nothing he could do about it. Pam would merely have to learn that she couldn't have a murder every night, with dinner. Not even if she did know a detective and—Mr. North looked across the room at Dorian and Bill—a lady who was, apparently, going to be a detective's wife.